Sue & family
Love ya Big.
Phil .10

Barriers

MID L. STUTSMAN

WestBow
PRESS

WestBow Press™
1663 Liberty Drive
Bloomington, IN 47403
www.westbowpress.com
Phone: 1-866-928-1240

First published by WestBow Press: 01/04/10

ISBN: 978-1-4497-0020-1 (sc)
ISBN: 978-1-4497-0021-8 (hc)
ISBN: 978-1-4497-0019-5 (e)

Library of Congress Control Number: 2010920065

Printed in the United States of America
Bloomington, Indiana

This book is printed on acid-free paper.

Israel

Genesis 12:1-3 Now the Lord had said unto Abram, get thee out of thy country, and from thy kindred, and from thy father's house, unto a land that I will show thee: and I will make of thee a great nation, and I will bless thee, and make thy name great; and thou shalt be a blessing: And I will bless them that bless thee, and curse him that curseth thee: and in thee shall all families of the earth be blessed. KJV

Chapter One

Anne Sheridan shivered as the commuter flight from Eilat to Tel Aviv headed into the Israeli skies and turned north, but it wasn't the liftoff that sent chills through her. She focused her attention on the man who sat one seat ahead and across the aisle. It was his eyes. They were mesmerizing, dangerous.

Dangerous... The thought startled her. She remembered him staring at her when they stood in line to board the plane earlier. Flattered, she had smiled back, but he had turned away with a perplexed look. Hardly a typical reaction. Thinking about it left her unsettled.

After being admonished by her late husband, she had learned to analyze strangers for her own protection and felt confident in her ability to pick up on anything illusory. Now, for the first time, her stomach twisted like a pretzel into one too many knots. She wasn't sure what she felt. *Something about the way he...*

"Such a pretty name." A voice nudged its way into her thoughts. It was the Jewish woman in the seat next to her, who had introduced herself earlier as Rachael Milchan. She patted Anne's hand.

Anne smiled out of politeness, but the dark, intense presence of the stranger wouldn't let her go. *What is it about him?* She searched for the elaborate Star of David suspended from a silver chain around her neck.

"What a lovely *Magen David* you wear." The woman spoke a little louder, her English heavy with Israeli inflection.

This time the sound of her voice got Anne's full attention. She turned to face Mrs. Milchan, "I'm sorry?"

The woman pointed to Anne's necklace. "Your Star of David is very old, *nu?*"

Anne looked down and fingered the opal set in the middle of the pendant. Touching it had a comforting way of connecting her to reality.

"Yes. It belonged to my mother. It's the only thing I have left of her." She released a catch in the silver hexagram and lifted the gem to reveal a black and white photo.

"Ah, a locket." Mrs. Milchan leaned closer.

Anne turned the picture so she could see it better. "My mother, Yona. She was from Haifa."

"You look a lot like her. So, you are *Aliyah?*"

"Yes, I am." Anne pressed the opal into the star to secure it.

"Good. Good." The older woman patted her hand again. "Yes. I am thinking it is always good when a Jew returns to live in *Eretz* Israel."

"Yes, well, making *Aliyah* has been a dream of mine since the death of my parents, but I wasn't able to realize it until this last year. I'm going to live in Haifa."

"Your parents?" Mrs. Milchan made a clicking sound with her tongue. "I am sorry to hear this." She brushed a wisp of hair from the side of Anne's face. "Your red and blonde highlights look so natural," she said, changing the course of their conversation. "And such lovely eyes." She leaned over and pointed out the window at the Mediterranean waters defining Israel's coast. "Beautiful, like the sea. And you are not married?"

This wasn't the first time Anne had wished for her mother's dark hair and eyes. "My grandmother's father was Irish, Mrs. Milchan."

"Of course he was." This time, she squeezed Anne's hand and didn't let go. "Call me Rachael. We are friends now, *nu?*" She looked thoughtful then. "From Ben Gurion in Jerusalem all the way to Eilat. Now we are flying back to Tel Aviv, and from there you must drive to your destination. You are taking the long way around to Haifa, I think."

Anne broke into a grin at Rachael's candid observation. "I guess I am. My friends in Jerusalem called the moment I arrived from America. The apartment they helped secure for me wasn't ready to move into yet, so I decided to spend some time in Eilat to work on my writing until it was."

Rachael stared at her. "So. You *are* single. And a writer!"

By now, Anne decided Rachael's bluntness was harmless and her offer of friendship genuine. "Yes, well..." she wrapped her hands around her carry-on purse, which masqueraded as a mini suitcase and thought about how best to answer. "I *was* married, but my husband died in a car accident. Now I am here. I hope to do some research for my latest novel." *Among other things,* she thought with a twinge of guilt.

Anne watched the man ahead of them turn his head their way. She kept him in sight as she leaned closer to her new friend and lowered her voice, "I'm especially interested in the Israeli Defense Force and their intelligence divisions. I want to know more about spies and double agents."

Rachael's hand flew to her throat. "Oh my! What is this you are writing?" She glanced around and whispered, "Be careful, Anne. This is not some romantic game to play, especially with the IDF. My son is in the military. He has had many a narrow escape. Intrigue can be a dangerous thing, can it not?"

Oh, if you only knew. Anne bit down on the left side of her lip…a nervous habit from childhood that had formed a curious but permanent dimple.

Rachael leaned back in her seat and looked at her. "You should meet him, my dear. He is a major, and he is *very* handsome." A smile then played across her face. "Yes, and I think my Ari would like you very much!"

Though embarrassed by her teasing, Anne wondered if Rachael's Ari would have access to the information she needed. Meeting him might not be a bad idea.

They continued their conversation until a light came on overhead, indicating it was safe for them to remove their seatbelts. Rachael winked at Anne. "I will be right back."

Anne grinned, but her smile faded when the man in front of them sprang up from his seat.

✡ ✡ ✡

The hot summer wind picked up errant grains of sand and sent them scudding across Haifa's airstrip. Without warning, they lifted here and there into miniature whirlwinds. When the wind tired of them, they fell back against the pavement and snaked along, looking very much like the feared desert adder.

An anxious major of the Israeli Defense Force tore his gaze from the mesmerizing swirls of sand and shaded his eyes against the sun, just low enough in the sky to send out a blinding ray of light. His jaws clenched as he waited for the Israir ATR commuter flight from Eilat. He checked the position of his anti-terrorist unit, tense and weapons ready. Even the wind seemed to quiet down and pull back as though waiting.

The officer thought about his orders. The sensitive situation had required months of planning. Everything was in place, and they had this one opportunity to uncover a traitor in their midst. He had close friends on board the plane, who were willing to put their lives in danger for the greater good of Israel. Men who wanted peace more than anything else but who felt they had little hope of realizing it in their life times. And yet, they never gave up trying.

He knew nothing could go wrong with this operation. Desperation marked time in Israel these days when it wasn't popular to be a Jew in the eyes of the world. This was especially true as they sought the best way to deal with militant Arabs who violently demanded their right to possess the ancient land of Israel and annihilate the Jews.

"G-d of my fathers, shall evil prevail against the innocent while we stand by and watch? Help us, HaShem. Give us the cunning to outsmart our enemies."

He blinked, suddenly convicted by how long it had been since he'd offered up any semblance of prayer. Too much was at stake to mess this up with a flippant attitude. Closing his eyes, this time in true humility, he prayed in earnest for the safety of the mission.

✡ ✡ ✡

Anne gripped the catch on her seat belt and watched several Arab men shove the flight attendant to the back of the plane. She willed her heart to stop its erratic thumping as she listened to the terrorists discussing…what? If only she had learned more Arabic than just *"hello, goodbye, thank you, and go in peace."* From the sounds of it, these weren't the current words of choice.

Rachael had barely left her seat when five men stood and drew weapons from their jackets. In a flurry of orchestrated moves, they gained access to the cockpit and forced the co-pilot to the back of the plane. One of the terrorists now guarded the door, his gun held to the pilot's head. Anne's mysterious man from the seat ahead announced in English and Hebrew that they were Palestinians, who were taking charge of the plane.

Passengers from the forward seats now stumbled to the back to join the co-pilot. They voiced their anger and fear until the leader shouted for everyone to shut-up. Silence hung like a menacing cloud while the Arabs collected cell phones and laptops.

Anne twisted in her seat to find Rachael. When she saw her, the older woman shook her head. Her eyes issued a warning, and Anne turned back around and hugged her purse. The plane banked just then, and she could make out the curve of the coastline below. The seaport of Haifa stretched out beneath her and embraced the Mediterranean Sea with Mt. Carmel vigilant high in the background. It was obvious they weren't going to Tel Aviv.

She closed her eyes and breathed a prayer, *"Aba, I know you didn't bring me all this way, fulfilling my heart's desire, just to let me disintegrate into a trillion pieces at the hands of terrorists. I'm not afraid to die; I just meant to actually walk through your Holy Lands, not view them momentarily from the sky..."*

A loud shriek and the sound of a scuffle rudely interrupted her discussion with the Almighty. Her head jerked to the muffled sound of a gunshot that sent one of the Arabs sprawling into the aisle next to her. The bullet passed through him and lodged in Rachael's empty seat, missing Anne by inches.

The victim cried out as he grabbed his right side. At the same time, Anne's hand flew to her mouth to stifle her own cry. The shooter, whom she guessed to be an air marshal, received a blow to the back of his head for his failed heroism. When he slumped forward, two Arabs shoved his body up against a bulkhead.

Anne set her purse down before she released her clasp and moved to Rachael's seat. She leaned forward to get a better view of the red stain spreading through the victim's shirt.

The Arab who appeared to be in charge shouted at her and motioned for her to stay where she was while he knelt to check out the wound. When he stood, he warned, "Unless you are a doctor, you will not move."

Anne's Irish temperament threatened to surface. His demeaning attitude made her teeth hurt. "I've had emergency paramedic training. At least let me see if I can help him."

The injured man clutched her hand. Without waiting for permission, she twisted her hair into a knot at the nape of her neck and slid to the floor. She unbuttoned his shirt and folded it away from the area. The blood oozed without pulsing, which meant the bullet hadn't hit an artery. She pressed down on the wound and looked up at the leader. His dark eyes held hers with a look she didn't understand. "Please," she implored. A sense of urgency bypassed the sickening feeling creeping into the pit of her stomach. "We need to stop the bleeding before he goes into shock. Can I have the first-aid kit?"

His intense eyes never left hers as he gave an order to the attendant in fluent Hebrew. Anne tensed when he called one of his men over and handed the gun to him. Her cheeks flushed warm under his gaze. She looked down at his comrade, in obvious pain, when someone yelled at her, "He is a terrorist. Let him die." But she refused to take sides. In a moment of compassion, she brushed the gleaming black hair away from his eyes. He was young, mid-twenties, she guessed. When she laid the back of her hand against his cheek, he gazed up at her with those same beautiful eyes and the same strange look as his commander. *Do you just not trust me?*

An outburst in Hebrew from one of the passengers startled her, though it didn't take an interpreter to explain his anger. She looked back at Rachael, but her new friend turned her head. *I'm only trying to help. What is wrong with you people? He's a human being.*

The young man exchanged words with the leader. When he struggled to get up, she snapped back from her frustration. "You can't move."

It was then the flight attendant appeared and thrust the medical kit at her. Anne asked the leader if she could stay and help. He nodded with a look that took her breath away, and she quickly focused on the flight attendant. "We need to hurry before the plane lands. Do you understand?" The woman answered her with a flood of angry words. Anne grabbed her pendant; the leader grabbed the attendant's arm and had her sent back with the others.

Without hesitating, he knelt and opened the medical kit, sending another shiver through her. "Tell me what you want done."

Avoiding his eyes, she took in a deep breath. "*I will not fear what men can do to me. Help me control this shaking, Father,*" she prayed. "Open a large gauze pad. Pour antiseptic over it. When I lift my hand, apply direct pressure to the wound before the blood flows again. Keep the dressing in place…any disturbance could rip the blot clot open and start the bleeding again." Her orders came out in an authoritative rush, and the one who once threatened life now obeyed without question.

"Now, put petroleum jelly on the bottom of another pad; it will keep air from entering the wound." She placed the second pad on top of the first one and quickly secured the dressing with medical tape. "Roll him onto his side. Carefully."

The Arab pulled the shirt away from the wound. As she watched him, Anne had the feeling he had done this before, but she didn't have time to reflect on it. They worked together in uncomfortable silence.

With the young man's back tended to, she relaxed just as the plane hit the runway. The sudden movement knocked her off balance and slammed the small of her back against the solid edge of the seat. She cried out from the pain and would have flown forward with the next lurch of the aircraft, had the leader not reached out to steady her. With his help, she managed to brace her legs against the base of the seat across the aisle.

Bending over the injured Arab, she wrapped her arms around him for protection as the plane rolled down the runway of Haifa's airport to the designated parking lane. She took in deep breaths to still her heart and shook her head. *This simply can't be happening.*

As soon as they came to a stop, the leader sprang to his feet amid a surge of commotion. He was once again the terrorist in command. Anne had to shout to get his attention, "He needs medical help I can't give. You can't just leave him like this…we don't know what damage the bullet did inside."

"He will live," came the curt reply.

The anger and fear on the passengers' faces showed no room for sympathy or compassion, but the other terrorists stared at the injured man and back at their leader until a loud argument broke out. Anne watched the Arab in charge motion for quiet. He kept his voice controlled, even. She wondered if he was trying to convince them to follow through with their plans in spite of their fallen comrade. He ignored her, but she heard an edge of frustration in his voice when he gave instructions to his men.

Now that they had landed, the terrorists forced the head pilot to the back of the plane to join the passengers. The leader faced her.

"What do you intend to do with us?" she asked, aware that her actions may have given her an advantage. Her only hope was to keep it that way, and she quickly prayed for wisdom to put it to good use.

He nodded toward the cockpit. "That depends on whether or not our demands are met for food, supplies and safe passage back to our village in Gaza."

"You are endangering human lives for food and supplies?" Her voice was little more than a whisper. When he didn't answer, she pressed him, "What if they won't cooperate?

"They must," came the reply from the one who appeared desperate enough not to want the alternative any more than she did. She suspected he would go to great lengths to assure that it *did* happen.

He knelt beside the injured man and spoke in Arabic, his voice soothing, comforting. Anne wondered if he was telling him to be brave or promising something he couldn't deliver. She took the opportunity to glance sideways at him, so intense and handsome, yet fierce and warrior-like. Was it fear making her heart race when he turned to her? She'd never felt so confused.

He looked thoughtful before asking, "What is your name?"

She fingered the shirt of the man in her lap before she found the courage to lift her chin and return his gaze. "Anne." She cleared her throat, "Anne Sheridan."

"My name is Rashad Sayyid." He nodded toward the young man, "My brother, Khalid."

"Your brother?" Anne squeezed her eyes shut. Rashad's hand, strong yet gentle, closed over hers. She clenched her fist, but she couldn't bring herself to pull away from his touch.

"He will live, thanks to you." He lowered his voice, "You are a very brave woman, Anne Sheridan."

A swirling sensation kept her from opening her eyes. *I feel sick, not brave.* She would have said as much, but one of the men yelled from the cockpit. When Rashad stood to answer, the anger in his voice made her forget her nausea.

"What is it?"

He squatted back down beside his brother and studied her for a moment. "They are stalling. We informed them of my brother's condition and what you have done, but they are waiting us out. Now I am afraid we must take drastic measures." He paused as though testing her reaction, "We have a saying: an eye for an eye."

"No!" The implication of what he said surged through the pit of her stomach again. Anne glanced past him at the passengers, held at gunpoint. She reacted without thinking and grabbed his sleeve. "If all you want is food and supplies, you'll undermine what you're trying to accomplish." When he reached for her hand, she realized her mistake and let go.

He looked away. "We must be taken seriously or the one responsible for shooting my brother will have to pay for his deed."

"You can't be serious. I'm sure he didn't mean..."

"He should not have been so foolish."

Anne searched for and grasped the pendant. "Then let me take his place," she blurted out.

"You do not know what you are saying." He looked half surprised, half amused.

"I'm serious," she fired back at him with her newfound courage. "My life for his." She hoped what she had seen earlier in his eyes would force him to reconsider.

"No." Rashad stood. "It is out of the question."

"Then let the others go and keep me as your hostage. You can use me to bargain for your demands."

He squatted beside her again. "Do you think you are important just because you are an American?" he mocked. "This is not one of your Hollywood movies."

"I meant what I said." She watched him run his hand through his thick wavy hair, black and gleaming with sweat.

His jaws flexed, and his dark eyes narrowed. "Why are you saying these things?"

"Because," Anne said, reeling in her indignation with a silent prayer, "my life is in God's hands. I want no more innocent blood spilled. I have influential family members in America, and they have money...it could help with negotiations."

There's that look again. She hoped he could see she was serious. Leaning forward, she gently touched his arm. "Please let them go. I'll personally deliver your message. Allow me to talk to the authorities."

His silence encouraged her. "Rashad," she pleaded, "Let me negotiate. At least let me try. Khalid needs medical attention now."

Khalid reached up and placed his hand on his brother's arm. "Rasha," he gasped. The sound wrenched Anne's heart.

"All right," Rashad said, nodding toward the cockpit. "You have one chance to make this work." He stood again, and Anne dared to hope, despite the dark warning in his voice.

Chapter Two

" **M**ajor, they have taken hostages. Here is a list of their terms and the passenger manifest."

Ari Milchan took the transcript from his aide. He did little to mask his anger when his eyes rested on a familiar name. *Of all the times for you to be traveling, Ima.* Hopefully his mother would keep her wits about her and not get into any trouble. He loved her, but there were times...

"They also have a wounded man aboard, Sir."

The major lifted his head. They had taken every precaution for this not to happen. "Do you have details?"

"Only that he is one of the terrorists. They are requesting immediate help for him."

"Try to get a name and details," Ari ordered.

"Yes, Sir." The young man hesitated before he turned to leave, "And, an American woman has aided them in administering medical help."

"A what? Of all the foolish, irresponsible..." He reached for his beret and slapped it against the palm of his hand. The fact that things weren't going as planned was the least of his worries. If an ill-informed American got involved, it could ruin the whole operation. He ran his hand across the back of his neck, but the looks from the men under his command made him check his personal feelings. He turned away and quickly put his beret in place.

"American or not...we will not give in to them," he muttered. "Somehow, they must be forced to surrender."

Voices hushed. He saw the glances exchanged throughout the unit. What he thought of Americans and terrorists was no secret to any of them.

✡ ✡ ✡

Laying a pillow under Khalid's head, Anne slid out from under him and accepted the leader's hand. The blood cursed its way to her legs and feet. When her knees buckled, his hand slid to her waist to steady her. At the same time, his free hand brushed the back of her head, releasing the dark auburn waves from the knot she had made. Emotions charged the atmosphere as she sagged against his chest, and he paused before he pulled his hand away from the silky strands.

Embarrassed by her vulnerable position, she took a step back and cleared her throat, "Can I take a second to use the restroom?"

Rashad nodded, but the moment she reached for her purse, he grabbed her arm. Anne jerked it back, but he didn't let go until she relaxed and opened it. Her unguarded defiance in the clash between their wills left her shaking as she thought about how many ways it could have gone wrong. She clutched her purse, thankful that she and the contents were safe, and hurried down the aisle.

Running water in the sink didn't drown out the harshness in the voices outside. She stared at her reflection in the mirror and fought back the tears. *What am I doing? I'm in a no-man's land.* Her husband had trained her to know how to handle herself in emergency situations, but she had never encountered a scenario like this one. She splashed cold water on her face and steeled herself for the unknown outcome of her actions.

The passengers all turned to look when she emerged from the facilities. One of the women cast angry insults at her, along with poorly aimed spit. Anne moved away and sought out Rachael, who looked upset but was kind when she spoke, "She is angry because you have befriended our enemies. Some people think you are in league with them."

Anne bit her lip. That much was obvious. She turned to address the pilot, "I'm being allowed to contact the authorities outside. I'll remain as their hostage until their demands are met."

Rachael gasped. Whispers rippled through the crowd. The head pilot spoke up, "I cannot allow you to do this. You are only an American, and if anything should happen..."

"I am a Jew!" She quickly lowered her voice, "I'm sorry," she apologized. "I think I've earned their trust for helping the leader's brother. Besides, it's already settled."

"Anne, do not be foolish." Rachael grabbed her arm and whispered in her ear, "The pilots are talking. Something is dreadfully wrong here. These men had weapons...they think they had inside help."

"I wondered about that," Anne whispered back. "But right now things are as they are. I must do this...time is critical." She saw the tears well up in Rachael's eyes. "*HaShem* will be with me." Anne hugged her friend and placed her purse in the woman's hands. "Here, please. It's important that you keep this safe for me. And, don't worry...I *will* return for it."

Aware that all eyes in the plane were on her, Anne hurried to the cockpit. With a headset on, her voice shattered the silence. She identified herself and spelled out the terms for releasing the passengers, beginning with Khalid's medical care.

She listened to the reply from the control room and stifled her indignation. "I am not representing America," she replied. "I have completed paperwork for *Aliyah*, and that makes me a Jewish citizen. And at the moment, I am the *only* one onboard who is being authorized to negotiate."

✡ ✡ ✡

Anne's demands sent a courier scurrying to the major's side. "Sir, the American is in touch with the tower and negotiating terms for releasing the passengers."

At this, Ari Milchan broke into a run and entered the control room. He read through the transcript. As he placed a headset on, a determined female voice came through loud enough for everyone in the room to hear.

"No, *you* do not understand." The calm in her voice seemed strained. "The leader's brother is critically wounded. If you don't act at once to comply with their terms he could die, and they will seek revenge, starting with the marshal who is responsible for his injury."

Ari broke into the conversation, "May I ask whose authority you are acting on, Mrs. Sheridan?"

"And who is this?" she countered.

"Major Ari Milchan."

He heard her suck in her breath, "Major, do you know that your..."

Ari clenched his teeth and cut her short, "I am well informed that my mother is a passenger on this flight."

There was a pause before she answered, "Then let me further inform you this is of my own initiative. I will take the place of the passengers and stay with these men as their hostage until we arrive safely at their destination."

Ari thought through the best way to handle this setback. He listened as Anne pleaded, her voice softer with emotion. "Major? Please, they say they only want food and medical supplies. They have acted with honor toward me.

The shooting was an accident, and I don't want anyone else to get hurt. At least help the one who's been shot, or I'm afraid there *will* be an incident."

Ari lowered his voice as well, "You need to understand that we are not in a position to act without authorization. And their demands may be a shield to hide their true agenda."

This time there was a spark of indignation when she replied, "It is *you* who must understand. Time is critical right now, and I think you're wrong about their motives."

"I hope you are right, Mrs. Sheridan." Ari closed his eyes to gain control. He then signaled his men.

✡ ✡ ✡

Anne removed the headset and ran her hand over it. Her sigh took flight and carried another prayer Heaven's way.

Rashad leaned against the doorway. He spoke without looking at her, "Do you know this major's name?"

"Milchan, Ari Milchan." She watched hardness sculpt the leader's face. "You know him!" As soon as the words were spoken, she wished them back.

His face came within inches of hers. His dark eyes flashed. "Do not meddle, Anne Sheridan. You will live longer."

Anne swallowed hard. "May I check on your brother?" She forced herself to return his gaze until he nodded and stepped back to allow her through. When she entered the cabin, she scanned the faces of the passengers. Some of them turned away, but most of them looked at her, mistrust evident as they stared. When Rachael motioned to her, she carefully stepped over Khalid. "I spoke with a certain Major Ari Milchan," she told her. "He said he's needs authorization before complying with the terms. I thought you'd want to know."

Rachael smiled her gratefulness, but her eyes glistened with more than just tears at the mention of her son's name. It was pride born of love and confidence in his military capabilities. Watching her made Anne ache for her mother.

Rachael cupped her hand around the side of Anne's face, which only intensified the feelings of loneliness. Feelings she thought she had buried with her parents. "I am praying for you," she said and gave her face a pat.

"Thank you." Anne bit her lip to keep back the tears and returned to the young man on the floor. When she knelt to feel his forehead, his eyes fluttered open and he touched her hand. "Are you thirsty?" she asked, making drinking motions until he stopped her and nodded his head.

"I understand English."

She looked around at the others, "Do all of you?"

"Most, yes."

A frustrated sigh escaped her lips. They understood Hebrew and English and she understood nothing. She called to one of the Arabs near the galley and told him to put ice chips in whatever clean cloth he could find. The terrorist waited for a nod from Rashad. "Bring a glass of water with it," she added.

Anne dipped the ice filled cloth into the glass and dabbed it over Khalid's parched lips. "I'm sorry this is all I can do. You shouldn't drink anything until you get medical help." He hadn't gone into shock yet, an answer to prayer, but she knew he needed expert help… and soon.

She wondered at her involvement in the dangerous scenario now playing out before her. Rashad might think she was brave, but right now she was terrified. She thought through the situation, but it held no way of escape. *"Aba,* she prayed, *I think I've gotten myself into something I can't get out of now, without a miracle."*

✡ ✡ ✡

Major Milchan discussed the situation with headquarters and it was decided they would go ahead as planned. He gave the command, "Get the smoke bombs ready."

Soldiers moved quickly in response. From the orders given, every man knew his place and what was required of him. The importance of timing didn't need to be explained to these elite combatants, who were trained specifically for this type of operation.

He grabbed the headset and waited for his captain's signal. If he could stall the terrorist's for just a few more minutes, the success of their strategy would be assured. Mrs. Sheridan turned out to be an unforeseen hindrance to the well-rehearsed mission, but it was decided her participation could work to their advantage. With the unexpected injury of the Arab, the stakes had just gotten higher, and she needed to be unaware of the importance of the part she now played in all of this. Nothing else could go wrong.

If only his mother wasn't on board. At least it didn't appear that she was involved in any way. Still, he wondered how Mrs. Sheridan knew about her. Leave it to his *Ima* to have made friends with an American. Her trust knew no bounds…a trait he was thankful he had not inherited.

He kept his eyes on his captain and brought his thoughts under control. For now, he had to concentrate on getting all of the passengers out safely.

✿ ✿ ✿

Rashad motioned to Anne when the call came through. She held up the glass of water, and he had one of his men take her place. "Like this. And don't let him drink any of it," she ordered.

Back in the cockpit, he watched Anne's eyes while she negotiated. Her demeanor throughout this ordeal was one of true trust in her God. The courage she exhibited, when he knew that deep inside she had to be afraid, drew his admiration. There was something about her that grabbed his heart and wouldn't let go, something that make him question his actions.

Her presence in the beginning could have upset his mission and might have had dire consequences, but he sensed at once her sincerity. She was as beautiful as she was brave, but it wasn't just her beauty that made him dig deep within his memory for why she seemed familiar, why he had agreed to her involvement in all of this. As he stared, her eyes lit up, and she turned to face him. "They have the supplies!"

Rashad grabbed the headset. "No tricks, Major, my men are desperate and will not tolerate any deception. Make sure you are careful in your moves."

He glanced over at Anne when he answered, "We have tried negotiating your way. We need these supplies now, not months after your superiors go through all of their committees and then deliver only a portion of what we require."

"No," he snapped. "The passengers will be released when the last of the supplies are safely aboard, not before." Rashad slipped off the headset and yelled orders to his men. He cast a concerned glance Anne's way before leaving the cabin.

Chapter Three

Anne stayed in the pilot's seat of the cockpit. Through the front windshield, she watched Israeli soldiers scurry across the runway and form a vanguard. A distinguished man appeared at the front and returned her gaze.

"Major Milchan," she murmured. "Your mother had the handsome part right." She turned, forgetting she wasn't alone, and would have stood, but the Arab in the co-pilot's seat motioned for her to stay put.

From her position, she could see boxes headed to the rear of the plane. She heard Rashad speak, heard the door open and the steps being lowered, saw Khalid hurried off to a waiting ambulance. Less than forty minutes had passed…minutes that had seemed like hours. The time factor was critical, but she believed God was in control of everything, even time. Though she couldn't pin point why, her heart had gone out to these two Arab brothers. She breathed a prayer of thankfulness when she heard, "You are free to leave now," spoken in English and Hebrew.

Rashad ordered the passengers to line up at the door. He shouted at them again when they held back. Still, no one moved. This time Anne stood. The Arab again motioned for her to sit down, but she challenged him by stepping up to the doorway. When Rashad called her name, the guard lowered his gun. A nod from their leader, and his men parted to let her through, but the look on his face made her heart sink.

"They are afraid they will get caught in a crossfire and refuse to leave the plane," he said.

She took a deep breath. "Would it help if I led them out?"

He searched her eyes. "I am not sure…"

"I can stand at the end of the steps until they're escorted to safety. You have my word."

He complied but warned, "I will be right here, behind you."

They moved to the door where he relayed Anne's willingness to go with them to the tarmac. At his nod, the men lowered their weapons. No one moved.

Without hesitation, Rachael called from the middle of the group. She pushed her way forward, took Anne's arm and faced them. In true Israeli fashion she identified herself. "I am Major Ari Milchan's mother."

She looked at Anne and tapped her forehead. "What are they thinking? Ari would never fire on his own mother! These men could have killed us all by now. Why should they wait and shoot us in the back after their demands have been met? Besides, look at the might of our army. They would never get two feet off the ground." And Anne was sure that was exactly what she told everyone in Hebrew.

When Rachael finished her speech, she spun around with Anne still attached and descended the steps. The moment they reached the pavement, Anne hugged her friend and told her to continue across the airfield. She held onto the handrail of the steps and watched the frightened passengers follow. The last of the group to exit was the flight crew. The pilot nodded when he passed her. She couldn't tell if his look was one of pity or thankfulness. At this point, it didn't matter.

With a prayer in her heart, she sucked in her lower lip and started up the ramp, knowing her fate now depended upon Rashad's integrity and God's protection. She felt for the *Magen David* when she saw the leader standing behind the door with his weapon trained on her, but he lifted it the moment their eyes met. She took another step, just as a sudden movement below caught her attention.

From beneath the plane, a soldier rolled out and hurled something past her. A second soldier grabbed Anne and pulled her down the steps, as smoke poured from the open door. It all took place so fast she didn't have time to react.

"Stay down!" The soldier yelled at her over the gunshots and the shouts of more soldiers who swarmed the steps.

Angered now by the realization of what was taking place, Anne got up and ran to the steps. Two more soldiers grabbed her and pulled her to the side of the field out of harm's way. "Let me go!" she yelled. She continued to resist until she found herself face to face with Ari Milchan.

"You! You promised them!" She hurled her accusation with the venomous force of a spitting cobra and wrestled free from the soldiers. But before she could run for the plane again, Ari grabbed her arms. She beat against his chest, pouring her anger into each blow. The more she fought him, the more his grip weakened any attempt to get away. Her balled fists lost their momentum. Her body went limp with resignation.

✡ ✡ ✡

War had prepared the major to deal with enemy resistance, not with a woman, who now sobbed within his arms. Holding her brought on feelings he thought he had overcome. The fragrance in her hair coaxed long forgotten memories from hidden places in his heart. His discipline and training left him at the precise moment he needed them most. He felt the warmth of Anne's face against his chest and fought the urge to wrap both of his arms around her.

Shocked by the onslaught of conflicting emotions, he looked around at his men, all of them occupied with taking the prisoners off the plane. There was nothing left for him to do but keep his arm around this woman, who had nearly upset the whole mission, and march her to the terminal.

Ari steered Anne through the commotion inside. He scanned the crowd. Medical personnel checked out passengers at their requests. The flight team stepped into rooms to be debriefed. He saw no one close to help him out of his predicament.

It was then a hand touched his arm, and a familiar voice came to his rescue. "Ari…let me." His mother held out her hands, and he released Anne into her capable care. Relieved, he spun on his heels and returned to the tarmac to oversee the handling of the prisoners.

A young soldier saluted him when he approached, "They are all accounted for, Sir. The traitor has been apprehended in Eilat." The major acknowledged. He cast a fleeting glance Rashad's way. The Arab maintained his defiant demeanor, his glowering eyes concealing any recognition, but Ari knew his message had been conveyed. There would be time later to sort out all that had transpired. In spite of the mishap, the operation had gone as planned. In time they would know whether or not they had accomplished their goal.

He stepped aside as the media arrived and let them assume their usual role of misinterpreting the circumstances. He watched them enter the airport and single out passengers to interview. The story would be front-page news by morning, making it that much easier to implement the second phase of the operation.

The sirens quieted down, but lights still flashed around the airstrip. Rashad thought about Khalid, now on his way to a Jewish hospital. It was the only part of the plan that had gone awry-- a minor setback that would be remedied as soon as word got around of their daring exploit. Once they escaped their Israeli captors, orders were to make it to Gaza City, infiltrate the Hamas Party and gain the new leader's confidence. If their plan worked, in time they would be causing more harm than what little had come about from this staged hijacking. His only concern was that they might not be allowed to stay together because of Khalid's injury. If that proved to be the case, he had to believe God would lead him to another operative who could be trusted. A lot depended upon the man headed their way.

He glared at the major, who took determined strides toward the group of Arabs. Soldiers stood at attention, their weapons trained on the terrorists as they waited for transportation. When the two leaders' eyes met, Rashad thought back to their brief years together at the University in Jerusalem. Life had not been kind to either of them, but especially to Ari. Both of them had lost family members to violence born of hatred. Ari's suffering came at the hands of terrorist suicide bombers. Rashad and Khalid lost all but their father's parents in Israeli retaliation strikes. Their faith defined their lives and gave them the ability to go on. But bitterness over the loss of those he loved defined Ari's life and left him without hope. They were once friends who shared the same ideals about peaceful relations between their two races. Today, they stood on opposite sides of a barrier. Enemies...for now.

✡ ✡ ✡

Rachael hovered around Anne like a protective hen until soldiers escorted the young woman into a room. During the interrogation and debriefing, she sat outside looking the part of a nervous mother. Her own daughter, Hanna, had been killed at a checkpoint near the Gaza Strip while on duty in the army. During a routine check, she had reached out in compassion to an Arab woman, not realizing there was a suicide belt concealed beneath her garb. Less than a year later, Rachael had breathed a sign of relief when her husband, Leon, and their son, Asher, had returned from active duty in the IDF. But her joy turned to grief after she learned they had boarded an Egged bus targeted by terrorists. 23 innocent lives had been lost that day and over 110 wounded. Asher died instantly. Leon succumbed to his injuries on the way to the hospital. After that she had loved Ari's wife, Rani, until her horrific death--the result of a suicide bomber attack in the *souk* she frequented.

Rachael couldn't explain why she kept doling out her love, only to lose it time after time. But as long as it was there, she would share it. Anne had won her heart on the plane. She would do all she could to see her through this unfortunate and untimely ordeal. *Not that any event like this in Israel is timely. I have lived here all my life. An everyday occurrence, true, but never timely.*

With the same spirit of determination and defiance shown by her peers, she had learned how to handle the fact that Arabs clamored for their demise with hatred and contempt. It was that way before, it was that way when Israel had become a nation, and it continued to be so. Like the younger generation, she wondered if peace would ever come to fruition, even while she prayed according to Psalm 122:6.

An hour had passed when Anne finally emerged. Rachael greeted her with a hug, "Such an ordeal, Anne. You must stay with me tonight." She waved away any protests. "I know you have your own apartment waiting for you to move into, but you have been through enough today without trying to set up housekeeping, *nu*?"

When Anne answered with a feeble, "yes", Rachael put a protective arm around her and led her away.

On their way to the parking lot, several passengers from their flight stopped them. One of them, who spoke English, told Anne how grateful they were for her courage and welcomed her to Israel. After all that had happened, Anne showed no pride in her accomplishment. She ducked her head, clearly touched by their sincerity. Rachael was impressed.

One older lady held out a hand-embroidered scarf. Anne refused, but the insistent woman grabbed Rachael's arm and asked her to translate. "Take it, please. This is nothing compared to what you have given me. I have a little longer to live, and life is precious these days in Israel."

Holding tightly to the scarf, Anne put her arms around the woman. "*Toda reba* (thank you very much)."

"*Be`vakasha* (you're welcome)," came the tearful reply. She touched Anne's face. "*Shalom.*"

Rachael wiped away her own tears. *Such emotion and drama in one day.*

Ari ran toward them when they reached the taxi. *And here comes more. He is probably furious with me.*

While Anne got into the cab, Ari pulled her aside. "I am not sure I want you taking Mrs. Sheridan to her apartment. I will have one of my men escort her there."

"Ari." Rachael put her arm through his and walked farther away. "Anne and I have become friends. I cannot abandon her now."

"Friends? Are you serious? Since when?"

"We became acquainted on the flight."

"So. You have known her for less than a day, and now you are friends?"

"Yes, and I have asked her to come home with me."

When his mouth flew open to object, Rachael moved her hand to his cheek. "Now, now. I have made up my mind. The girl has been through enough today, *nu*? She does not need to try to make it through the night all alone in a strange new city. She barely speaks our language, Ari."

"You do not understand the situation, *Ima*. She..."

"She what? Let me tell you what she did. She stood up to those terrorists. You would have been so proud of her courage. I saw her shaking with fear, but she never backed down. Our people need more *ometz* like this! Maybe we would not be in such a way as we are. Maybe the Arabs would not be taking over our land and making our leaders cower like ghetto Jews in the holocaust."

"Calm down, *Ima*. I just think..."

Rachael turned them both around before he could finish and proceeded to march back to the taxi. He started to protest again, but she kissed the side of his face and told the driver to take off as soon as she got in the car.

Chapter Four

Anne tried her best to take in all of the scenery on the way to Rachael's home, but most of it blurred into darkness. She did notice they were on an incline. Relaxing against the seat, she let the arms of gravity pull her into a comfortable hug, which made it hard to listen to Rachel give a detailed account of their surroundings. Sleep tugged without mercy on her senses while the older woman chatted on.

At some point, they turned into a promenade. "Is this not so lovely? If you like the ocean, you will find the Port of Haifa has some of the most beautiful beaches around."

Anne caught a glimpse of the water before Rachael's voice faded and her eyes drooped shut again until she heard, "Oh look, Anne!"

Rachael's exclamation pierced Anne's sleep. She jerked awake and grabbed her pendant, only to find they were driving once more.

"Look out your window. The Baiha'i shrine is a major attraction, not that I should recommend their religion, but look at those gardens and the steps. It is very hilly and steep around here, but you get used to it. Often I take walks to the promenade…"

Anne wanted to listen, but her mind failed to cooperate. The next thing she knew, they were parked in front of a house somewhere on the summit of Mount Carmel. Rachael helped her out and paid the driver after he deposited their luggage at the doorstep.

"Are you hungry?" she asked as soon as she closed the front door behind them.

"Terribly," Anne said. "But can I just rest a bit first?"

"Of course. What was I thinking? Your body protests what happened today, *nu?* And I think of food. " Rachael led her down a hallway and opened a door. "You can stay in here tonight. It used to be Ari's bedroom, but he has his own home in Nesher, not far away."

Nothing about her surroundings registered. Anne dropped onto the bed before Rachael finished turning down the sheets.

✡ ✡ ✡

Rachael let Anne sleep while she prepared a light supper. She glanced now and then at the large suitcase and a smaller travel case--the extent of her belongings, Anne had told her. It looked as though she meant to stay for a mere week instead of moving to Israel to live.

She continued to cut up green onions, cucumbers and tomatoes while she thought about their conversation on the plane. Anne said she had only her grandparents after her mother and father had died, and that "they were not terribly close", as she had put it. Her husband died later in a fiery car crash. Anne thought both accidents seemed suspicious but couldn't prove anything. After that, she sold their house and belongings and applied for *Aliyah.* She appeared determined to start fresh in Israel. "I don't even want to look American," she'd said. "I want everything to be Jewish, including my clothes."

Rachael looked around at her own two-bedroom house. She had purchased it after Leon's death. Ari lived with her until he married Rani. Although Mount Carmel was considered an elite district, she had found this modestly priced house and liked the view. It was a welcomed change from the memories that lingered in their home in Gilo, a suburb of Jerusalem. She wondered if Anne had any idea of the cost of living on this side of the world and what it would take to furnish an apartment. It wouldn't be easy. Times were hard, not just with the economy, but with everything happening around them. The rocket attacks on southern Israel didn't help matters. There was talk of war with Iran. Rachael shuddered at all that would mean for her and her tiny country surrounded on all sides by Arab or Muslim nations. Had Anne taken any of this into consideration?

She added olive oil, lemon juice and spices to minced parsley and mint, along with the chopped vegetables. In a larger bowl, she lightly tossed the mixture together with cooked bulgur. Anne did mention that her parents had left her a sizable inheritance, and that her grandparents were quite wealthy. But, even with money enough to start over, she found it hard to imagine how the young woman would survive, since she was a stranger to the land and its language. *It will take more than just being frugal. It will take commitment. It will take…*

"Listen to yourself, Rachael." A quick taste of the *tabouli* had her adding more salt. "Such a worrier you are, and you have not even known her for a whole day. She is a grown woman, capable of making her own way. Look how she proved it today." She stirred the salad one more time, but when she turned to the table, she nearly dropped the dish.

Anne stood in the doorway of the kitchen and stretched, giving no indication she'd heard her soliloquy. "Sorry. Did I scare you?" She walked over and wrapped her in a hug, an endearing gesture that touched Rachael's heart. "I'm glad you insisted on bringing me here. And something smells delicious. I'm starving."

Rachael grinned. "It is almost ready. Would you like to freshen up? Maybe a shower?"

"That would be nice," Anne admitted, "but I don't want to impose. You've done so much already."

"No, no, not a bother. I already took mine while you were sleeping. After all we have been through today, I wanted to feel clean again, you know?" She walked down the hall to the bathroom and opened the linen closet, where she pulled out a large bath towel and a washcloth.

Anne took them and kissed Rachael on the cheek. "Thank you."

That was it. In Rachael's mind, Ann had become more than a friend…she was like a daughter. She thought of Ari on her way back to the kitchen and clasped her hands together. *Who knew?*

✡ ✡ ✡

Ari paced in his bedroom after receiving a report from Intelligence on Anne Sheridan. He regretted over and over having handed her into his mother's care at the airport.

I should have known better. His mother would adopt a terrorist if she thought that feeding him and giving him a place to stay would change his ways. He had a hard time thinking along those lines. *It is not enough that they chant our demise, but they manipulate the media and gain the world's approval and sympathy. How do we fight people like that and win?*

He picked up the picture frame on the dresser and ran his hand over the photo of his family. His father, his older brother, and his younger sister… gone. He missed them. *Arab terrorists and their random acts of murder. They do not care who they kill as long as they are Jews or Christians. If innocent Arab civilians could somehow separate themselves and be free from their dictates, maybe the world's aid would actually fund desperately needed supplies, instead of more weapons for war.*

His thoughts continued down the same path as he turned over the picture of his wife, Rani. Feelings of loneliness and grief washed over him as he thought back two years when he had come home after spending weeks in intensive undercover training. She had wanted him to go with her to the market, but all he wanted was to relax. "I will not be long then," she told him and kissed him goodbye.

Twenty minutes later he heard the blast and ran in a panic toward the market area. The dread in his heart mounted as he fought his way through the blood-splattered madness of sirens and screams--the carnage nearly more than he could bear. And then he saw her. In the midst of it all, Rani gasped for air and twitched in agony beneath two other mangled bodies.

Ari fought the memory of holding her torn and shredded body as she died in his arms. His feelings had teetered on the edge of bitterness, with despair not far behind. It had taken a determined will for him to go on with his life. Being involved in Intelligence kept him focused on defeating his enemies to the point where nothing else mattered. *I know you would not approve if you were here, my love, but it is what I have to do.* He closed his eyes and kissed her picture, before placing it face down on the dresser.

He grabbed his jacket then and headed for the door. Like it or not, he had to have a talk with his mother before this matter with Anne Sheridan got out of hand.

✡ ✡ ✡

Anne pushed the *tabouli* onto the flat whole grain bread with her fork and took a bite. "Ahh, real Mediterranean food." She savored the mouthful and closed her eyes in an effort to make the moment last.

A dish of sliced avocados drizzled with limejuice, along with another dish of olives, sat by her plate. A bowl of figs, dates, and pomegranates perched at the edge of the counter not far from the table. She eyed the bowl of chicken and grape salad and reached for another pita.

"It's as if I was meant to live here," she sighed. "Thank you for fixing my favorite salad."

Rachael laughed out loud. "I am feeling you *were* meant to live here, child. And you are welcome. Sophia, my sister in Chicago, makes it for me when I visit. I am glad it is your favorite as well."

"Do you visit often? "

"Ken. I mean, yes. You may notice the more I am around you, the better is my English. It happens when I am in America with Sophie, too. I visit her every year for a whole month. Before I retired, it was a nice vacation away from teaching.

"How often does your sister come here to visit you?"

Rachael sat down and dished up some *tabouli*, the sorrow in her eyes evident when she answered, "Not very. She moves to Chicago when she was young and, um, impressionable. Her views, shaped over the years, have become biased."

Anne took a drink of water and cleared her throat. "My mother spoke of self-loathing Jews who have a liberal viewpoint of Israelis and the way they deal with Arabs. It seemed to bother her, but she never would say why."

"I guess that is how you might say it. Sophie thinks we have changed, we are aggressive, oppressive. She will not come back, so I must visit to her, if I want to see her. I do not think she would feel that way if she lived here all this time, but she listens to news, and they paint slanted picture of the so-called Palestinians' plight." She folded her hands in front of her and shook her head. "And my Sophie has a very much soft heart."

"Not all American Jews think that way...I don't."

"No, but enough do. They make a difference, you know? Newspapers and magazines buy up the lies about their own people and print it as truth."

Anne reached over and touched the back of Rachael's hands. "They sound like some of the Jews who were carried away to Babylon. After living in exile for seventy years, they were too established and comfortable to want to move back to Israel and help rebuild Jerusalem and the Temple. They had no connection to their birthplace. And didn't the same thing happen with the Israelites when they fled Egypt in the first place? They found themselves in the wilderness and suddenly, all they could think about was the food and stability they once had, even though they were oppressed. There are some who can't seem to grasp an understanding of God and His higher purpose. This land doesn't mean anything to them. It is just a place that is a stigma and casts a bad light on them. They can only see what's going on through humanistic eyes."

Rachael turned her hands over and grasped Anne's. The tears that threatened in her eyes now twinkled "You give me hope, Anne. Maybe you should write for the newspapers here."

"You mean the ones that aren't liberal?"

"Indeed." Rachael's joy soured into a wry smile. "You see the irony. I guess they are just as bad, *nu?*" She let go of Anne's hands and took a bite of salad.

Anne thought about the direction their conversation was taking and ventured an observation, "You said, so-called Palestinians..."

Rachael lowered her fork and cocked her head. "You do not know? They were never calling themselves Palestinians before the '67 war. The Romans called our land Palestine. Everyone living here is a Palestinian before we become a state. Syrians, Lebanese, Iraqis, Jordanians. Jordanians…such a joke. The British gave them our land west of the Jordan River, and suddenly Arabs become Jordanians. It is a, what you call a political tool, a myth to make legitimate their claim to our homeland. I know. I was not just teaching history, Anne. I lived here when an Arab was an Arab. Even the few who stayed here after we became a state did not call themselves Palestinians until Arafat makes it so."

"I guess I did read something along those lines. It's just that everyone calls them Palestinians now."

"And so you see how the myth is simply lies the media makes into Arabic truth. They had nothing here but scattered villages until Jews bought waste land, cleared swamps, built cities, planted trees and crops, and the Almighty made the desert to bloom. All that before we became a nation. Look what we have done since. Now all of a sudden they claim the land and we are called, called "occupiers". G-d forbid. But the world believes them. The world believes the lies."

The pain in her eyes made Anne sorry she had asked. Rachael looked embarrassed then. "Listen to me going on. You must wish we talked about something else, eh?"

"I don't mind. I researched all of this, but hearing it from someone who lives here puts a whole new light on it. I feel bad asking questions, though, if it upsets you."

"You can ask questions, all you want," Rachael said, waving her hand in the air. "And if I get excited too much, you can stop me, *nu?*"

They both laughed. Anne decided to take her challenge. "So…what about dividing Jerusalem?"

"*Feh!*" Rachael scoffed. "Do you know Mohammed turned his back on Jerusalem and commanded his followers to do the same? They pray toward Mecca with their backs to Jerusalem. Never was it a holy site to them. They desecrate our Holy Temple with their mosque to um, to humiliate us when they conquered the land."

She slammed her hand on the table. "We should have razed it to the ground when our soldiers took back the Old City in the '67 war. Some wanted to, but their commander negotiated with the Muslims. Once again the land and Holy Temple mean nothing to him or our leaders, and we have now the problems you see. East Jerusalem is a, a neglected, ruinous slum when we get it back. That is how much Muslims cared when they had control."

She pressed her hands to her face and sighed. " Oh, Anne, I am sorry," she apologized. "You must think I am not liking Arabs. I have Arab friends. It is their leaders who demonstrate to us they do not want peace. Nothing we give them will be enough…they simply want to be destroying us."

Anne scooted grapes and chunks of chicken back and forth with her fork. A door for sharing about *Yeshua* as Messiah begged to be opened, but she didn't know Rachael's heart well enough to know if she would hear and understand. She sat in silent contemplation until a sharp rap at the door made them both jump.

✡ ✡ ✡

Rachael shook off the sadness that had come over her and answered the door. When she saw her son, she greeted him with a motherly hug. "Come in. You are just in time to eat with us."

Ari grabbed her arm. "I did not come to eat, *Ima*. I need to talk to you. It is very important."

Rachael removed his hand and playfully cuffed his face, "Pfoo, pfoo, what can be so important that you cannot eat with us, eh?"

When he opened his mouth to speak again, she put a finger to his lips and nodded her head toward the kitchen area. She lowered her voice, "You know Anne is here, Ari. Do not be rude. Be careful what you say."

"And you know I would not have come over unless it was important."

"Anne is my guest," Rachael insisted. "This is not a good time. Just come in and have something to eat with us."

When he hesitated, she took him by the arm and steered him around a partition of solid wood panels, which separated the kitchen from the entry. She saw Anne take a quick drink of water and slosh it around her mouth before she lowered her hands into her lap. *Oy, that bulgur…it has such a habit of clinging to teeth.* Rachael smiled at the emotional current in her kitchen--so palpable. It was just as she had suspected. Whatever was so important to Ari would have to wait.

✡ ✡ ✡

Ari took one look at Anne, wearing a tank top under a long sundress, and nearly forgot why he'd come over. Even with her hair wrapped up in a towel, she was beautiful. Her cheeks colored when she saw him, and she seemed nervous. Feeling awkward all of a sudden, he cleared his throat. "Mrs. Sheridan."

"Major."

It was obvious his mother didn't miss a thing. She smiled as she pointed to the chair across from Anne, and Ari knew exactly what she was thinking. He'd heard her say it too many times: "*If those two were not made for each other like Adam and Eve, I know nothing about love.*"

Since Rani's death, she had been on the look out for another woman for him, even though he insisted he never wanted to marry again. She was not a real matchmaker, but she always said she knew him better than anyone. Not that she did. Still, she was his mother, and he simply stopped arguing with her for the sake of keeping the peace. Better her than a professional *Yenta*. G-d forbid.

He sat down and looked at the food, glad that she had offered again. He decided to wait until after they were done eating to talk to her.

Rachael got another plate and silverware and set them before him. "Eat, Ari. We do not get to be together as often as we should like, *nu?*" She filled his glass. He saw her wink at Anne and groaned inwardly.

While his mother made small talk about their earlier conversation about Palestinians, he ventured a sideways glance at Anne. Their eyes met, and he had a feeling she was analyzing him.

What are you thinking? Why are you really here? His questions were answered when Anne suddenly stood and excused herself, saying she needed to write down what had happened earlier, before she forgot the details. She emphasized the last part and avoided his stare. *So that is it. You are holding a grudge.*

When his mother scooted her chair back, Ari placed his hand firmly on her arm and frowned. Rachael remained seated and told Anne to call if she needed anything.

Anne's jaw flexed before she smiled sweetly at his mother. "Thank you, Rachael."

She looked him in the eye, "Major."

He merely nodded. It wasn't a secret that she blamed him for the outcome of the hijacking, but there was nothing he could do about it now. She didn't understand. He watched her disappear into his old bedroom. Why it made him uncomfortable, he wasn't sure, but he had a hard time brushing away the image of her sleeping in his old bed.

He turned to his mother. The disapproval on Rachael's face clearly showed her frustration with this turn of events. Ari leaned closer, "*Ima*, it is dangerous for you to get involved with Mrs. Sheridan right now."

When she started to protest, he held up his hand. "I cannot explain. Keep your contact with her minimal, by phone preferably, if you can. Try not to cause any suspicion on her part."

Rachael's eyes grew misty. Ari leaned over and kissed her cheek. He whispered in her ear, "Please trust me. You know me. I would not tell you this unless it was serious. Develop a headache tomorrow. I will come over and take Mrs. Sheridan to her apartment."

Ari waited for her response, which didn't come. She certainly knew how to make him feel guilty. He squeezed her hand. "It will be all right. Soon, I hope." He kissed her cheek again. Still, she said nothing.

When he stood, she motioned toward the food. "You did not eat so much."

That was more like his *Ima*. He stuffed chicken salad into a pita pocket and headed out the door.

✡ ✡ ✡

While listening to Rachael's chatter, Anne had watched Ari down the chicken salad and tabouli as though eating his last meal. Definitely a bachelor, she had surmised, but she wondered why such a good-looking man would be unmarried? His dark eyes, framed by long black lashes and perfectly formed eyebrows, captivated her. Tan, lean, strong, it seemed odd that he would be single. Then she remembered their first encounter and smugly concluded he probably couldn't get along with a woman long enough to form a relationship.

Scenes from the incident on the plane surfaced then, and any enchantment she had earlier about his good looks dissipated when she thought about what he had done. She had never formed much of an opinion about the Arabs who lived in and around Israel before that day. Her initiation into the conflict left her unsettled. The anger and hatred shown by both sides shook her to the core of her being. *Yeshua's* words in Matthew about hate translating to murder made her realize just how much His teachings were needed here. She ignored a gentle nudge by the Holy Spirit about her feelings toward Ari, and justified them as righteous indignation.

With that settled, she unzipped her leather purse containing her small laptop and journaling material. She sat on the bed and recalled the ordeal on the plane and the scene later at the airport. It was something she wished she could erase from her memory. At the same time, she didn't want to forget any of it. Parts of it already seemed muddled and confused.

After she opened her computer, she paused for a minute and glanced at the icon her late husband had placed there the night before his fateful accident. It was a mystery she desperately wanted to solve, but she hadn't figured out the password yet. *Do I really want to know what secrets you locked away, Daniel?*

She stared at it for a second before shaking free from her thoughts. She guided the pointer away and brought up her Word documents. But instead of starting a new page, she looked around the bedroom. Until now, she hadn't paid much attention to her surroundings. Was she slipping? Her heart said "no".

It's because I trust you, Rachael. The thought brought on a smile. It had been a long time since she had allowed herself the luxury of trusting anyone. She drew in a deep breath and simply enjoyed Rachael's decorating scheme. Pale lavender walls emitted a calming sensation. She ran her hand across the satiny bedspread with stripes in deeper shades of lavender. Embroidered violets scampered across the tops of the pillow shams, and a single picture of a waterfall with wild flowers in the foreground, graced the wall. Simple and efficient, yet it all reflected Rachael's loving care. Anne let out a contented sigh. *"Thank you, Aba, for this blessing."*

Her eyes rested on her computer and she remembered why she had opened it. She typed what had happened during the flight and then stopped. The sight of Rashad standing in the doorway of the plane and nodding to someone beyond her before the turn of events came to mind. The only one behind her was Major Milchan with his forces. Her imagination would have run with it, but Rachael knocked just then.

"Anne, do you need anything?"

She got up and opened the door. A quick peek toward the kitchen revealed empty chairs. "Your son left already?"

Rachael cleared her throat as though she would answer, but simply nodded. After what she had seen at the table, Anne surmised there hadn't been an amiable parting between the two of them. She shut her computer lid and slipped her arm around Rachael. "Then you need some company, *nu?* Got any chicken salad left?"

The next day, Rachael sat on the couch with a splitting headache. It was after Ari had called. She told Anne he was on his way over to take her to her apartment.

Anne scowled. *I don't think so, Major.* She didn't mention she had other plans.

Rachael patted her hand. "Would you get the morning paper for me, Anne?"

Pictures from the hijacking dominated the front page. Rachael read it to her and said it talked about her involvement and stated that her efforts had, in fact, focused the government's attention on the impoverished village with the promise that food and medical supplies would be delivered after all.

Cheered that something good had come of the incident, Anne cleaned up the kitchen and did breakfast dishes in spite of Rachael's protests. "It's the least I can do for all your help and hospitality," she insisted.

As soon as she finished, she sat on the couch beside the older woman who looked pale. Anne took her hand. "Is there anything else I can do before your son gets here?"

Rachael shook her head. "Just be safe. You will be all alone, and I will not be there to help you."

Anne smiled at her maternal ways, "I'll have my friends help me. I just have to call them and see when they can drive over."

"Why did you not want to find a place close to them in Jerusalem? Is it because of your mother living here?"

"No." She thought about what had drawn her to Haifa. "I love the water. The beaches and hillsides are more interesting to me than being in a big city. But there is something else, something I can't put my finger on. I think there is a reason for me being here, one I hope to discover as I get acquainted with the area."

They heard a knock at the door. "It is probably Ari," Rachael said. "Could you please turn off the light? It is bothering my eyes."

Anne gave her friend a hug. "*Shalom*, my dear Rachael. Thank you for being so much like a mother to me. I'll call when I get settled."

Rachael placed a hand over her eyes. Anne turned off the light, but not before she saw a tear slide down her cheek.

Ari had let himself in and walked past her to look in on his mother. He kissed her forehead and whispered something, but she waved him on. Anne watched with interest. There was a definite bond of love between them. *At least he's capable of feelings.*

Out in the kitchen, Ari reached for her bags, but she got to them first. "I'm not helpless."

"So I have noticed." He looked as if he wanted to slam the door. Anne held her breath, but he let it close on its own.

She marched past him and put her bags on the back seat. "You can take me to a car rental agency," she informed him. "I'll find my own way home." *No way are you going to know where I live.*

Ari let the trunk lid fall. Anne braced herself when he walked over and put his hand against the door. His face nearly touched hers, revealing the anger in his eyes. "You can despise me all you want, Mrs. Sheridan. You and all the rest of your meddling American friends who know nothing about what is going on over here."

Anne's hand connected with his face hard enough to leave her shaking. Ari clenched his jaw and turned away. He got in the driver's side and took off before she could close the door. She hung on, shocked at the sudden outburst that went against all she believed, but she jerked on the door until it latched and bit down hard on her lip.

Neither of them said a word the short distance to the small rental building. Ari made no attempt to help with the bags and drove off as soon as she set them down on the sidewalk. He never heard her pathetic attempt at an apology. A lump formed in her throat and she blinked back tears when the owner came out speaking Hebrew.

✡ ✡ ✡

Ari had Anne's apartment watched day and night. Her friends, Phil and Martha, drove up from Jerusalem to help her find furniture. They made trips to the market and grocery stores, trips to the Grand Kenyon, one of Haifa's largest malls. She stayed in Jerusalem with them and visited Ein Karem. It mattered little where she went. He made sure eyes watched and reported on her every move. So far, he saw nothing of a suspicious nature in anything she did. He was beginning to think there was no basis for the Mossad chatter about her.

Summer lingered. Another month and *Rosh HaShana* would be upon them. He stopped in to see his mother and find out if she had heard anything new. She greeted him with a smile and the wave of a doughy hand. "Coffee's hot," she offered.

He grabbed a cup. "So. How is Miss High and Mighty?"

"Ari!" Rachael turned back to the floured mass on the counter. "Have you no shame? Where is your compassion?"

"Compassion? Oh, *Ima*, really."

She picked up the rolling pin and faced him. Ari looked at her face and then at the wooden cylinder, poised in the air, ready to connect with her free hand. He waited for the smack. It didn't come. This was more serious than he thought. Stepping away, he backed up to the table and sat down. While she stood there, he studied her features. She stayed in shape, which made her look younger than most women who were in their late fifties. Her now graying hair curled softly around her face, but he did notice more lines forming at the corners of her eyes. She called them laughing wrinkles. *I wish you were laughing now.*

Rachael lowered the rolling pin and placed it on the counter as Ari stared. With a deep sigh, she wiped her hands on her apron and joined him at the table. "Anne calls me everyday to let me know how she is doing. Everyday she drives to the beach and walks along the shore. The whole day, Ari, like you used to do."

He sipped his coffee and conjured up the mental image of Anne he had gotten used to seeing. "You sure do make good coffee, *Ima*." The rolling pin would be making a loud noise for sure if she found out he had Anne under constant surveillance and already knew everywhere she went.

His mother sighed again and slowly stood, never taking her eyes off him.

"*Ima*, I..."

"Ari," she interrupted. "She is hurting, and she is lonely. This is her land, her heritage, and yet she feels like a stranger. She told me the Arab on the plane had been gentle and kind when he tended to his brother. That he had admired her willingness to lay aside the animosity between our two people by putting her life at risk to help. You, I am afraid, have not been so kind."

Ari's fist came down on the table. Coffee spilled over the edge of the rocking cup. "What do you expect? She is not from here, not a part of this. She has no idea what these butchers get away with. She is, she is an American!"

"She is a Jew!"

"Fine, *Ima*!"

"Ari," Rachael sat down again with her hands folded in front of her. Tiny bits of dough fell to the tablecloth as she rubbed her thumbs together. "She is no *meshugeneh*. She told me she was coming here to write about the IDF and terrorism."

Ari acted surprised as he leaned forward and covered her hands with his, "She is a journalist?"

"No, she said she was doing research for a novel she is writing. I think it has something to do with the deaths in her family. She has not had an easy life, you know."

He relaxed and picked up his cup to take another drink. Over the rim he saw his mother still watching him. *You are not through with this, are you?*

"So?" He said it slowly.

"So, she is intrigued with danger and is a romantic."

Ari chewed on this new bit of information about Anne. His mother had never been wrong about a person. With all of his research, he had felt confident in his assessment of the woman. Now he wasn't so sure.

Rachael stood again. "I am afraid for her. She says to me she feels like she is being watched."

"Hmmm." He finished his coffee and scooted away from the table. "What is it you want me to do? She is stubborn and independent. She would be furious if she found out I was checking up on her."

"Talk to her then. It might make her feel better to know you are concerned. Maybe she will open up to you."

"You know I have tried talking to her already," he scoffed. "All it got me was a slap across my face."

"So try harder, *nu*?" Rachael tended to her dough after he kissed her goodbye on the cheek and called after him, "And this time, do not get so close."

✡ ✡ ✡

Rashad ran his hand over the metal shape beneath his shirt and searched the darkness. He hated waiting. It had been six weeks since he had been transferred to the jail. He stared into the black night through the bars and replayed the incident on the plane. Anne's features flooded his mind. Everything about her reminded him of someone, but the sound of keys unlocking his door stopped his thoughts.

"Ari! Finally." The two men embraced. Rashad held his friend away from him. "Have you found out anything more about Anne Sheridan? You are still keeping an eye on her, right?"

"Of course."

"Well? How is she doing?"

He watched Ari's face. The answer was apparent, and he took a secret delight in thinking about the fiery green-eyed beauty standing up to the major. "She is a handful, is she not?" His chuckle didn't seem to improve the major's mood. Anne had nearly botched their attempt to catch the traitor who had allowed them to smuggle weapons on board the plane that day. It was his fault. Something about her had urged him to allow her to be a part of their plan. Despite the fact that they had to improvise, they still had pulled it off. The Palestinians hailed Rashad and his brother as heroes. Khalid had miraculously healed from the gunshot wounds with no complications. Now they could implement the second phase of their mission...going undercover for the IDF and Mossad deep in Hamas territory.

Ari hit him over the head with an envelope. They both sobered when he removed his beret and sat down. "This is getting more complicated by the day, Rasha. You do not have to take this assignment." He handed the envelope to him.

Only Khalid and Ari called him Rasha, and only when the situation was serious. Rashad opened the official documents. His breath escaped through his teeth in a hissing sound as he read. He thought for a moment before answering, and then he tapped Ari on the arm with the orders. "But this is why I am here, is it not? Besides, I have an obligation now. It has become a family matter, and I am next of kin."

Their eyes locked. Ari rubbed his hand across the back of his neck. "I am not understanding."

Rashad held the paper out and underlined a sentence with his finger. He stopped when he came to an Arab's name. "He is my mother's brother." He watched the connection sink in.

Ari shook his head. "Unbelievable." He looked at Rashad. "I am not comfortable about the methods we will have to employ in order to accomplish this. I would hate to see anyone in your family get hurt."

Rashad didn't have to be told how dangerous it was for everyone involved. "It will not be easy, but we must go through with it. You know this as well as I do."

"I guess so." Although Ari agreed, there was a pained look in his eyes that Rashad knew all too well. When he stood, the two friends embraced again. "We have the word out that you and Khalid are being moved...be ready tonight." He adjusted his beret and paused before leaving, "Make it look good."

Rashad acknowledged with a salute. "And you, my friend, guard your heart," he whispered after Ari was outside.

Rashad took up his watch at the bars again. He wanted to give in to the emotions he had suppressed when seeing his family's name on the orders. His training told him to keep them locked away for the time being. He trusted his life and the lives of the remaining members of his family into God's care and keeping. There were no coincidences, his grandparents had always told him. Everything happens for a reason. They had taught him and Khalid about Jesus at an early age. Thanks to them, this latest development would simply be a greater exercise of his faith.

Something moved in the dark. Rashad felt for his gun and took a deep breath

Chapter Five

Anne kicked off her sandals and stood on the Haifa beach, watching the seagulls circling overhead. She tossed pieces of her bagel out onto the sand and waited for the shrieks. The birds, anticipating a hand out, sailed in and dove for the tidbits. Amid the ruckus, a lone juvenile caught her attention. He stood to the side, the wind ruffling the down on his spotted breast.

She tore off several more chunks from the bagel and threw them into the mêlée, keeping one back, which she slyly pitched to the loner. He grabbed it up and took flight to avoid the scolding and pecking of his superiors over his insolence. "Yeah, I totally know how you feel, Buddy." She ripped up the rest of the bread and hurled it at the squabbling birds.

"Bad bagel?"

Anne's hand flew to her neck. She whirled around and faced Ari Milchan. A number of replies crowded into her mind, but she left them there, bouncing around and slamming into each other, while she eyed him in silence.

Ari held up his hands and backed up a step. "Anne, I think we… I mean, I would like to talk to you. I realize we got off to a bad start and my mother thinks…"

"You're back peddling, Major."

"Back peddling?"

"Spinning your wheels." Anne brushed the crumbs from her hands. She looked at him then and shook her head. "You don't have a clue, do you?"

Ari said nothing. Anne wasn't sure if his look of ignorance was feigned or real. She stooped to pick up her sandals. "What do you want to talk to me about, Mr. Milchan?" Her attitude shocked her conscience into action, but she ignored it.

"Mr. Milchan?" Ari mumbled. "Seems a bit formal. Are you not comfortable calling me by my first name?" He followed her to a bench.

She set her sandals down between them and turned to face him, "You are not a comfortable man to be around."

"That is harsh."

"But you aren't disputing it."

"No," he agreed. "I guess not."

Anne squinted. Was he trying to make her feel guilty?

Ari looked away and they both watched the waves snatching pockets of sand, taking them out to sea and then depositing what was left on the next venture in to the beach. The mesmerizing motion added more wrinkles in the sand at the edge of the water.

The major seemed far away in his thoughts. Anne eyed him with guarded interest. Maybe she had misjudged him. He was, after all, protecting his people. Still. She examined her fingernails and brushed sand from the cuticles.

"I…I know why you come here." The Major's voice, hesitant, almost timid, was bantered about by the wind. "These are the same waves I have stared at time and again, trying to make sense of life and the brutal slaying of my wife."

"What?" She had heard him, but was taken back by his statement. His look pierced her heart.

"This was the only place where I could get away and think. The solitude was comforting, as odd as that sounds. It did not mock me. It just listened. Listened while I cried, ranted and raved, cursed and spit out all of my frustrations."

Anne's lower lip trembled. She felt the familiar sting in the corner of her eyes, but she sat motionless, not wanting to disturb the moment. Would he tell her more?

He stared at her for a moment before speaking again. "Your eyes are beautiful, like the ocean. So different from the warm brown of… She died in my arms, you know? My wife, Rani."

Anne couldn't move.

"It took me a long time to acknowledge it was her blood soaking into my shirt. I just held her, not wanting to let her go. This was the only place that made sense to me afterwards…the waves coming and going, stealing the sand and bringing it back in a kind of rhythmic give and take. The constant lapping eventually wore down my anger, the same way it wears down and changes the shoreline."

The anguish showed in his face. Anne touched her neck where it tickled and saw wet spots on her fingers. She turned away and closed her eyes, breaking the spell.

He stood then. "Would you mind walking with me?"

She did mind, but he had aroused her curiosity. Besides, he held a wealth of information that she needed. She didn't see any problem using him the way he had used her. She brushed away the guilt about having such thoughts and picked up her sandals.

They walked quietly together until he broke the silence, "You do not say much."

"You are the one who came here wanting to talk."

He stopped and faced her. "You are still that angry with me?"

It was hard to come up with an answer. Anne couldn't believe he didn't get it. She looked down.

He spoke again when she didn't respond, "I am beginning to wonder if you need to slap me again before we can become friends? I can take that a little easier than talking to myself."

Anne sucked in her breath and let it out slowly. "What do you want from me? My forgiveness? What you did with those Arabs, or Palestinians, or whatever you want to call them, was despicable."

"I know. You have already made your feelings clear on that. And yes, I do want your forgiveness."

"You used me!"

"I did not know you then. You were just a meddling American who was interfering with a serious situation."

"I am a Jew. A Jew!"

"I know that now, Anne. I am sorry. I do not know what else to say. There are things you cannot understand. And for your own safety, I am not able to offer you any more of an explanation."

Anne's throat tightened. She bit down hard on her lower lip. Ari's nearness, his willingness to make things right made it tempting to let down her guard. Yet, she still didn't trust him. She looked at the waves and relived their last time together when her hand had connected with his cheek. "Slapping your face before didn't seem to elicit your friendship. What makes you think it will now?"

Ari threw up his hands.

Ann shifted her sandals to her other hand. "Look, just what is it you wanted to talk to me about?"

"You know what? Forget it. Not a thing." He turned and walked away. "Go ahead and hold your petty little grudge, Mrs. Sheridan, but you had better be on guard…this land is no fairytale!"

"You're telling me!" Anne dropped her sandals and slipped them on before she started down the beach. After a few minutes, she picked up her pace. She refused to look behind to see if Ari was still standing there. She didn't care.

✡ ✡ ✡

A lone figure leaned against the corner of a small café, on Dado Beach, chatting casually with the owner while he kept his eye on the woman just down the way. He bought a drink and took it to the nearest table.

The sun played with the thin clouds overhead and teased the sweat from his face. He gulped down his cold juice and crossed his legs before retrieving a bag of crackers from his coat pocket.

Relaxing with his back against the table, he broke the crackers into small pieces and tossed them to the eager shore birds, while he watched the woman he had been sent to keep an eye on. Someone approached her then, and he sat forward and took notice. He wished now that he had chosen a different table so he could hear what they were saying. Considering who they were, it could be valuable information. *And the more valuable the information, the greater the reward for me.*

He hesitated. Moving closer would put him in an awkward position. He watched the two of them walk away in opposite directions, obviously not happy with each other. Disappointed, he dumped the rest of the crackers on the ground and stuffed the bag back into his pocket.

He stepped aside to watch the mob of gulls descend on the free meal. Their squabbling made him weigh the consequences of his decisions of late. He had once valued loyalty over wealth, but one bombing had changed his life and his allegiance. It didn't matter that the people he worked for had warranted reasons for their retaliation. Some day they would know how much pain those actions had inflicted upon him, and they would pay.

I have nothing now, he thought, in an effort to appease his conflicted conscience. *I have lost everyone I ever loved. And no one cares, so why should I?*

With his head down, he flicked his cigarette into the sand and hurried to his car. His contact would hear of this meeting right away and pay him well no doubt, even without knowing what the conversation was between the two of them.

What he did now was deceitful, but it was the nature of his work. At least he still had work.

✡ ✡ ✡

Ari walked for a ways before he turned to watch Anne stride down the beach. Suddenly he thought of a million things he wanted to say to her, but she broke into a run. She'd never hear him now above the wind. He kicked at the sand on his way to the parking lot.

There was something about her that wouldn't let him push her aside. She wasn't just another case to be taken care of and filed away. Part of him wanted to be near her, wanted to break down the wall between them, wanted her to know and understand him, but every time they had come together, it had ended badly. A sigh of regret escaped his lips. He made the mistake, however, of going over their meeting word by word. By the time he reached his car, he was furious again for thinking he could get through to her.

His Rani had never been so stubborn…at least, not that often. She had been headstrong, yet there had never been the tension between them that he felt whenever he was around Anne. He pictured his wife, a dark skinned beauty, whose natural coloring didn't need the sun to enhance it, but his thoughts stayed on Anne.

He had seen her tear escape, and followed its path to her suntanned neck. Her skin glowed, radiant and soft, enhanced by the beautiful *Magen David*. He blinked away the image, wondering why he was once again comparing Anne to his dead wife.

Rani had been so alive and Jewish, her love for the land so intense and devoutly patriotic. Her passion for the *Tanach* kept him on his toes and careful to observe all the holidays, even when he wasn't home to celebrate them with her. She made *Shabbat* special with her quirky habit of decorating as though the Rabbi from Jerusalem was going to stop in at any moment. He teased her about it, but he loved her for all her effort and creativity.

You may live here now, but just how Jewish are you, Anne? Thoughts about her spun around in his mind as he headed for home. At one point, he pounded the steering wheel, unable to pin down what it was about Anne Sheridan that drove him crazy.

✡ ✡ ✡

The dark narrow streets of Old Jerusalem teemed with crowds, jostling their way to separate destinations, but Achmed, an Israeli Arab, slipped through the throngs like an invisible figure from the past. When he reached a small tobacco shop, he hesitated for a moment to scan the people milling around. As soon as he entered the building, the owner escorted him to the back room. He hoped his information would give him direct access to one of the most feared Hamas leaders in the land. Then, maybe, it would be easier to decide his destiny.

"So, Achmed, you are sure of this? Major Milchan and Mrs. Sheridan? You saw the two of them together?"

"Yes, yes." The middle aged Arab tugged on his moustache. "This Mrs. Sheridan, she was alone at first, feeding the shore birds. Then, when the major walked up to her, they went over to a bench and sat down. She put her sandals between them. Very strange. I think it was meant to be a signal. They talked for awhile, and then he stood and she picked up her shoes and followed him for a ways."

"Could you hear what they were saying?"

"No, I tried to get closer, but they talked very quietly. Secretively, I am thinking. Though she did get excited when they parted. They acted as though they did not like each other. It was a cover up…of this I am sure."

"Hmmm." Atif, a tall Arab, robed in a traditional *thoub* and wearing a checkered *kaffiyeh*, reached into his pocket and pulled out several Nis. After handing them to his informant, he patted him on the back. "Well done, my friend, but more information will bring more compensation, and perhaps a visit to someone more important."

Achmed bowed low and backed out of the room. "May Allah bless you," he crooned. Though disappointed he would have to wait to meet the Hamas leader, he was more than happy with the transaction. He hurried away from the tobacco shop, contemplating his next move.

From his position across the street, he waited until he saw the robed figure slip through the side door into the alley. He tried to follow, but Atif disappeared without leaving a trace of his whereabouts. The informant slapped his Fedora against his linen trousers.

What are you doing? Whose side are you on? He put his hands to his head and tried to clear his mind. He had to decide soon, or he knew he would end up on the wrong side for the wrong reasons. Being an informant was dangerous business, especially if he wasn't really committed to what he believed.

What do I believe? He shook his head and headed back to Haifa to see if he could to find out more about Mrs. Sheridan.

Anne paced back and forth in her apartment. Pangs of hunger attacked her. She ignored them and rehearsed out loud everything she wished she would have said to Ari. When she came back around to the sofa, she flopped down and folded her arms. It was a waste of time to fret about him, she decided, but as she relaxed, her conscience left her feeling guilty. She thought through their meeting once more. *Why is it so hard to forgive you, Ari Milchan?*

She had spent the rest of the day at the beach, wandering along the shoreline in the welcomed silence. Now the apartment seemed too empty and quiet. She toyed with the idea of calling Rachael, but changed her mind. When her stomach growled again, she thought about the shops close to Ben Gurion Boulevard. Some of them stayed open late. She slipped a jacket on and walked to the café down the street.

Unrest in the Wadi Nisnas district with the Arabs, and a failed bombing attempt the week before, had security on high alert. Soldiers patrolled both sides of the streets in pairs with their rifles slung over their bulletproof vests. They had survived the rocket attacks by Lebanon in 2006, so this was nothing, Rachael had assured her. Keeping that in mind, Anne walked unafraid, breathing in the sights and sounds. Haifa at night took on the beauty of a controlled light show.

A group of uniformed guards gathered at a coffee cart. They seemed to be in good spirits, in spite of the tension in the air. She grinned when they raised their cups and greeted her in Hebrew, "*Shalom. Erev tov.*"

"*Shalom,*" she replied and thought, *I would love to have a good evening. At least something better than what happened this afternoon.*

The café was still open. She could see a small crowd gathered around outside. Her stomach complained, and she hurried toward the enticing aroma drifting out into the street. But before she got there, a young teenaged boy appeared from a side street and walked straight toward her. As he approached, he avoided eye contact. His hands shook when he grabbed at the front of his shirt. She looked back over her shoulder at the band of soldiers absorbed in a moment of camaraderie, and something warned her heart. "Terrorist!" she cried out.

Someone in the crowd yelled "*Mehabel,*" to the soldiers, and people panicked.

"Get back. Get back!" The confused youngster stopped. His hands trembled violently. He hesitated and looked around before he ripped open the front of his shirt.

"Explosives!" Anne's scream died away as a shot rang out, and the frail body slumped to the ground.

In the confusion of sirens and the crowd running in all directions, she rolled over and crawled to a street lamp. Darkness closed around her like a vise when she pulled herself up. Gasping for air, she kept her arms around the pole and doubled over. As soon the spasms passed, she ran for her apartment, while soldiers cordoned off a space around the body for the bomb squad to work.

✡ ✡ ✡

Ari Milchan stood at his kitchen window with a cup of coffee in his hand. He stared past his neighbor's homes in the Haifa subdivision of Nesher. As hard as he tried, he couldn't get Anne out of his thoughts. He called the agent watching her apartment and told him to take the night off. It wouldn't be the first time he had taken over the job of watching her through the night.

"Who am I kidding?" After the death of his wife, Ari asked to work with one of the IDF's intelligence units and vowed he would remain alone the rest of his life. Now the wall he had built around his heart had a breach in it. His training said to fix the opening fast before the gap got any wider, but the more he thought about Anne, the more he wasn't sure he wanted to seal it off.

If I could just get her to talk me. He had yet to gain her trust and get answers to the mysteries surrounding her late husband. The fact that his government was interested in her left him feeling uneasy. It was no secret that corruption started among those at the top and filtered down, which made it hard for him to know who to trust.

He lifted the coffee cup to his mouth and made a face. Had he been thinking about Anne that long? When his phone rang, he put it on speaker and took his cup to the sink.

"Major, there has been an incident near the Hashmura café in the Old German Colony on Ben Gurion. A would-be bomber was taken down before he could detonate himself."

"Anyone hurt?" Ari poured his lukewarm coffee down the drain and reached for his coffee pot. It was still hot.

"No, Sir. Soldiers there said a woman warned them and then disappeared."

"I am on my way." Ari filled his travel mug and grabbed his keys. He fired off orders to secure the area as he got in his car and backed out of his driveway.

"Yes, Sir. No, wait… two of the soldiers are saying the mysterious woman looked like Mrs. Sheridan."

Coffee sloshed over the edge of the mug and into the cup holder when Ari hit the brake pedal. "They are sure?"

"They seemed to be, Sir. She greeted some of them right before it happened as she headed toward the café."

The major leaned down to pick up the lid to the mug. "Lieutenant? Call Major Yitsak. I am stopping by Mrs. Sheridan's apartment. She may have gone back there."

"Yes, Sir."

Ari made sure the lid was on tight this time and switched to his headset before he pealed out of his driveway. As soon as he got to Anne's apartment, he screeched to a stop behind her jeep and jumped out of his car. He bounded up the steps and pounded on her door. When there was no answer, he ran around to the backdoor. It was locked.

His mind raced. She would have had time to get up the hill, but there was no sign of her anywhere. He checked the doors on her jeep and hit the handle. "Ah, Anne, what have you gotten yourself into now?" He threw up his hands and walked back to his car.

✡ ✡ ✡

Achmed waited in the dark across the street from Mrs. Sheridan's apartment. He had followed her home after the incident with the suicide bomber and had held back, staying out of sight until Major Milchan left.

Good thing too, he thought, as he hurried back to Jerusalem to relay his information. Working for both sides had gotten risky. When he reached the little tobacco shop, he ran in and nearly knocked the owner down. "Where is Atif?" He placed his hands on his knees and bent over to catch his breath.

The shopkeeper looked over his shoulder. "Where he always is."

Achmed hurried through the doorway into the back of the shop. He searched the dimly lit room and found Atif sitting at a table with two other Arabs. The informant shifted from one foot the other, wiping sweat from his face. His eyes gleamed with anticipation.

Atif rose from his chair and stood in front of him with his arms folded. "You have news?"

"Yes, yes! But you must hurry. Mrs. Sheridan just drove away, and she took a suitcase with her. A trip, I am thinking."

"Anything else, Achmed?"

"Major Milchan. He came to her house, but she would not answer the door. She waited until he was gone and then hurried away in the dark. I am thinking she does not trust him. Perhaps she has much to hide, eh? And the major," he continued, "he was clearly upset. Frantic, even. When he finds out she is gone, he will search for her, no doubt."

"Well done." Atif reached into his pocket. "Locate her. Jamar will want to know exactly what she is up to. But before you go, he wants to talk to you."

He pulled out his cell phone. There was an unmistakable look of warning on his face when he handed it to the informant.

Achmed wiped the sweat from his forehead again. He ran the back of his hand across his upper lip and coughed to clear his throat.

Chapter Six

"Major, Mrs. Sheridan has not been back here. I sent some men to search the side streets, but no one has seen her since this all happened."

Ari accepted a cup of coffee from the soldier and slumped against the café wall. His trained eyes, accustomed to the darkness, scanned the area. It was already cleaned up and back to normal. It was the Israeli way. They would never let anything, especially the senseless acts of terrorists, interfere with their way of life. Never again.

He sipped his coffee and tried to imagine where Anne would have gone. Had he been at her apartment, instead of wasting time thinking about her, he might have prevented her from going down town. Once again he had let his feelings get in the way of doing his job.

Ima… Maybe she was on her way to see his mother. He reached into his pocket for his phone, when he caught sight of a small light across the street in the alley. Three times, in measured succession, it blinked and then stopped.

Ari set his cup down on the small metal table next to the wall and walked toward the darkness, his hand tense at his side. A quick glance over his shoulder assured him there was back up if needed.

"Careful, Major," came a hushed voice. Ari recognized it at once. He relaxed his hand and slipped into the shadows.

Rashad put his penlight away. "She is gone."

"Were you here then?"

"Unfortunately. It happened too fast to avert. But I followed her home."

"I was just there."

"I know. She waited until you were gone, and then packed up the jeep and drove away. Someone else was lurking in the shadows, but they slipped away before I could get a good look."

"Probably my informant." Ari thought for a moment. "Packing means she plans to be gone for a while. She is running away. We met on the beach today and it did not go well. Then this..."

"Ari, I would alert the check points. She probably wants to get as far away as she can."

"Eilat."

"That would be my guess. Take care, my friend. This complicates matters even more, especially if someone else is on to her. Khalid and I are waiting to hear from Jamar...we might not be able to help out."

Ari grabbed Rashad's arm and pulled him into a strong embrace. "I know. Be careful, the both of you." As soon as he returned to the café, he sent out an alert and called his informant.

✡ ✡ ✡

A light haze framed the horizon and faded into the pale blue morning. While the concrete and roadside rushed by the open windows of her jeep, the world ahead advanced toward Anne in slow motion. She blinked rapidly to shake the heaviness pulling on her eyelids.

All at once the haze lifted, and the sleepy landscape came to life. A patch of green glowed, the sand sparkled, and her heart would have caught sight of her surroundings and wondered at the beauty of them, but for the relentless fear pursuing her.

She passed a few Bedouin shanties, visible now in the light of dawn, and a peculiar feeling gripped her heart. The enchantment of the landscape vanished.

A checkpoint appeared up ahead. "There is no escaping this," she groaned. She gripped the steering wheel when the soldier scanned her identification and papers and passed them to his counterpart. To her surprise, they merely exchanged glances, and allowed her through. She drove away with her heart pounding in her ears. Only when the roadblock grew smaller in the rear view mirror, did she breathe again.

She thought about Ari. Had she really fooled him last night? Once again guilt nagged at her conscience, and once again she wished she had driven straight to Haifa when she'd first landed in Israel. None of this would be happening. "Not that I can change things now," she argued out loud.

The sun, no longer shy, warmed her left shoulder. Anne reached for her hat. She glanced down at the map bouncing on the seat beside her and rested her hand on the folded paper, giving it a pat. The last thing she needed was to get lost out here. Signs appeared up ahead for Eilat and she relaxed. Oh, how she loved Israel. She had forgotten that all the major signs were in English and Arabic, as well as Hebrew

Eilat--the resort city of the south. It could have been an obscure village for all she cared...it was as far from Haifa as she could get on her own. The fact that it was her initial taste of Israel when she had first arrived from the States made it seem secure, somehow.

"So far, so good," she whispered into the wind. Her stomach growled, and the thought of food brought back scenes from the night before. She shook her head, trying not to remember, but the image of the scared young boy, crumpling to the ground, hit her hard.

As soon as she had reached her apartment, she leaned against the cupboards and slid to the floor, too sick and upset to even cry. Now her emotions surfaced and culminated in a flood of tears. "Abba, to see that young boy so conflicted."

She cried until her throat was too hoarse to utter another sound. From the day she had arrived in this land of her dreams gone awry, she had held back her feelings, hoping that things would get better. It felt good to get it all out now. She took a long drink from her water bottle. For now, she was just thankful Eilat was not too far away.

✡ ✡ ✡

Anne made herself breathe when the glistening white town, hugging the blue sea, came into view. It sat like a shining treasure at the end of a desert colored rainbow. She headed for a fueling station and filled up her jeep. On her way out, she grabbed a brochure and got her bearings. She couldn't wait to get settled into a nice quiet room.

It was early in the week with not much going on. She found the hotel she wanted and went inside. According to the brochure, the one she decided on claimed to have a panoramic view. She walked to the lobby doors and gazed out at the scene before her.

Palm trees huddled in groups and whispered ancient secrets. Serene waves caressed the shoreline, much to the delight of a kaleidoscopic rainbow of wind surfers. Then there was the sky. She focused on the line where the horizon and water fell into each other's arms in a lover's embrace of unimaginable blues, and turned to the desk clerk, "Panoramic is the best description you could come up with?" The young lady only smiled. Anne pushed the doors open and strolled outside for a better look.

From the moment she had arrived, the color of the surrounding mountains stayed in constant motion, changing from rose to deep purple to greenish gold at the slightest whim of the sun and clouds. *This isn't panoramic; this is breathless. And this is a much better location than what I had before.* She hugged herself and squished crystals of warm sand between her toes before she went back in to get settled.

As soon as she lowered her bags to the plush carpet, she secured the door to her room on the second floor and glanced around. "Nice," she whispered, congratulating herself. It was luxury in a big way.

"Of course it's nice," she said and laughed to herself. "I've picked the perfect hotel with a *panoramic view!*" Once again, thanks to her parents, Anne had more than enough money to cover her expenses. At times like this, she was definitely appreciative. She only used it for emergencies; the rest of the time, she lived off her own savings. This was one of her more urgent emergencies.

She drew back the curtains and opened the glass doors out onto the balcony, where she filled her lungs with the salty air. Suddenly tired, she flopped down on the plump cushions of a chaise lounge and closed her eyes. The cares of her first two months in Israel escaped with her sigh and took flight on the Mediterranean breeze.

She would have dozed, except she remembered grabbing mail on the way out of her apartment. It took a moment before she convinced her body to get up, but after she found what she was looking for, she returned to the comfortable recliner.

"Bill. Bill. Junk, already. What's this?" The rest of the mail fluttered to the deck as she held up an envelope and inspected the return address.

"Bethlehem?" Although addressed to her personally, she didn't recognize the handwriting. Anne tapped the envelope on its side and tore it open along the stamped edge. Two sheets of thin paper and a picture slid out into her hand. One look at the picture and she decided to take a walk on the beach.

✡ ✡ ✡

Anne stared at the letter in her hands. Angry and confused, she sat on top of a table, resting her feet on the bench. Nothing made sense. She couldn't believe her mother would have kept the truth from her. The letter remained in her hand and she tapped it against her thigh, keeping time to the sound of the waves.

What was it Ari had said? A kind of rhythmic give and take? She wondered what he would think of her now if he knew that she embodied everything he hated? A Jewish American Arab. She unfolded the paper and reread the letter from her father's parents.

"Dear Anne,

May you be well and safe. Please forgive that we must have someone else write for us this letter. It is a trusted friend who will keep it as secret as it has been kept from you all these years. You see, we have been silent on this matter, honoring the wishes of your mother's parents. But after reading of your heroic actions on the plane, we can no longer keep from you what you should know.

In 1973 our son, Yasir, visits in Chicago, America. That is where he met and fell in love with your mother, Yona. They might have been happy and stayed there, but she was a Jew, and her parents forbid she should see him.

Their love stayed strong--stronger than racial and religious rules forced upon them, and they eloped, coming to Haifa to marry. They spent two weeks in Eilat, happy and in love. Unfortunately, their happiness died too soon.

Three months later during the Yom Kippur War, the car they were driving came under gunfire and crashed. It killed your father. Your mother escaped, barely alive. David Sheridan, the man you have known as your father, drove by when it happened, and he risked his life to rescue her.

They were both of them taken to a hospital, and it was there she found out she is pregnant with you. Not wishing to be a burden to us, she moved in with family in Haifa and got a job. When David recovered from his wounds, he found her and they married.

What you do not know is Yona came for a visit to us before returning to America. You were one year of age and she wants us to see our grandchild, Yasir's daughter. She tells us also of fears she had about his death, fears that have us now worried about you.

We hope this will not be of a shock too much to you, and you will find in your heart a way to call us. The days here are filled with violence and danger, but we would risk a meeting just for a sight of you.

We have also more pictures of your mother and your father, Yasir.

We send this in our love, Anne
Namir and Qasim Yusha"

She stared at the picture again. Her father's dark, handsome features reminded her of someone, but she struggled with the images that came to mind. She folded the letter and placed it back into the envelope. *Another question*, she thought, disappointed that she seemed to be getting more of them instead of answers in her search for the truth.

Rachael nearly had her convinced she just imagined that someone always followed her. This new information gave her reason to believe it was true. Now she wondered if it had something to do with her real father. *There's one way to find out.* She placed the envelope in the pocket of her sundress. When the chance came, she disappeared into the midst of a group of sun worshippers and turned back to the hotel. She hugged the outside walls and hurried around the side and into the back without stopping.

Anne looked to make sure no one had followed her and ran up the stairs and down the hall to her room, She managed to smile at the couple walking toward her and got out her card. Once inside, she locked the door and leaned against it. Her alert eyes scanned the room.

With a silent prayer, she stooped and looked under the bed before creeping toward the bathroom. But she was so caught up in the suspicion and suspense of the moment that she forgot she had no way to defend herself.

Slowly she pushed the door open and waited. Nothing happened. She stuck her head in and glanced around. In a bold move, she pulled the shower door open, unmindful of the fact that she had her back to the room--a mistake she would never make again.

A clicking sound made her spin around. Her eyes fastened on the curtains hanging across the balcony doors. For a frantic moment she couldn't remember locking the doors. The handle clicked again. She dove for her phone on the bed and yelled, "This is an emergency; get me the police!"

She heard the sound of footsteps running across the balcony and threw back the curtains, just in time to see a head of dark curly hair disappear over the balcony. Shaken, she eyed the hotel phone on the dresser. The temptation to call the desk vanished once she weighed the consequences of having the military or police involved.

The ordeal left her weak-kneed. If the letter was true, and her real father was an Arab, he could just as well have been a terrorist or even a traitor. She had to call her grandparents, but not until she could find a way to lose her stalker. She packed her bags and waited for night.

✡ ✡ ✡

After Ari got confirmation of Anne's arrival, he made the necessary arrangements to catch a plane to Eilat the next day. The last time he'd taken any semblance of a leave had been for Rani's funeral. He prayed this wouldn't be for the same reasons.

The hour and fifteen minute long flight would get him there before noon. He hadn't heard from his informant since the night before. Hopefully he still had Anne under careful surveillance.

Once again, without his permission, his mind wandered to their first encounter. Although thoroughly annoyed at her insolence, he had secretly admired her tenacity and courage. She had been a little wild cat when he'd grabbed her and kept her from running back to the plane. Unafraid and willing to risk her life, her passion had kindled his own until he uncovered her true identity. The discovery left him in a personal quandary.

He looked out the window at the coastline fading away to desert hills and struggled to set aside his feelings in order to solve the mystery surrounding her. There was more at stake now than just national security.

His phone rang. It was *Ima*--the one person he didn't want to talk to just then. His mind argued; his heart won out. Ari did his best not to sound annoyed when he answered. As much as he loved his mother, she had a habit of calling at the wrong time about the wrong things. Today, however, she had his attention. "What about Anne?"

Chapter Seven

Ari hurried off the tarmac. A car pulled up beside him and stopped. He leaned his head in the passenger's side when he recognized the driver. "Biny? What are you doing here? Thought you were still in Europe?"

Binyamin Feldman, Ari's partner, patted the seat beside him. "Marni missed home. Shira and her fiancé asked us to come down here when we got back. They are in a panic about last minute details for their wedding. I tried to get a hold of you yesterday, but got a busy signal each time." He lifted his sunglasses and looked at Ari, "Your informant called. He told me you were on your way. That is how I knew you would be here. Said to tell you he has lost track of your Mrs. Sheridan."

"Lost her? She is a woman--an American who has never been in Israel before now; how can she just disappear the way she does?" He got in the car. "Besides, why did he call you? I have had my phone on."

Biny pushed his sunglasses down on his nose again, "Said he tried but could not get through. Probably when you were on the plane. Ari, have you lost your mind? What happened while I was gone?"

Ari drummed his fingers on the dash as he stared out the windshield. "It has gotten complicated. I do not expect you to understand, but I need to do this."

"Sounds like this is getting personal. And you know I do not trust this guy. You need to be careful."

"I just learned I cannot trust him either. This is why I am here. And it is more than personal, but right now I am going on a hunch. I need to do this,

Biny. I took a week off, and if I come back with the information I am after, General Elon will not think twice about how I did it."

Biny frowned. "What about Rashad and Khalid?"

"They are keeping me in the loop whenever they can call."

"Well, I hope for your sake you know what you are doing. We will be here the rest of the week if you need me."

Ari hit his friend on the shoulder before he got out of the car. "Not to worry. Give my love to Marni and Shira."

✡ ✡ ✡

After he found his rental car, Ari drove to a small building in the middle of a sandy parking lot on the east edge of town. Dov Stedman, the owner of Red Sea Jeep Safaris looked up when he opened the door. Ari held up his hand. "Stay where you are," he said.

Dov sat on the edge of a desk, swinging his good leg in time to some hidden tune in his head. "Ari, my old friend," he scoffed. "I can get around as well as you can." He stood and the two friends embraced. "What brings you to Eilat? You are too dedicated to your work to be taking time off for pleasure I think, eh?"

Ari laughed but didn't answer. Dov sat back down. His left leg had been badly injured in the second Intifada. After he had been dismissed from the army, time and prosthetics had given him a new lease on life. Eilat provided the perfect place to merge his love for photography and adventure. Pictures of his trips shared wall space with his framed photographs.

Ari looked around at some of the pictures of the Negev. "I see you still enjoy taking tourists on trips into the wilderness." He walked over to one particular photograph and stared at the haunting colors of the Red Sea at dusk. Venus nestled close to the crook of a silver crescent moon in a cerulean sky. "This was always Rani's favorite."

He turned to his former army buddy, "I need your help."

Dov stopped swinging his leg. "This sounds serious." He motioned to one of the chairs next to his desk. "Sit. Please."

Ari took a seat and ran his left hand along the back of his neck before he answered, "Remember Daniel Weis?"

Dov sucked in his cheeks and nodded.

"His wife is here, in Israel. Anne Sheridan? You may have read about her in the news."

"The name sounds familiar, but I am not following you, Ari."

Ari paused and thought about how best to tell him what he wanted to do without being too specific.

"Wait a minute." Dov squinted. "Do you mean Sheridan? As in David Sheridan's daughter? She married Daniel?"

"I am afraid so."

Dov let out a low whistle and grabbed his schedule. He thumbed through a couple of pages and looked up. "She booked a day tour for the day after tomorrow."

"I know." Ari sat forward, "Dov, I need a really big favor."

✡ ✡ ✡

Dressed in a Bedouin *medraqah*, the bronze skinned guide leaned his arms on a boulder, while he concentrated on the map spread out in front of him. He stroked his trimmed beard of three-days growth and pulled the *kaffiyeh* closer around his face.

So far the lovely woman walking his way had seemed preoccupied on the tour and had barely acknowledged him. That was fine, but he put his sunglasses back on, just in case. He didn't need any complications right now, and he knew she could prove to be a dangerous distraction should he let down his guard. Ignoring her, he lifted his water bottle to his lips and drank deeply when she stood next to him. He could see her shade her eyes as if to survey their surroundings.

"Beautiful view. Hamed, is it?"

The guide stopped drinking. He watched her turn around slowly and lean against the boulder. She kept her gaze on the others resting in the shade when she whispered, "Or is it, Ari?" She twisted her head slightly to look up at him.

"I do not know what..."

"Of course, you don't," Anne cut in, "and I'm not going to blow your cover, Major, but I want to know why you've had me under surveillance and why one of your men broke into my room."

The back of Ari's hand came across his mouth and he carefully replaced the cap, tucking the bottle into his pack. "You are treading on an adder's den, Anne Sheridan. Or, should I call you Mrs. Weis?"

Anne glared at him and fumbled with the chain holding her *Magen David*. "I want to know what's going on," she demanded.

"Careful, Anne. Keep your voice down. I had no idea your room was broken into, but it seems as though you have been keeping some secrets as well, true?"

Anne's cheeks colored. She let go of the pendant and shoved both of her hands into the pockets of her safari jacket. "It wasn't enough that your government had my husband killed. Now you try to pretend that you're protecting me?"

Ari nodded to Dov and leaned closer to Anne. "I said keep your voice down. I did not say protecting you, I said watching you. You have no idea what is going on, and you certainly are not making it easy for me to do my job."

Just then Dov cornered a scorpion and had the others gather around. Ari knew he had seen his signal. Before Anne could protest, he grabbed her arm. "Stay with me. And be quiet." He pulled her behind the boulder and half dragged her up a rocky trail.

"Are you part Ibex?" Anne worked hard to stay in shape, but she struggled to keep up. "How can you run in that robe? Where are you taking me?"

They followed along the edge of a deserted canyon road lined with massive boulders, until Anne stopped and bent over. "Give me a minute." She struggled out of her backpack and let it drop in the sand.

Ari urged her on when he heard two vehicles headed their way. Something was wrong; there was only supposed to be one jeep coming to pick them up.

"Get down!" He ran back and pushed her behind the boulders as two jeeps raced by and pelted the area with flying rocks and sand.

✡ ✡ ✡

Anne hid her face in Ari's chest and felt his arms tighten around her. He exhaled slowly, and the warmth of his breath sent a shiver down her neck. After the jeeps disappeared, she watched him check the area. When he looked down, their eyes locked in a moment of shared relief. He rolled away, but left his arm crossed over her.

She felt the erratic beating of her heart against his arm. He turned toward her, moving his hand to her collar, where he shook the glittering specks of sand away from her shirt. "Are you all right?"

Anne trembled, unsure if his nearness or the imminent danger had her shaking. She didn't understand him, didn't know what to say. She just stared.

"Anne." Ari touched the side of her face. She saw the question still framed in his eyes but couldn't speak.

"C'mon," he coaxed. He got up and pulled her to her feet. When he brushed some sand from her hair, she shivered again and turned her head.

Ari cleared his throat and stepped back. "We need to get moving."

"I don't understand," she said.

"This is not easy for me, Anne, but right now, I just need to get you to safety."

She looked at him, confused. Was he talking about his feelings? "I don't... don't understand what's going on. Why am I in danger, and why should I trust you?"

Before he could answer, she heard a vehicle coming back up the road. Ari grabbed her backpack and steered her to a larger group of rocks.

"Climb." He pointed to a series of ledges above them. Anne scrambled up the steep sandstone wall, with Ari helping her when she needed. When they got to the second ledge, he motioned for her to hide behind a pile of fallen rocks.

She heard the vehicle stop below them and held her breath. Someone shouted in Arabic. When she peered around the corner, she saw a gunman sitting beside the driver of the jeep. Ari tensed, and for the first time, she noticed his weapon. He squeezed her arm and held his finger to his lips.

Through a crack in the rocks, she saw the one Arab throw his gun down and jump out. He walked around and finally pointed past their location. The jeep backed up, but then it stopped. The driver must have seen them, because he grabbed the machine gun and started spraying the face of the cliff with bullets. Some of them ricocheted too close for comfort.

"Keep your head down," Ari warned as he inched commando style to the edge of the cliff.

She closed her eyes and buried her head in her arms, but not before she saw him steady his weapon and fire. She stayed that way, caught between bewilderment and fear, until he called her name.

"We need to go." He held out his hand and helped her climb down to the road and into the jeep. He kept his weapon trained on the second Arab and made him tie up the injured driver before he forced him into the driver's side. They hadn't gone far back up the canyon when he lowered his gun. The driver abruptly left the road and took off through the rocky hillside.

Anne bounced in the seat beside Ari as they drove further into the harsh terrain. In all the commotion and confusion, she hadn't had time to process what had happened. Now questions flooded her mind as she glanced at the driver. The *kaffiyeh* hid the side of his face, and from behind, she couldn't get a good look, but there was something about him that disturbed her. Why had Ari holstered his gun? Was she being abducted? His actions back in the sand confused her, and she felt he owed her an explanation.

"Ari, what's going on? Why did you just leave the other Arab back there?" When he didn't answer, she pressed him, "I want to know what's happening. Who is after us?"

His reluctance to talk riled her. Daniel had said it made the green in her eyes spark with a warning that told him not to push her anymore. Ari must have noticed. He hesitated before he faced her. "I will tell you later. I promise."

He seemed sincere. Frustration gathered in the corners of her eyes as she battled her emotions.

Ari framed her face with his hands. "Trust me, Anne. Please. I only wounded the other Arab. He is a terrorist and my driver tied him up and informed the Eilat police. They will pick him up. My driver is a friend. And now we are going to see another friend until I can get this sorted out."

She listened to the deep flowing sound of his voice. His pleas stirred her emotions. His touch stirred her heart. Did she dare trust him?

When she closed her eyes and nodded, he turned to the driver, and she heard him speak in Hebrew. It was a question...something about his brother.

Rashad climbed the hillside of al-Jin, sandwiched between two Hamas guards, their bodies indistinct in the deepening shadows of twilight. His alert eyes scanned the area, taking in all he could before total darkness hid the surroundings.

He thought back to the day before and hoped his brother was able to find Ari and Anne and get them to safety. The order to report to Gaza headquarters had come through on the short wave when they had started down the canyon and could not be ignored. A second jeep picked him up and they exchanged drivers. It was their prayer that they wouldn't be separated on this mission, but he alone had been summoned. All he could do now was hold fast to his faith in God and pray for Khalid's safety.

There had been no time to warn Ari, but he trusted his friend would find a way to protect Anne and get her back to Haifa. They had served together in Intelligence for five years now, and he loved him like a brother. If anyone could do it, he could.

A hand on his shoulder stopped his thoughts and made him focus on his location. The leader they called Atif steered them into a clump of bushes and trees, and the four men disappeared into the darkness. He followed the guard and ducked inside a stone doorway, where they walked down a short passage leading into a dimly lit room. Three men squatted around a small fire, drinking dark Arabic coffee and filling the room with cigarette smoke. When Rashad approached, they scrambled for their guns.

Atif greeted them in Arabic. "It is well. This is the brother we rescued from the Jewish infidels." He slapped Rashad on the back. The men slung the rifles over their shoulders and lifted their cups in a toast to Allah and victory.

Rashad held up his hand and shook his head when offered a cigarette. Atif took it and jabbed him in the side. "What is the matter? Afraid you will die from cancer?"

He forced a smile. "No. It clouds my judgment. And if I am going to meet Jamar, I want a clear head." His answer started a lively discussion among the men. "Well spoken," said one. The others nodded in agreement.

Atif lifted the coffee pot from the fire and poured the dark liquid into a cup. He sipped it with a thoughtful look.

One of the men with a rifle squatted down in front of the fire. When he looked up at Rashad, the light from the flames danced in his eyes, revealing several jagged scars across the side of his right cheek. He kept his gaze on the newcomer but directed his question to the one in charge. "What are our orders now, Atif?"

Taking his *kaffiyeh* down, the leader draped the material around his neck and threw one end over his left shoulder. He ran his hands through his hair and locked them behind his head. "Now we take him to headquarters. Jamar is waiting."

"All of us?"

Atif nodded and finished his coffee. "We stop in Bethlehem first." He poured the last of the pungent liquid into the cup and handed it to Rashad.

Chapter Eight

Anne heard barking before the Bedouin camp came into sight. Two dogs with black and white markings ran toward the jeep. Three more stood guard just outside the goat hair covered tent.

Two young boys and a little girl ran around the tent poles. They stopped to stare at the approaching vehicle. Sweat and sandy dirt smudged their faces, but their eyes sparkled with laughter. Anne smiled back.

Beyond the tent, she saw large flat rocks protecting a small spring. Green trees and plants crowded around, vying for a share of the precious moisture. The water sparkled, teasing her parched throat. She turned her attention back to the children and noticed a man of impressive size get up from the pillows inside the center section of the tent. With his flowing Bedouin *medraqah*, he looked like someone straight out of the **Lawrence of Arabia** movie.

"Ari!" He came near when they stopped, and the major jumped out and embraced him.

"You have downsized your camp, Moshe." Ari looked around and nodded toward two women squatting beside a fire. "And had more children, I see."

Moshe nearly choked. "Not mine. They are my brother's children. And, yes, it is getting harder to pick up and move with any speed when the officials come around. We are being pressed to join others in concrete compounds, Ari. Even my brother thinks about it. You know I cannot do this."

Anne looked on with interest as Ari placed his arm across the Bedouin's shoulder. "I know. I wish there was another way, my friend."

"You are a good man, Ari Milchan. You do not come around often enough." He looked in the direction of the tent and swept his hand toward the pillows. "I hear you are busy with more pressing matters. You look like it, too."

"And how is it you know what I am busy with?"

Moshe smiled and winked. "I have my ways of finding these things out. You know this."

"Yes, well, be careful. Some of these *things* could get you into a lot of trouble."

The Bedouin sobered. "I am always careful. You know this as well."

Ari said no more; he merely smiled. He looked back at the jeep and motioned for Anne and the driver to join them. Moshe waited until they walked over and then called out to the women.

Anne watched the dark hooded figures head for the spring and return with a jug of water each. The younger girl made an aromatic tea, tossing in a handful of cloves and other spices, while the older woman, she supposed to be Moshe's wife, busied herself with frying flat bread. The smell made her mouth water.

Ari spoke to the driver, who remained outside to keep watch. Moshe followed his guests into the tent and gestured toward an elaborate wool rug. After they were seated and served drinks, Ari introduced her, "Moshe, this is Anne…Sheridan."

"Sheridan?" Moshe's question hung in the air.

Ari's nod brought on a moment of awkward silence before the Bedouin bowed his head toward Anne. Her cheeks warmed when she returned his greeting. Did they think she wouldn't notice the looks they had just exchanged?

"Moshe and I have been friends for many years," Ari explained to her. "He and I served together during the Lebanon War."

Anne glanced at Moshe, who leaned back on a pillow. "Yes, and somehow we both managed to come out unscathed."

"Only because you are an expert tracker and sniper."

"You saved my life too, do not forget." He addressed Anne then, "So, you are American."

He said it as if he already knew, but something about him disarmed her suspicions. "I am Jewish as well," she said and took a deep breath. "And now it seems I have Arab blood flowing through my veins." Her voice broke with emotion, and she pressed the back of her hand against her lips.

When she pulled the letter from her jacket, she saw Ari and Moshe exchange unmistakable looks of surprise. "I found this the other day in my mail. It's from an Arab couple who say they're my grandparents. They want to meet with me. I haven't had a chance to call them, but I will as soon as I get back to Haifa." She bit her lip and handed him the envelope.

Moshe got up and laid a leathery hand on Ari's shoulder. "I will leave you two alone and see how our evening meal is coming along."

Ari grasped his hand in reply and then opened the letter. He read, while Anne covered her face and wondered if she had done the right thing.

✡ ✡ ✡

"Do you think she gets our letter?" Namir wrung her hands as she looked out the window at their once quiet neighborhood. Her fearful question met with no response from her husband, Qasim. He walked over and rubbed her back while he thought about all that could have happened to keep his granddaughter from hearing the truth.

"We must trust that she did. We must believe and be patient and hope that God will keep her safe. There are, no doubt, many reasons why she has not called." He wrapped his arm around her and patted her reassuringly.

"I want just to see her. I want to hold my son's daughter once again. She is all we have of him."

Qasim squeezed his wife's arm and kissed the side of her face. "I know, Mamma, I know."

A knock at the back door startled both of them, and the fear in Namir's eyes matched the pounding of Qasim's heart as he helped her to a chair and walked slowly to the door. He cleared his throat. "Who is it?"

"It is Rashad, *Baba*."

The Arab's hand shook as he unlocked the door and let his grandson in. He drew the young man into his arms and kissed both his cheeks. "Rashad, so many bad things happening here have us jumping every time there is a knock at our door."

Namir was already at his side and soon wrapped his warm embrace, but he quickly pulled away and shushed them with a finger to his lips. Looking around, he pointed to the windows, and Qasim hurried to close the blinds.

Satisfied, Rashad herded them into the middle room and sat close to the two relatives so they could all whisper. "I am short on time. Anne is here in Israel, and she is in grave danger." His grandmother covered her mouth but listened without a sound as he spoke.

"I know you will want to see her, but you must not try to contact her in any way right now. I came here to warn you in case someone comes to question you."

His grandparents looked at each other and Namir put her head down. Rashad grabbed Qasim's arm. "What is it?" The sorrow in his grandfather's eyes filled him with dread. "Tell me."

"We saw the article about her in the paper, and we wrote her a letter by Khalid's friend, Daoud, and sent it to her home."

"When?"

"Five, maybe, six days now."

"What did you tell her?"

Namir lifted her head and whispered. "Everything." Rashad let go of his grandfather's arm and covered his face.

"Rashad you were in prison when news of Anne made the headlines. That is how we found out. We could wait no longer to get in touch with her."

Namir touched his hand and he looked at her. "*Sitti,* what exactly did you tell her?"

Qasim cleared his throat. "We told her about her father and how he met her mother. We send a picture of them together."

"Nothing more?"

"Yes. Yes, there is more. We told her also about the accident. About David Sheridan rescuing Yona." Qasim took a deep breath. "And that we are worried about her safety because of what her mother had heard concerning Yasir's death."

"Did you tell her what those fears were?"

"No." Namir hung her head.

Rashad breathed out a sigh of relief. "At least I can shield her from that." He took his grandmother's hand. "What is done is done, but whatever you do, do not try to see her."

"But our number...we told her to call."

"If she calls, I think you should not cause any more suspicion than is necessary. Let her know you are concerned, but say no more about her father's death."

Qasim put his arm around Namir and nodded. Rashad stood and embraced them both. "I have to leave before I am missed. You will hear things. Do not believe them. Just remember who I am."

At the door he hesitated. "I have no idea when I will see you again. Be safe and keep us in your prayers."

The old couple locked the door after him and held each other while they prayed for their grandchildren.

✡ ✡ ✡

Ari finish reading and thoughtfully folded the letter. When he handed it back, Anne slid it inside the envelope and asked the question he knew was coming. "Does this have anything to do with what's going on?"

It was clear he would have to give her an answer. Just how much he should reveal nagged at his heart more than his conscience. He leaned toward her and took her hands in his. "Yes." He waited, watching for Anne's reaction. She didn't move, didn't say anything. "Anne, it is complicated."

"I want to know everything."

Ari cleared his throat. His eyes never left hers. "We believe Daniel was a double agent. The ones who are after you are likely after any information he may have purposely or inadvertently given you."

"A double agent? I knew something was wrong when he…" She grasped her *Magen David* and looked up. "You speak as though you knew Daniel. We who? Who is after me? I…I think I do have information on my laptop. I just don't know how to get in to read it. I'm not sure I want to."

Ari didn't hesitate. "Do you trust me?"

"Answer my questions first, Ari."

He let go of her hands and sat back. "Daniel served in Lebanon with me and with Moshe and Dov Stedman. We are not sure yet who is after you, but we have an idea that it is a leading Hezbollah figure who is taking over the Hamas faction in Gaza."

When she remained silent, Ari continued. "Anne, the information you may have could bring destruction to this country on a scale never before known. It is vitally important we get to it before our enemies do."

Anne placed her hands over her face. She let out a frustrated sigh and pushed the sides of her hair behind her ears. "My laptop is locked up in my hotel vault." She bit down on her lip. "I changed hotels, by the way, after I realized I was being followed."

Ari suppressed a smile. "Of course you did." He leaned forward again. "We need to get back to Eilat…tonight."

She looked up at Moshe who had just entered. Ari got up and pulled her to her feet. "Moshe, we can not stay."

"I know. Do what you must." He motioned his wife and daughter over.

Ari shook his head. "I am afraid there is no time. We have to get back to Eilat."

Moshe's wife smiled and handed Anne a lidded basket filled with food and drink. When Anne thanked her, she put her head down and stepped back.

Ari pulled Moshe into a hug. "Thank you."

"What can I do to help?" Moshe dismissed his wife and took Ari aside. "Ari, these are dangerous times. Do you know who you can trust?"

Ari thought for a moment. He motioned the driver over. "Khalid, radio in and cover for the incident back in the canyon. Tell them you were ambushed, but you managed to escape, and get the jeep back before you arouse suspicion.

Anne has not yet figured out who you are. To protect her, I think it is best to keep it that way, at least for now."

He looked at his friend. "Moshe, Anne and I are endangering you and your family. I can call Dov to come pick us up. We were on our way back to his office when this all happened."

Moshe put his arm across Ari's shoulder. "I can take care of myself and my family. It is you I am concerned for, especially now."

Ari looked around. Darkness was settling in around them. "Khalid will drive us to the road. Dov can pick us up there, and you will not have to be involved. I will be fine." Ari knew by the look on Moshe's face he wasn't convinced. He grabbed the Bedouin's arm. "Stay alert."

Khalid started the jeep while Ari called Anne over. He saw her exchange worried glances with Moshe. Then, disregarding Eastern customs, she threw her arms around the Arab and hugged him. She looked at him and said softly, "Be careful, Moshe. And thank you."

Moshe took hold of her arms and held her away from him, clearly touched by her sincerity. "And you be safe, little *Zuhra*."

When Khalid drove up, Moshe helped Anne into the jeep. Ari heard him tell her, "May you be protected as you seek the truth." His own heart echoed the Bedouin's sentiments.

✡ ✡ ✡

Rashad hurried through the night with four other members of the Hamas team. The leader knocked on the door of a cement blockhouse in Gaza City. While they waited, Rashad put his hand against the doorway and marked it with a small piece of charcoal he retrieved from his pants pocket. He let it slide to the ground and stepped on it. When the owner answered the door, he wiped his hands on his pants and entered with the others.

Money exchanged hands between the leader and the owner of the home as he led them to the kitchen area. He bowed with a quick *"Allah Achbar"* and retreated to his bedroom.

The Arabs moved the table and chairs and pulled up the rug beneath. A trap door opened, and Rashad climbed down the steep steps and entered the crude tunnel. Weapons and supplies lined the edges of the already narrow dirt walls. He crawled carefully, committing everything he saw to memory.

The tunnel led to a large storeroom. He looked around at fertilizer bags, wires, and pipes--the usual supplies for making bombs. A stack of boxes with Russian markings got his attention. AK47s and ammunition boxes were stacked away from the wall, which meant they were hiding something more important in the space behind. A missile, perhaps? Or rocket launchers?

He followed the others through a connecting tunnel big enough to stand up in. *"Lord"*, he silently prayed, *"be with me. Give me the grace to uncover the plans of these men so intent on destruction and hatred"*.

A deep rumbling sound filled the air. Dirt and sand filtered down on their heads and the leader broke into a run. Rashad was right behind him.

Chapter Nine

When they reached the dirt road, Ari and the driver said their goodbyes. Anne got out and watched the deepening shadows cover the ancient Edom Mountains, wondering at this new turn of events in her life. Danger didn't just pop up randomly. It seemed to anticipate her every move. She closed her eyes. *"Now what, Yeshua? Please guide my steps."*

She turned when Ari touched her shoulder. "Ari," she said, "Moshe called me something."

"Zuhra. It means a star. Venus, actually. He was saying you are a bright and beautiful light in the darkness." He cleared his throat and handed her his cell phone, "Dov should be here in less than 30 minutes. You can use this to call your grandparents."

Anne handed it back. "I have my own phone."

He wrapped his hand around hers. "No one will be able to trace mine."

She hesitated, her mind racing with the implications of his warning. Ari squeezed her hand again, "Call now, before Dov gets here. And Anne, tell them you are staying in Eilat."

The tears she had been trying to hold back formed when she pressed the "on" key. A blue light lit up the darkness, and she struggled to take the letter out of her pocket and read it.

Ari took the shaking paper from her. "Let me dial it for you," he said, his voice kind. He handed the phone back to her when it started ringing and turned to walk away, but Anne grabbed his arm. Her heart insisted it was time he knew something else about her. "Please stay," she begged, as she heard someone saying hello in Arabic.

"This is Anne. Anne Sheridan." She waited and hoped they spoke enough English to communicate.

"I'm happy to hear your voice, too. I know very little Arabic, except that a friend taught me how to say *sitti* for grandmother and *baba* for grandfather."

"Yes, I am safe. I'm with a friend in Eilat. I wanted to let you know I got your letter."

"I want to see you, too, *Sitti,* and learn more about my father, but I've been told it is not safe right now."

Anne ran her hand across her eyes. "Are you in danger because of me?"

"I understand, but when you talk about God's protection, does that mean you're Christians?"

"Yes, I am, too."

"Since I was a baby? *Baba*, was my father a Believer?"

"Both of them were? So that's why my grandparents disowned her and are so distant."

Ari touched her arm. He pointed to the lights coming up the road.

"I have to go now. I'll call again when I get back to Haifa."

"I love you, too. Be safe."

She handed the phone to Ari just as a small European car stopped. The headlights dimmed. Ari opened the passenger door and shook the driver's hand. "I owe you, Dov." He pulled the seat forward and helped Anne into the back.

Dov turned around and greeted her while Ari stored their backpacks in the trunk. "You have been through a lot today, *nu?*"

"Yes, too much, I'm afraid. Thank you for your help, Dov." Anne leaned against the headrest and closed her eyes when they started down the road. Exhausted, she listened until the hum of the Fiat's engine grew faint.

✡ ✡ ✡

Headed back to Eilat, Ari sat in silence, lost in his thoughts. At one point, he saw Dov glance in the mirror at Anne, and when he looked over, Ari said, "I'm surprised she lasted this long."

"What now?" his friend asked.

He was thoughtful for a moment. "I just want to get her back to Haifa safely, but there is something we must do first."

"You are welcome to stay at my office for the night," Dov said.

"I was hoping you would offer. But I need another favor. We need to leave Anne's jeep in Eilat."

"So. You are welcome to my car as well. We will trade, if you will explain to Havah, and I am not in trouble, eh?"

Ari chuckled and hit Dov on the arm. "Deal. I will take on Havah any day, you coward." He looked back at Anne. The gap in his heart had grown wider. At the same time, a fear, greater than any he had ever known, threatened to destroy his feelings. He saw the lights of Eilat appear and wondered at what Anne had disclosed in her conversation with her grandparents. Did they even have a chance?

He touched the side of her face when they arrived at Dov's office. She opened one eye and sat up in a panic. "Ari, something's wrong."

He hushed her, "We are at Dov's...you were probably dreaming."

Dov led them to the back of his office. He checked his watch. "Ari, I should probably get home. Havah is used to me working to a certain hour. I do not want to cause any suspicions."

He swept his hand around the room, which looked like a small efficiency suite. "Make yourselves at home. I will come by early. Will that give you enough time to accomplish your mission?"

Ari looked at Anne, who nodded her head.

"Good. I will see you in the morning then, and you can take my car back to Haifa."

Dov turned to Anne. "You will find some of my Havah's clothes in the dresser. She keeps them here in case she needs to stay and help me. She is a little taller than you, but I am sure you will find something of use if you want to change."

Anne smiled and thanked him.

Dov hesitated at the door. "Ari, if you need anything, anything at all, do not hesitate to call me."

Ari took his hand. "We will be fine, Dov. Thank you for everything."

"Yes, well, I guess you know how to stay safe. So. I will see you in the morning, *nu*?"

✡ ✡ ✡

While Ari and Dov talked, Anne sat on the edge of the bed and surveyed her surroundings. She peeked into the bathroom and noticed the window was too high for her to reach. The window over the kitchen looked accessible. She stopped. Everything Daniel had taught her about self-preservation came back during moments like this. He had once told her that knowing she could take care of herself made him feel better since he was gone so much of the time.

The questions she'd asked herself then, and had quickly dismissed as foolish suspicions, now became clear.

While she thought about it, she looked through the dresser drawers and found a pale blue-green sweater and a pair of gray slacks. She fingered the soft cashmere and ran her hands over the pants as she listened to Ari and Dov say their good-byes.

As soon as Dov drove away and Ari had closed and locked the door, she held up the clothes. "Are you sure he meant what he said? I really would like to change."

"I am sure he did. I know Havah," Ari said. "She would not mind, but it is getting late."

"I know." She ducked into the bathroom, where she unlaced her military-style boots and changed out of her safari jacket, white shirt and khakis. The shower looked tempting, but reality reminded her there wasn't time. She put on the new outfit and opened the door.

Ari walked in from Dov's office, and she heard him suck in his breath. His reaction made her blush. "Anne, it is after one in the morning, we should probably get your computer now."

She knelt down to hide her embarrassment and cuffed up the slacks. When she stood, she wiggled her bare toes and raised her eyebrows. "Can we walk to the beach first? There are some things I need to clear up about Daniel before we get it."

Ari seemed conflicted. He reached his hand behind his neck and looked away.

"Please?" Anne pleaded. "I want to walk barefoot in the sand and listen to the waves and get my bearings after all that's happened today. And it's really not that much farther to the hotel."

He nodded his head in an unconvincing manner, but it was enough for Anne. "Thank you!" She grabbed his hand and unlocked the door before he changed his mind.

✡ ✡ ✡

Earlier in the day, Achmed had roamed the public beach in Eilat, muttering to himself after losing track of Anne. He had tossed broken bits of crackers to the shorebirds while he tried to imagine where she could have disappeared. She reminded him of the eels he had tried to catch when he was a boy. Just when he thought he had caught one, it would slip from his grasp and wiggle away. "Who ever taught her to be evasive did a good job," he fumed.

He knew she had gone on a Jeep Safari for a day trip, but she had never come back. Jamar would want to know where she was, but he didn't have any answers for him. He thought about his conversation with Hamas' dreaded new leader. The amount the Arab had offered him to spy for them was more than tempting. The hard part was staying one step ahead of the Mossad. He tugged at his moustache, still conflicted about his duplicity.

He had to find that woman. The fact that Ari hadn't contacted him, made him suspicious. The major was another one who was hard to keep track of, but Achmed had pushed the thought aside and concentrated on Anne.

He wondered around town the rest of the day, searching for a clue, watching to see if she would come back on the sly. His efforts turned up nothing on either of them. Frustrated, he decided to go back to his hotel and eat a late meal at the restaurant in the lobby. When he got up from the table, he filled his pockets with packages of crackers and a leftover roll, before retiring to his room.

After an hour of switching channels on the TV, he took a long hot shower. *Where are you, Mrs. Sheridan?* Still wrapped in a towel, he stretched out on the bed and went through the events of the week. It was hard to shake off the guilt of what he was doing now, but he was committed and knew he had to follow through. A quick glance at his watch showed it was nearly one in the morning. He closed his eyes, but thoughts swirled through his mind, making sleep impossible. He came back to Anne and the Jeep Safari. Had she simply used it as a decoy in order to get away, or was the owner in on her disappearance as well?

He rolled over and stared at his jacket. When he had first arrived in Eilat, he had seen the owner bump into Anne in the lobby of her hotel. Dov Stedman had introduced himself and handed her one of his brochures. They had talked for sometime, and it seemed innocent enough. Unless...

Achmed sat up and got dressed. He grabbed his jacket and took a walk in the general direction of the Safari office.

✡ ✡ ✡

Ari and Anne strolled in silence toward the beachfront. The sound of water lapping against the boats in a nearby marina mingled with the laughter of late night revelers and gave the night a peaceful feeling of normalcy.

Once they were past the bright lights of the Vegas-style hotels and restaurants, the dark outline of the hills and the silhouettes of palm trees surrounded them like a protective hand. Brush strokes of starshine through the night sky made the scene seem surreal.

Ari argued with his heart, afraid of what Anne would ask him. The matter concerning Daniel was a sensitive issue. He had to be judicious in what he disclosed. On the other hand, he felt he owed an explanation to the wife of the man who was once his friend and one of Israel's most trusted agents.

There was also the matter of how he felt about Anne. If he let the gap in his heart widen any more, the protective walls would crumble and leave him defenseless, and that could prove to be dangerous to both of them.

As they walked, he could only guess at what she was thinking. Had he told her too much already, or did she know more than she let on?

They reached the end of the boardwalk, and when they stepped onto the sand, Ari grabbed both of Anne's hands and turned her toward him. "Anne, I am unsure exactly what you want."

Anne pulled her right hand free and touched his lips with her fingertips. "It's all right. I just need to know if my husband was already a traitor when he married me. I believed in him then, Ari. It's important to me."

Not knowing what to say, he looked away and nodded.

When Anne brushed her hand across her eyes, he took her face into his hands and kissed her with a passion that made her push away. "Ari…"

He pulled her back and put his face next to her ear. "Be still, Anne," he whispered, "we are being watched."

He felt her relax and leaned his forehead against hers. "I need you to do exactly as I say. Exactly, do you understand?"

"Yes."

"Then say goodbye and walk away. Go back by the way of the marina, duck out of sight and wait until you hear from me or from Dov. I am going to call him now."

"But what about you?"

"No 'buts', Anne. I know what I am doing."

He kissed the top of her head. "You are strong. I know you can do this. Go--now."

Ari let go of Anne and watched her walk away, knowing he would have to deal with the ache in his heart at a later time.

The Safari office was closed and dark. Achmed wagged his head as he walked toward the beach, his steps slow and deliberate. *What am I going to tell Jamar? Should I call him now?* He took out his phone and flipped it open. His fingers hovered above the buttons just as he happened to looked up and see a couple on the beach. He gasped, nearly choking, and turned his face away.

"I might have known," he muttered. When he reached the corner of the next building, he ducked out of sight and called Jamar.

"She is on the beach with the major. Should I follow them?"

"Yes, of course. Perfectly clear, Jamar."

"But this woman is crafty, I am not sure I can get the laptop on my own."

"How will I know when your men are done with the major?"

"Yes, Jamar. I am on my way."

"No mistakes, I understand." Achmed wiped the sweat from his face, and put his phone away.

"How could I have been so stupid?" His anger grew. "He has had others watching Mrs. Sheridan all this time. And most likely me." He reached beneath his jacket and felt for his weapon. At least if something went wrong, he had a gun. With that much confidence mustered, he set out on his mission.

As soon as he saw Mrs. Sheridan walk away from the major, he did what he did best--he followed.

✡ ✡ ✡

Ari's kiss left Anne dizzy with confusion. The attraction between them was undeniable, but it also seemed wild and untamable, like the wilderness from which they had just returned.

She didn't know what he had picked up from her conversation with her grandparents, but she knew that being a Messianic Jewish Arab from America wasn't in her favor as far as a long-term relationship was concerned. She searched her heart. Did she care?

And then there was Daniel. How could he have betrayed her trust? More importantly, she needed to know just how involved in espionage he had been, and how serious the material was that she had uncovered. Ari seemed to be protecting her from something, but what?

Her questions came to an abrupt halt. She had reached the end of the beach, and Ari was nowhere in sight. Anne cleared her head and broke into a run toward the marina. A party on one of the larger sailboats spilled over onto the main pier. It would provide the perfect cover.

Her mind raced through all the scenarios she could imagine, along with the ways she could escape, should she run into trouble. *Ari was right*, she thought. *I can do this. Daniel trained me well.*

She stopped for a moment to uncuff her pant legs before joining the group. Down on one knee, a sudden realization brought her hands to her face. *"Daniel's knowledge is not going to help me, Yeshua. I've not been able to do anything right on my own so far. Please guide me through all of this. I need Your wisdom. I need Your strength."*

When she opened her eyes, she saw what she needed just within reach at the edge of the dock. She picked up the empty pop can and sauntered over to the party.

✡ ✡ ✡

Rashad sat in a small room in Jamar's house in Gaza, listening to a conversation on the phone. He had been called in for a meeting with the leader, but as soon as they had greeted one another, Jamar said he needed to take the call that had just come through.

When he mentioned Ari and Anne's names, Rashad prayed for wisdom. He knew exactly where this was leading, and the timing couldn't have been more fortuitous. Recognizing the Lord's hand in the situation, he prayed for cunning and bravery. The only way to defeat this man was to outsmart him. It wouldn't be easy. He was educated and intelligent; he was also ruthless, which made him even more dangerous. *"But I have You, Lord. You kept me safe in the tunnels. Now I feel like I am in the lion's den; please send angels like You did for Daniel."*

Jamar stood silent for a moment after setting the phone on his desk. He looked at Rashad. "You heard my conversation?"

Rashad nodded.

"And you know of these people I just mentioned?"

"Yes."

"I am told you had contact with this Mrs. Sheridan during your siege of the plane in Haifa."

"I did. And this major, Ari Milchan, was in charge of the rescue operation, which got my brother shot and ruined our plans."

Jamar walked around to the front of the desk and sat on the edge just inches from Rashad. He ran his hand across his mouth and stared across the room without saying anything. Rashad took the opportunity to study the new leader of Hamas who took great care with his outward appearance. Expensive suits, manicured beard and moustache, hair styled—not your typical terrorist image. It was a well-known fact that he was Syrian, but when asked about it, he would wave his hand in the air and raise his dark eyebrows. "We are all Palestinians in our hearts, are we not?"

His image disarmed Western diplomats. His education and eloquence drew the admiration of the Western media. But Rashad saw beneath the charismatic façade to the glittering eyes, like those of a King Cobra. Cold, heartless, even with his own kind. Those who were close to him behaved wisely in his presence, or they were never heard from again.

Jamar rubbed his chin and spoke then, "What can you tell me about your involvement with Mrs. Sheridan?"

Rashad took his time answering. "She told me nothing personal, but I gained her trust and sympathy, I think. She seemed very eager to help my brother and me. It did not make her very popular with the other passengers, though." He looked back up at Jamar with smug confidence. "I also think she was attracted to me, if that is of interest to you."

Jamar laughed and placed his hand on Rashad's shoulder. "What others have told me about you seems to be true."

He walked around to his chair and sat down. "If that is the case, then I believe I have an assignment for you."

Rashad leaned forward. "What do you have in mind?"

Chapter Ten

Anne stepped over a young man passed out on the pier, and entered the thin cloud of smoke hovering about the rest of the crowd. Her assessment had been correct--everyone had been drinking far too long to notice she was new. She blended in, speaking what little Hebrew she knew, while keeping an eye on the street beyond.

The sailboat's teak deck and polished brass fittings and trim all reflected the elegance she had been used to back home. The people, in their late twenties and mid-thirties, were definitely well to do. But the temptation to envy them vanished when she looked at the emptiness in their eyes. *"They seem to have everything—everything except You, Lord."* How she wished she could spend some time in this beautiful place and reach out to these people.

Dov's call brought her back to reality. Anne gave him her location. She inched toward the edge of the pier, but as soon as she saw his Fiat screech to a halt, she broke into a run.

"Have you heard from Ari?" she asked, when she reached the car.

"Just get in," Dov said, without looking at her. He sped away the moment she sat down. She grabbed the dashboard and hung on to the door until she could get it closed. His phone rang before she could ask him again.

"Yes, she is safe." He looked around. "Where are you?"

Anne peered into the darkness trying to focus, but the adrenaline rush left her breathless. Something more than just the excitement of the moment made her feel uncomfortable. Dov's demeanor had changed. He seemed nervous. She saw him look in the rearview mirror.

"Okay, I see you."

As soon as they stopped, Anne pulled her seat forward. Ari jumped into the back. "We need to get your computer, now."

Fighting a feeling of dread, Anne took them to the hotel and retrieved her belongings. She wrapped her arms around the laptop as they made their way to Dov's office. Once inside, she held back when Ari reached for the case. Their eyes locked for a moment before she handed it over. She wanted to tell him she was afraid but couldn't find the words. There was nothing to go on but the knowing in her heart that something threatening, something sinister loomed before them.

Ari misunderstood her actions and kissed the side of her face. "Everything will be fine."

Dov handed Ari the keys to his car. "You know, you said this was sensitive information. You might want to transfer it to a flash drive. It would be safer. In fact, I have one you can use." He unlocked his desk drawer and handed the device to him.

Ari looked up at Anne. "Once you give me the password and I transfer the files, I will have to scrub your hard drive. Do you have your files saved online?"

Anne barely heard him. Dov sat on the edge of the desk, whistling and swinging his leg. Something warned her heart again. "I'm sorry?" she stalled.

"Your files. Anne, are you all right?"

It was the song! She recognized the tune as the same one Daniel whistled when he worked late at night in his office. Anne squeezed Ari's arm. "My files are saved. Can I just give you the password? I need to use the bathroom."

As soon as she shut the door to the back room, she opened the window over the sink and crawled out. When she hit the sand, she called Ari's cell phone.

"Ari, watch out for Dov..." A loud commotion broke out and Ari's phone went dead. Anne heard gunshots and started to run, but a hand came over her mouth and something hard jabbed into her back.

"I think you will not be going anywhere, Mrs. Sheridan, except with us."

Someone slipped a hood over her head and fastened her hands behind her back with tape. She prayed desperately for courage and willed herself to remember her training, but a hard shove sent her sprawling to the sand. Her efforts to resist were quickly subdued as more tape bound her feet together. She managed to keep her wits about her until a hand touched her waist. When she screamed, another hand clamped over her mouth again. She fought the urge to bite down.

"Settle, Mrs. Sheridan. I just placed a belt around your waist with a bomb attached. Any sudden movement on your part and it will go off. Do I make myself clear?"

Anne's muffled "yes" prompted her captor to remove his hand.

After that, she was lifted up and then lowered into a container. She explored it with her hands. It was a box of some kind, big enough for her to sit at an angle with her feet stretched out to the opposite corner.

She fought a wave of panic and lightheadedness, just as a hand shoved her head down and pulled the hood off. At the same time, the top of the box closed over her. Two small slits had been cut into the cardboard above her for airflow.

Anne propped herself up against the box and refused to think about the belt around her waist. She recited one of the first verses in Isaiah she had committed to memory. *"No weapon formed against you will prosper."* She whispered it again and again, until she felt calm enough to think.

Then a still small voice spoke to her heart. *"I will be with you. Trust Me."* She took courage. As she thought through her circumstances, Daniel's checklist automatically surfaced again. She shut out the desire to go over it. It was clear her survival wouldn't come by her own wisdom and strength. This time, her faith would have to take her beyond anything she had believed for in the past.

Renewed by the knowledge that the Lord would be with her no matter what she had to go through, she placed her ear against the box. As near as she could tell, there were two people. She recognized one of the voices.

How could I have been so foolish? She clenched her teeth together and made herself listen. Nothing much was said, but after a short drive, they stopped. The door opened and her container was shoved around. From the sounds, she imagined more boxes being loaded. Time passed, adding to her frustration. Finally, a woman's voice said goodbye before the door slid shut again.

They were driving now, on a highway, she surmised. *Where are you taking me?* She thought about Ari and bit her lip.

✡ ✡ ✡

Achmed sat sideways on the passenger seat of Dov's van. He looked at the cardboard box in the back of the vehicle. "Jamar is not going to be too happy about the mess we left behind."

"You worry too much. I cannot imagine he will mind the loss of two men, especially when we have what is important."

"You are sure they got the major?"

"I saw Ari go down when the bullet hit his head, but even if he is not dead, it will look like I was captured, so no one will suspect me."

"What about her? Why did we have to bring her along?"

"Are you stupid? Why do you suppose? She did not give the right password to open the computer files."

"And if she does not talk?"

"Jamar seems to think that will not be a problem."

Achmed slapped his forehead. "Like he thought not telling me you were in on this all along was not a problem?"

"You talk too much. He told you what you needed to know when it was the right time. If I were you, I would drop it, Achmed. Informers and spies are plentiful enough on Jerusalem's streets nowadays."

Dov was right. Achmed fell silent for a few minutes before speaking again. "So, how is it you are in so good with Jamar?"

Dov snorted, "*Oy*. You *are* an idiot. You ask too many questions."

Achmed turned to face him. "It is not often I meet Jews who turn against their own people." The informer knew his words stung.

Dov sucked in his cheeks and glared at him before he spoke. "Jamar and I grew up in the same neighborhood close to Old Jerusalem. Our families were friends back then, and he and I played together with a young boy named Daniel Weis." He turned and jerked his head toward the back. "Daniel married our little Miss Sheridan."

Achmed stared at the box again and processed all of this new information as Dov continued.

"Daniel and I were always sympathetic toward our Arab friends, so whenever he would come across information he knew would give them an advantage against the Jews, he would contact me, and I would get a hold of Jamar. Unfortunately, Daniel got caught by the Mossad and was conveniently eliminated before he could relay the information that he had come across. It was something extremely important. Now everyone seems to think he might have transferred that data to his wife's computer before he was killed."

Dov looked sideways at Achmed. "That is why our little American beauty is so valuable. She may know more than we first thought, in which case, Jamar thinks he has just the right man who can persuade her to reveal her secrets."

✡ ✡ ✡

Anne pieced together some of the conversation between the two men. Part of the time it was confusing, with both of them speaking back and forth in Hebrew and Arabic. Dov obviously was in charge, or so he sounded. She knew their names now, along with one other person named Jamar.

Dov also mentioned Daniel and the Mossad, and she understood just enough to confirm what she had already guessed. Dov must have been Daniel's contact in Israel for whatever information he got by way of his job.

Jamar sounded like an Arabic name, so it was likely he was the other side of the equation. The word, 'friends', had been used when Dov spoke of himself, Daniel and Jamar. Childhood friends? That would explain a lot, but was it enough of a reason to make Daniel turn against his own country?

She had come here with a myriad of questions, but so far, her quest has gotten her deeper into trouble without yielding any answers, especially concerning Daniel. If the Mossad really did kill him, he had to have been compromising Israel's security in some grave manner.

She squeezed her eyes shut and thought about Ari. Was he Mossad as well? Could he have been instrumental in having Daniel killed? She didn't understand what Dov had said about him, which left her wondering now if he was in on the whole plot to capture her all along. The unbearable thought held her captive in a prison of doubt and heartache along with the realization that she *did* care about him.

Chapter Eleven

Ari groaned when he regained consciousness in Dov's office. His hand brushed against the left side of his head above his ear where a bullet had grazed his skull. What little bit of blood was there had already dried. The back of his head hurt worse than where he'd been shot. He sat up and felt a bump at his hairline. *Must have lost my balance and hit it against the desk when I fell.*

He looked around in the dim light and saw two men, lying on the floor. A quick check revealed they had been shot as well. Both were dead. Dov was nowhere in sight. He couldn't remember shooting anyone. Couldn't remember anything except Anne calling him.

Anne! He found his phone under the desk chair and dialed her number. A faint ring came from the back room, and he followed the sound to the kitchen sink. When he leaned out of the opened window, his vision blurred, but not before he caught sight of her phone half buried in the sand.

Ari pulled his head back in and leaned his arms against the sink until the dizziness passed. A myriad of thoughts ran through his mind. He remembered Anne saying something about Dov. Could he have been involved all this time?

Just thinking about it made his head hurt worse. He placed his hand over the throbbing lump and went outside to retrieve Anne's phone. When he picked it up, he noticed the empty spot where Dov's van had been. A call to Binyamin would have him there within a matter of minutes.

✡ ✡ ✡

The morning sun started its ascent over the Edom Mountains. Dov had passed the Timnah Valley reserve a while back, and he stifled a yawn as they continued to cruise along highway 90, going north. It would be several hours until they reached Jerusalem, where he was to hand Anne over to Jamar's men.

He had wanted to leave earlier, but loading the van with photos and squaring things away with Havah had set them back. They were well outside of Eilat now, hopefully settled in for a peaceful ride.

Jamar had promised there would be no problems, but Dov wasn't taking any chances. His army training had left him suspicious and guarded. He wouldn't be able to rest until Jamar had custody of Anne, and he had the money in his hands.

His fake abduction had been worked out beforehand to make sure he wouldn't be blamed. Not even Ari would have been able to figure it out and connect him to what had happened. Jamar would never find out that he had killed the two Arabs sent to assist in the kidnapping, since he made it look like Ari had shot them while trying to protect Anne.

He smiled, thinking how easy it had all been. *Maybe too easy.* His only regret was the loss of Ari's life and friendship. *Israel has lost a good man in you, my old friend.*

It was quiet in the van. He looked over at Achmed, who had curled up in the seat and had fallen asleep. No sounds came from the back. He glanced in the rear view mirror at the box, thinking Anne must have dozed off as well. With her hands tied behind her, she wouldn't be able to figure out that the bomb was not active and wouldn't go off, unless a stray bullet were to hit it. Dov knew Daniel had trained her well, but the idea of a bomb around her waist had subdued her in a hurry.

He laughed at the irony, when a sudden movement on the highway jerked him from his thoughts. In the few seconds he had taken his eyes off the road, several gazelles bounded across the highway in front of the van. He gripped the steering wheel and cranked it hard to miss them. In his haste, he over-corrected. The tires went off the pavement, and the van spun out of control.

Dov saw Achmed lurch forward. Wrenched from his peaceful sleep, his head slammed into the dashboard, and he was thrown through the windshield as the van hit the sand and gravel on the other side of the road, then turned and flipped over. It rolled several times before it came to rest on its top in the middle of the southbound lane. Anne's screams were the last sounds Dov heard before the light faded.

✡ ✡ ✡

Anne stopped screaming after the box flew out of the back of the van and came to rest in the middle of the road. Blue sky peeked through the torn flaps and she could see now that the bomb wasn't active. She rocked the box carefully until it turned on its side. Though sore from the initial impact, she rolled out onto the highway and stared at the mangled scrap of metal that had been her prison.

No one moved inside. She pushed herself to her feet and hobbled to the rear fender where she used a sharp piece of metal to cut through the tape around her wrists and ankles. Reaching around behind, she worked the clasp loose on the belt and let it fall next to the van.

She felt for the pendant and inched to the front of the van. One look at Dov revealed he hadn't survived the crash. Neither had her computer. Achmed lay in the coarse sand at the edge of the road on the other side of the van.

He moaned. Anne's first instinct was to run away, but her heart and training said to stay and try to help him. Rivulets of blood ran down the side of his face from a deep gash across the top of his head. She knelt down and checked his pulse. When he opened his eyes, she asked how he felt, but he grabbed her arm and pulled her close to his face.

"Leave, Mrs. Sheridan…hurry," he whispered.

"What?" Anne tried to remove his hand, but he wouldn't let go.

"You must…get away from here. If the major is still, still alive, tell him about Dov."

"Are you talking about Ari? What do you mean if he is still alive? Who are you? Who do you work for?"

"F--for Israel. Once." His hand gripped her arm harder. "You were… you were going to lead us to Jamar."

Achmed's confession took Anne's breath away. She sat down beside him, unable to grasp what he had just disclosed. "Ari was using me?"

"He would not have let…" His hand dropped from her arm as his body shook with pain.

"Achmed!" Anne grabbed his shoulders, but his body went limp and his head rolled to the side. She listened for a heartbeat, then closed his eyes and stood in a daze of heart wrenching emotions.

She brought the *Magen David* to her lips and tried to think. *"You are the only one I can trust now, Abba. What do I do?"*

It was still early morning, but the sun would start heating up the desert landscape soon. Thirst sent her searching for water Dov would have had along for the trip. She found a bottle still intact and stuffed it into her pants pocket.

More searching led her to Dov's gun. It hadn't been damaged and still had a fresh clip in it. She shuddered to think of having to use it, but she knew how.

Still barefoot from the night before, her survival instincts forced her back to Achmed's body. She removed his boots and socks. They were too big, but they would get her through the rough terrain if she laced them up tightly. She removed his jacket and paused for a moment to pray before hurrying across the road toward the rocky hillside.

A voice inside urged her to get away and stay hidden. It wouldn't be easy, but thousands of years ago God had taken care of those who had trusted in His protection, right here in this same desolate land. He wasn't bound by time. He was the same today as He was then. It was a matter of faith and trust.

As she ducked behind a group of pillar-like boulders, several popping noises ricocheted through the landscape. A loud explosion followed and sent her sprawling in the dust. She covered her ears and peered around the rocks to see a large fireball mushroom skyward. The van rocked as a second explosion destroyed any evidence of her horrific ordeal and those who had subjected her to it. She remembered the belt that had been around her waist. Only a direct hit from a bullet would have set if off.

There was no time to think about it now. It was best to escape to higher ground while the explosions concealed her movements. Halfway up, she turned and looked across the hazy landscape. A white blur appeared out of nowhere. She crouched low to the ground and rubbed her eyes. Moshe's good-bye echoed in her mind, *"And you be safe, little Zhura."* But when she looked again, pillars and boulders stood like solitary sentinels…none of them had sniper rifles slung across their backs.

She sought out an overhang in the rocky hillside. It would be a perfect place to avoid the sun. The terrain looked more like a hostile moonscape, but despite its intimidating nature, she felt at peace as she hid. Something about the barrenness produced a calm she had never experienced before. Moses and the Israelites walked this land. Elijah fled into the wilderness from the wicked queen, Jezebel. Suddenly the Old Testament came to life in her mind and filled her with an overwhelming feeling of connectedness. This was the land of her forefathers, promised to the Jews forever. It was her land.

When she reached for the bottle of water, her hand brushed against the pocket in Achmed's jacket, and it made a crinkling sound. She pulled out several packages of crackers and a dried roll and held them close. Her heart filled with tearful praise. *"Thank You, Lord, for providing water and bread in the wilderness."* "Oh Elijah," she breathed out, "things around here haven't changed much in all these years. But then, neither has our God."

Anne surveyed her surroundings to make sure there were no loathsome creatures before she folded the jacket to make a pillow. She would rest through the heat of the day and travel at night. The Lord had shown His love for her by providing food and drink. He would surely protect her as well. She closed her eyes and drifted off to sleep.

✡ ✡ ✡

While Ari waited for Binyamin, he analyzed the events of the night before. Something had spooked Anne. She had seemed reluctant to hand over the computer at first and then anxious to leave after he had asked for her password. Now that he thought about it, he remembered she had acted nervous when they were at the hotel to pick up her suitcase and computer. Had she been trying to tell him something then? He listened again to her warning about Dov, but his thoughts grew jumbled and disconnected. He put his head down and tried to stay focused.

When Binyamin arrived, he brought disturbing news. "A report of a fiery crash, several miles past the Timnah Reserve, just came through. It fits the description of Dov's van."

Ari felt sick. Biny handed him some pain pills just as his phone rang. It was Moshe.

"Ari, talk to me. I just destroyed a van that had been carrying Anne as a prisoner."

"You saw her?"

"Briefly. She has disappeared into the landscape."

"But, you are sure it was her?"

"Blue-green sweater, gray pants. Her actions were not of a normal woman in distress, my friend. I am thinking Daniel trained her to be evasive. And, I am thinking she is a valuable commodity to someone, eh?"

"Moshe, you know I cannot divulge details."

"You do not need to. I have enough information to piece together a theory. But you do need to get here soon. You are an hour away. I will keep looking for her."

"Moshe, were there any other survivors?"

"No, Ari."

Binyamin read the situation well enough to have his car ready when Ari came out of the building. Silence pervaded the ride up highway 90.

Ari searched his heart. His growing love for Anne had compromised their lives and had blinded his ability to perceive Dov's involvement. He thought about the computer as well. Moshe hadn't said anything about Anne having it with her. Just how much did he know, and if the information had been destroyed, would Anne be safe now? His government wasn't known for giving up easily when they were after something as important as this. Until now, they had taken their time until they could tell if she had been working with Daniel. Things would undoubtedly heat up after this. If only he knew who he could trust outside of his closest friends.

Binyamin got his attention and pointed to the smoke filling the air ahead. Ari decided now would be a good time to fill his friend in on the whole situation.

Chapter Twelve

The heat from the wreckage made it impossible to search for any evidence of the computer. Ari talked with the Eilat police, who arrived on the scene. To them he was just a passing motorist, until he flashed his credentials.

The driver had been burned beyond recognition. If the computer had been inside, it, too, would have been completely destroyed. Ari knew he would have to call headquarters now and everything would be out in the open about his involvement with Anne. This was not going well. He hated to think of the consequences. The last thing he wanted was to be reprimanded, or taken off the case, or worse, to be ordered not to have any involvement with her. He had to find something to go on and get to Anne as quickly as possible.

A thorough examination of the area showed there were no signs of a third person having been involved. She had left no trace of her whereabouts. Binyamin called him aside, "She has covered her tracks, Ari. That means she is afraid of being found."

"Afraid of what? Why would she not try to get a hold of me, or at least leave me some kind of a sign that she was okay?"

Binyamin lifted his sunglasses and looked around. "Achmed. Do you suppose she could have talked to him before he died? His body is off to the side of the road."

Ari stared at his partner. "You might be right. Anne is not stupid. If he had been alive and said anything at all to her, she could have come to the wrong conclusions. We need to find her before someone else does. Dov may not have been working alone."

"True, but to search this region could take days."

"Unless you have a friend in the area who is an expert tracker." Ari shaded his eyes against the sun and walked back to the police.

✡ ✡ ✡

Anne trudged through the night, using the stars as a guide, but even with her knowledge, it was hard to navigate through the hostile terrain. She didn't worry about covering her tracks anymore; her only concern was water. There was one package of crackers left, but with nothing to drink, just the thought of putting them in her mouth made her choke. It was the second night since the accident, and she knew the symptoms of dehydration. Common sense would elude her; delirium would set in next and rob her of making life-saving decisions.

Overhead a bright object caught her attention. It looked like an enlarged star in the Perseus constellation, though it appeared to be fuzzy. She rubbed her eyes in an effort to focus and lost her balance. As she stumbled, she slid on a patch of loose rock and fell into a narrow ravine.

The faint growls of an animal sounded overhead, but she was too weak to defend herself. She closed her eyes and breathed out the verses of Psalm 91 her mother had taught her from the Tanach:

"You, who dwell in the shelter of the Most High, who abides in the shadow of the Omnipotent, I say to you of the Lord who is my refuge and my stronghold, my G-d in whom I trust, that He will save you from the ensnaring trap, from the destructive pestilence. He will cover you with His pinions and you will find refuge under His wings; His truth is a shield and an armor. You will not fear the terror of the night, nor the arrow that flies by day, the pestilence that prowls in the darkness, nor the destruction that ravages at noon. A thousand may fall at your left side, and ten thousand at your right, but it shall not reach you. You need only look with your eyes, and you will see the retribution of the wicked. Because you have said, "The Lord is my shelter," and you have made the Most High your haven, no evil will befall you, no plague will come near your tent. For He will instruct His angels on your behalf to guard you in all your ways."

"Angels..." Anne murmured. She fell asleep and dreamed of lions.

✡ ✡ ✡

In the breaking light of dawn, something rough and scratchy tickled Anne's nose. She opened her left eye and peered at the knotted end of a rope dangling in her face.

Her mind moved in slow motion, and it took several minutes for her to think of looking up.

"So," she heard a voice say, "you *are* alive!"

She squinted at the blurred vision of Moshe and blinked. The effort to keep her eye open was too great. There was no strength to answer him.

"Anne, listen to me. I need you to help me. I cannot get you out. The passage is too small for me to reach you. Are you hurt? Let me know... nod or shake your head."

A sharp pain stabbed through Anne's left arm when she moved. She willed herself to open her eyes. "Water. I need...water."

The raspy sound of her voice echoed in her ears, but Moshe must have understood. He let down a bottle of water to her. "A few sips... no more."

Though her body screamed for her to drink it all, she let just a small amount of water trickle down her throat. Even then, she went into a coughing fit.

"Easy. Take it easy," Moshe coached. "Can you tell if you are hurt?"

Anne tried lifting her arm again. "My arm, but I think I'm okay," she said. Her voice seemed strange. For all the effort it took to yell, the sound came out as a hoarse whisper.

"Anne, if you can stand, I think I can reach down far enough to help you climb out. Take a little more water."

This time Anne managed a full sip. It hurt when she swallowed, but she took another one and then slowly got to her feet. Since she had fallen between two rock ledges, she used the hard surface to steady herself as she stood.

"You are doing fine, little *Zuhra*; go slow and easy." Moshe was stretched out on his stomach as he reached over the edge of the rock. His hands touched her shoulders. "Now, lift your arms up and wrap them around mine."

Anne did as she was told and bit her lip as pain surged through her left arm again. She pushed with her feet as he lifted her, and in a matter of minutes, was sitting beside the Bedouin.

Moshe poured some water over the end of his sleeve and gently wiped Anne's face. "Let me have a look at that arm," he ordered.

He helped get her arm out of the torn coat sleeve and felt for any breaks. "It is pretty badly bruised, but I think nothing serious. You are one blessed woman. You know that? I could not get close until I chased off that lion."

Anne felt for the *Magen David* and squeezed it. "There was…a lion?" She held her head and thought about her dreams.

"I think he meant no harm to you. It was as if he was protecting you. Very strange."

"Lion of the tribe of Judah."

Moshe leaned down. "What did you say?"

Her eyes blurred. She wanted to cry, but the tears wouldn't flow.

"Not to worry." Moshe patted the side of her face and took his cell phone out of his pocket, but when Anne saw it, she panicked.

"Moshe," she pleaded. Her voice squawked with every other word, "Don't tell… I need time. You're the only one I trust. Please."

Moshe looked surprise. "It is Ari," he said, studying her.

"Ari's alive? Achmed thought…thought he might be dead."

"I just talked to him yesterday. He is very concerned about finding you."

Anne quickly reached over and covered the phone with her hand.

The Bedouin took a deep breath, "All right." He held his finger to his lips. "Ari, I am close. I will call you soon."

He put the phone away and looked at her, "I think I should know what is going on."

Anne clenched her teeth. The last moments with Achmed surfaced and flashed through her mind. Moshe's hand covered hers when she shuddered. He encouraged her to take more water.

"Achmed, the man with Dov, said Ari was using me to help them find Jamar, some, some important Hamas leader. Said he worked for Israel." Her voice hovered at a whisper. She couldn't muster the strength to speak louder.

Moshe fell silent. Anne could only guess at what he was thinking and hope she had made the right decision in trusting him.

It took a moment for him to respond and stand to his feet. "Come on," he coaxed. "We will go to my camp. We can talk more when you feel better."

The Bedouin lifted her up in his arms as though she were an injured lamb. Too weak to resist, she rested her head against his chest and prayed.

✡ ✡ ✡

With the flap to the women's section of Moshe's tent tied open, Anne had a clear view of her surroundings. She reclined against large pillows and sipped the broth his wife, Nila, offered her. The Bedouin woman's nurturing ways had come to her rescue as soon as Moshe had taken her to the woman's side of the tent. After helping her clean up, Nila had given her a change of clothes.

Anne ran her hands over the beadwork on the simple *abayah*, which reminded her of a caftan her mother had worn when she was young. Emotions tugged at her heart. Somehow it seemed right to be wearing the Bedouin garment. She *was* part Arab. At the same time, she missed her Jewish friends.

Moshe walked over and stood outside the curtained-off area. Anne pushed up into a more upright position. "Moshe, I feel like I'm in limbo between two different worlds," she said, her voice stronger, but troubled.

"So you are, little *Zhura*. Come to the other side of the tent. We must have this talk. Ari is impatient, I am afraid."

Anne followed him and settled down into a cushion. When she realized he waited for her to begin, she swallowed. Moshe's affections for her were clear and honorable, but he had a presence that could be intimidating. This was one of those times.

"Before Dov's partner died," she said, daring to look at the Bedouin, "he told me to get away. I was confused, but he insisted. I think he said he worked for Israel once, which means he must have been a double spy or an informer who sold out." She watched Moshe's expression, but if he was surprised, he gave nothing away.

"After Achmed told me about their plans with Jamar, he said if Ari was alive to tell him about Dov. He must have thought Ari wasn't aware Dov was involved before that night. I just don't know what to think."

She waited for him to say something, but Moshe looked past her. The expression on his face had her scrambling up from the cushion.

"Get down," he hissed. He said something in Arabic and stood in front of her while Nila lifted the curtain.

Anne ducked into the women's side of the tent. Nila handed her a *burqa* and fastened the veil. Moshe's daughter, Jale, joined them and handed Anne some of her beadwork. They kept their heads down and threaded needles.

Anne held her breath as Moshe greeted two strangers. The conversation in Arabic eluded her. She clenched her jaws, once again frustrated that she couldn't understand.

She leaned next to Jale. "I need to know what they are saying," she whispered.

The young girl looked at her mother, who gave her permission. "They are searching for an American woman who might have been injured in a crash on the highway."

Jale continued to listen and bent her head closer to Anne. "Father told them he came across some remains left by a lion, but they do not act like they believe him. They keep asking if he knows anything about the crash."

Anne shivered and silently prayed for this family, put in harm's way because of her.

Moshe argued with the two Arabs, who insisted they would have to search his camp. His hand ached to grab the revolver shoved into a belt around his *medraqah*, but as he moved, he saw a glint of light flash in the cliffs beyond.

The Bedouin slowly lifted his hands and placed them behind his head. Then, before the men could react, he fell to the ground as two shots rang out. He rolled out of the way and pulled out his gun. When he jumped to his feet, he trained his weapon on the men, who were down on the ground, but the sniper's aim had been accurate. He held his hand up to signal it was clear and collected the Arabs' rifles.

"Anne," he called out, "It is safe now. Ari is on his way."

Anne lifted the curtain. She came to his side and stared at the men lying on the ground. "You're all right?"

Her concern touched him. "Yes, I am fine."

"How did you know?"

The Bedouin set the rifles against the main tent pole. "Ari and I had a system of communication we used in the war. He let me know he was in position, and I knew what to do."

She lifted her chin, and he saw a look of defiance flash through her eyes. "I can't face him yet, Moshe."

He understood. "Wait on the other side until Ari and I can talk. Listen to what he has to say, Little One, before making up your mind. I know he is not perfect, but the Ari I know would not do what this Achmed has accused him of."

Anne returned to the women's side and let the curtain fall. Moshe turned to greet Ari and Binyamin.

✿ ✿ ✿

Rashad sat on the edge of a bed in Jamar's house. He kept his hands over his ears and silently prayed. Years of committing passages of the Bible to memory had seen him through dangerous situations, but this was the worst.

It had been three days now without communication from his brother, Khalid, or any word from Jamar about Anne's welfare. It didn't help that the

IDF had stepped up their incursions and were actively taking out militant leaders in the area. The situation in Gaza had deteriorated into chaos. Jamar tried to keep control of his forces, while on the run from the IAF. During his absence, dozens of Fatah followers had been assassinated, and loyal Hamas troops guarded his house in anticipation of his return.

Rashad continued to wait. Any slip his part would jeopardize everything the Mossad had accomplished so far. Now he had to trust the Lord for protection, not only against the Gazans, who warred with each other, but also from the Israelis, who would see him as a terrorist. It was the down side of being undercover.

He thought about Anne. Her defiance on the plane had revealed a spark of true devotion to what she believed. He had loved her from the first and even more after he'd found out her true identity. Knowing she walked in close fellowship with the Lord made it easier to believe God would work out a way for the two of them to expose Jamar and his operation.

"It is in your hands, Father. I know You have a plan for our lives."

An explosion outside drew him to his feet. He prayed for his grandparents and sympathized with the many Christian Arabs in Gaza, who were now prisoners of Hamas…the ones who had not been driven out or eliminated altogether. *"All because of hatred for anything that is not a part of Islam. How can the world be so blind? We need You, Lord. The whole world needs You."* His heart wanted the madness to stop. He longed for peaceful times and the freedom to be with and enjoy his family and friends. If only he could get in touch with Khalid. Not knowing if he was safe was hard, but in moments like this, he had to rely on his faith in God to keep him sane.

Jamar's house rocked from another explosion. Rashad braced himself.

Chapter Thirteen

After Anne called her friends to come get her, she listened to the banter between Moshe and Ari and one other person. She bit down on her lip until it hurt. The Lord's protection from Dov and a lion faded into distant memory. Now, she could think only of what Achmed had told her. Moshe said he didn't believe him, but why would the man lie when he knew he was dying?

She clenched her fists in an effort to control of her emotions, but the sound of Ari's voice twisted her nerves and stretched them thin. He had used her. Confusion and exhaustion impaired her judgment. In an impulsive move, she picked up the sidearm she had taken from Dov's body and walked over to Moshe's side of the tent.

Ari stood as soon as he saw her. She took in a deep breath to steady the handgun and motioned for him to sit back down. "How far were you willing to go with this, Ari? All this time you were using me to help you find some leader named Jamar. Achmed told me everything."

"Anne, you do not understand."

"No, you don't understand. You destroyed any trust or feelings that might have been established between us. My computer is in ashes, along with everything it contained. All because of greed. Greed and bloodlust. Arabs seek to annihilate the Jews. Jews will do anything to survive. And too bad for the American woman who gets caught in the middle."

Ari held out his hand, "It is not like that, Anne. Let me explain."

"No! No explaining. No more manipulation. Moshe is the only person in this world I trust right now. He's the only one who has been honest. You might as well leave. I have nothing of value for this Jamar or your government. I am nothing of value now...to anyone. Just leave me alone."

Anne's hands shook.

Moshe got up. "You do not want to do this, Anne."

She blinked when he stood in front of her. He held out his hand, and she lowered the gun and gave it to him. The room blurred as she fumbled for his cell phone. "Thank you for letting me use your phone. My friends are flying down from Jerusalem. They'll be here soon with my jeep to take me back to Haifa."

She pushed aside the curtain to the women's side of the tent. Jale closed it behind her and held out her arms.

✡ ✡ ✡

It took half an hour to reach highway 90. Anne slept. The long drive to Jerusalem was sober and uneventful. Her friends, Phil and Martha, begged her to stay with them for a while, but she convinced them she was fine and would visit soon. They only knew that she had gotten lost after she wondered off from the Jeep Safari. If they found out anything at all about Dov on the news, she hoped they wouldn't put it together.

It wasn't until the next day when she was alone in her apartment that she allowed herself to think about all that had transpired. The pain of remembering spurred her to get dressed and head for the beach.

Sitting on the warm sand, Anne closed her eyes and listened to the waves. The sound of water crashing over water gave her a secure feeling, one that allowed her to face the harrowing experience she had gone through in Eilat. Now that the ordeal was over, certain parts had a dreamlike quality to them. She forced herself to remember and finished writing it down in her journal. All of her work had been stored on a secure website, and would be easy to restore once she bought a new laptop, but for now it was therapeutic to write it out by hand.

As the sun peaked in the sky, she stood and removed her jacket, stuffing it into a straw bag along with her journal. The sea lured her into the water until it lapped at the hem of her sundress. The warm breeze fussed with her hair and she tossed her head back and relished the feel of saltwater slapping against her skin. The rhythmic flow of the waves reminded her of Ari and the day before.

He had spoken to Moshe in Arabic after her little scene with the gun. Jale had quickly scooted close to her and interpreted. The one thing she related that Anne couldn't shake was Ari's warning to Moshe, "Be careful, my friend.

Her computer may have been destroyed, but I would not put it past Jamar to think she has knowledge that still could benefit his cause. You and your family could be in grave danger if these men revealed their whereabouts to him when they came into your camp."

Before they left, Ari mentioned he and his friend would take care of the bodies. Anne remembered slipping her arm around Jale, who had shuddered at the thought.

It was the moment of a lifetime for her, and she had used it later to witness to the family about her belief in *Yeshua* as the Messiah. They were just seeds, planted in the minds of these precious Arabs, but she knew God to be faithful to water seeds, no matter how small, and to bring them to fruition in His own time.

They had been quiet, as she shared about *Yeshua* being God's only Son. At the prompting of the Holy Spirit, she stopped. "I'm sorry. I didn't mean to..."

Moshe had interrupted, "Do you think this is the first time I have heard about your Messiah?" He looked at her, amazed. "I was in the IDF. I lived day and night with zealots, atheists, Messianic Jews and Arab Christians. I am weighing all these things, Little One, and one day I will come to a decision."

He then asked if Ari knew how she felt.

"I think he knows now."

"You are aware that his mother is a believer in your *Yeshua*?"

Anne was sure at the time the expression on her face gave away the fact that she didn't know.

"Does she know you are?" he asked.

She remembered stuttering when she answered, "I, I was waiting for the right time. It's not an easy thing to confront a Jew about. They can be...very unreceptive."

She could still see his amused smile. "Perhaps she is waiting for the right time to tell you." His smile turned into outright laughter, "Anne, you are so brave standing here, telling us Arabs about your beliefs; yet you quiver at the thought of sharing with those you deeply love."

The Bedouin then sobered when Anne had blinked away tears and told him, "I love you and your family just as deeply, Moshe."

Jale had inched closer and put her arms around Anne. Moshe pulled them both into a hug. "And you are in our hearts as well. Perhaps you will be given the right circumstances, soon, to share with Ari what you believe ...if it is that important to you."

He had released her, and Anne remembered the look in his eyes when she told him, "It is the truth, and the truth *is* that important."

Before she left, Moshe handed her phone to her. "Ari thought you might need this. I think, little *Zuhra*, that your *Yeshua* taught about forgiveness being as important as the truth, did He not?"

Her heart stung just as much from embarrassment now, as it had when Moshe had posed that question to her. And the way she had answered him meant she would have to follow through and make things right.

She wrapped her fingers around her *Magen David* and prayed for wisdom as she pictured the Bedouin family. A family she had come to love--a family the Lord loved. She prayed He would open their eyes to the truth.

A gust of wind broke into Anne's thoughts. The image of her friends faded as the waves splashed her dress. She sighed and turned back to the beach. Just as she bent over to pick up the straw bag, her phone rang. It was Rachael.

✡ ✡ ✡

Ari sat rigid before Brigadier General Elon, the head of Intelligence, who went through a stack of paperwork, page by page. When he was done, he slid it into a folder. He pushed back from the desk and looked out the window of his office before he finally spoke. "Our security branch went over Mrs. Sheridan's hard drive thoroughly and found nothing. It was completely damaged. Do you have any reason to believe she has, or might be, withholding vital information from the Israeli Government?"

It was a question Ari had anticipated. "No, Sir. She said she found the icon on her desktop the day after his death and was not able to open it." He watched the commander lean his elbows on the arms of the chair.

The general was silent for some time before he spoke again. He turned his chair around and looked Ari in the eyes. "What else did she tell you?"

Ari returned his gaze. "She told me about the circumstances leading up to her husband's accident. It was afterward that she discovered he had been on her computer. She came here looking for answers, herself."

General Elon's eyes narrowed. He scooted the chair back up to the desk. "Major Milchan, are you aware that your clandestine excursion with Mrs. Sheridan was without authorization? Not to mention the fact that it is costing the government a good deal of money to cover up for you and clean up the mess you made of this?"

Ari didn't flinch. "Sir, I felt it was part of my investigation to find her and make sure that she was not compromised by Jamar or any of his men."

"And yet, you did this without clearance and without letting me know what you were planning."

"I had leave, Sir. I thought I could persuade her to return to Haifa. I had hoped to gain her trust, and thought if she knew her life was in danger, she would confide in me."

The general's eyes sparked with unmistakable anger. "And yet, as a result of your actions, we have lost valuable secrets her husband may have obtained on the Iranian Nuclear Project. We know for a fact that he was a counter agent and passing information along to Hezbollah factions in Gaza. Now that his contact, Dov Stedman, is dead, we have also lost a crucial link that could have resulted in much needed leverage with the international community."

Ari maintained his posture and kept his eyes on his superior. "Sir, if you would just let me explain."

"I am not through." The general picked up the notebook and tapped it on his desk. Ari held back his disagreement with the general's assessment and waited.

"We have not heard from Rashad in several days, and his brother, Khalid, has been unsuccessful in finding him. I am denying your request to take surveillance off Mrs. Sheridan. If Rashad has failed, it is our belief Jamar may still try to contact her in an effort to learn if she has information that can benefit him. We need to find Jamar and take him out, and Mrs. Sheridan could still lead us to him."

Ari clenched his fists. Using Anne as bait? He wanted to stand and pound the table.

The general folded his hands. "Major Milchan, your involvement with Mrs. Sheridan Weis may have compromised your loyalty to this department. The recommendation is for you to disassociate yourself from her until this mission is completed. And by completed, I mean when we have captured or eliminated Jamar."

General Elon set the folder down and moved it to the side of his desk. "That is all, Major. You have your orders."

Ari got to his feet and saluted. "Yes, Sir." He suppressed the things he wanted to say in his defense and on Anne's behalf and walked out of the IDF Headquarters in Tel Aviv.

✡ ✡ ✡

Ari's orders didn't say he couldn't visit his mother. He called first to make sure Anne wasn't there and drove north to Haifa.

When he arrived, Rachael pulled him into the house and quickly closed the door. She pressed her finger against her mouth and motioned Ari to the kitchen counter. "Hi Honey," she said, while she wrote on a tablet: ***I think my house has been compromised.*** "Would you like some coffee?"

"Sure, Ima." Ari frowned as he wrote back: ***What do you mean?*** "Got any chicken salad?" he asked. "I am famished."

Rachael grabbed his arm, "Chicken salad. Oh, you know what? I need to go to the store. Would you mind taking me? I will get the things I need and make some for you as soon as we get back."

"Are you sure? I hate to be a bother."

Rachael squeezed his arm. "No. No bother. In fact, it *really* sounds good to me right now. I am so happy you like it. It is Anne's favorite, too, you know."

Ari flashed her a half-hearted smile. "Of course it is. Are you ready?"

"Just let me get my purse." Rachael picked up the tablet along with her purse and hurried to the door.

Ari went straight into interrogation mode as soon as his mother closed the jeep door. "What happened? Why do you think your house has been bugged?"

Rachael clutched her throat. "I went out for a drive this afternoon. When I got back, my neighbor motioned me over as soon as I got out of my car. She said she heard her dog barking right before I drove up, and when she looked out, she thought she saw a man sneaking around my back door."

"Your neighbor next door? Mrs. Levi?"

"Yes, you know how suspicious she is. Well, I just thanked her, and when I tried the door, it was locked, so I thought to myself, 'Crazy Orva.' I checked through the house just in case, but nothing seemed missing or out of place. Still, with all that has happened to you and Anne, well, I just…I just immediately thought that someone might be trying to tap my phone to get information on you or her through me."

Ari screeched to a halt in front of the little marketplace. "Ima," he said, turning toward her, "what do you know about what Anne and I went through? Have you seen her?"

Rachael lowered her head and looked at him sideways. "That is where I went. I called her, and she asked me to meet her at the beach. She told me what happened. Are you mad?"

Ari thought about what his commander has said earlier. "No, I am not mad at you. Get what you need for the salad. We can talk on the way back."

Rachael did her shopping in record time. As they drove home, Ari reached for his mother's hand. "When we get to the house, make me some salad, and we will carry on a normal conversation. I think the government would not go so far as to tap your phone, but we will not take any chances."

"So. Anne *is* in danger, is she not?"

Ari avoided her question. "I need to talk to her somehow, without anyone knowing."

He stopped the jeep in front of her house, "Ima, be careful what you say to her if she does get in touch again. Do not try to warn her. Just let me take care of this. Do you understand?"

Rachael fingered the bag of groceries she held in her lap. Ari touched her cheek, and she grabbed his hand. "When will it end?"

"When there is peace."

"Ari, there will be no peace until *HaMashiach* comes. Have you forgotten?"

"*Ima*, not now." She had told him many times, but it wasn't what he wanted to discuss.

Rachael searched his eyes, "I meant for Anne, Ari. When will she be free of this madness? Our government. The terrorists. It has to stop. It has to, before something dreadful happens to her."

"I know, okay? Ima, think. Did she say anything about her computer or what was on it?"

Tears formed in Rachael's eyes. "No, but she seemed so sad about what had happened. It broke my heart."

Ari pulled his hand away and opened his door. "Not to worry. I will find a way to talk to her today. Nothing will happen to her...I promise."

Chapter Fourteen

For two days, the IAF air strikes pounded the Zeitoun neighborhood of Gaza City. They targeted vehicles filled with explosives and took out several members of Jamar's elite fighting force. The leader's home shook with each explosion and Rashad knew he could escape and try to get back into Israel, or he could trust the Lord and stay for Anne's sake.

As he paced in his room, praying, one of Jamar's guards burst through the door. "Yella!" Rashad ran after him into the living room, where the Hamas gunman shoved the couch away from a trap door and scrambled down the ladder into a tunnel.

Rashad followed. *I should have known,* he thought, just as a missile hit. Debris fell down through the tunnel behind him, and he outran the cloud of smoke until he heard voices. Two tunnels branched into the main one. He grabbed the first man he found. "Where does this lead?" he asked in Arabic. The man was covered in dust. He bent over and coughed before he answered. "So fast...it happened so fast."

Rashad shook him again. "Where does this lead?" A hand on his shoulder made him jump, and he whirled around into the embrace of his brother.

Khalid pulled him aside. "Are you all right?" he asked, keeping his voice to a whisper. "It was too hard to get through to warn you about the strike."

"I am fine. What have you heard from Ari? Anne should have been here by now."

"Dov and Achmed are dead. Crashed the van somewhere in the desert on their way to Jerusalem. Anne escaped into the mountains, but Moshe found her two days later, after she had fallen into a ravine. She is back in Haifa. Seems her computer was destroyed."

Rashad put his hands to his head and tried to think.

Khalid stepped aside as a hooded Arab hurried past with his arms full of weapons. "This place is a mess, Rasha. You need to get out of here."

Dust settled over the two brothers, and Rashad wiped the back of his hand across his mouth. "The fighting between Fatah and Hamas has intensified. Jamar is in hiding. I wonder if he even knows about Anne. I heard him give instructions to Achmed the night he was supposed to have abducted her. Then it seemed as if hell itself broke loose here."

"It has. We need to get out now, while we can."

Rashad took hold of his brother's arm. "I need to stay. If Jamar hears about Anne, he will still want to find out what she knows. He will get to her no matter how many men Ari has watching her. I have to be here, Khalid. I am her only hope of surviving. Pray for me, and get word to Ari that I am all right"

Khalid removed his brother's arm. "Do you know how hard it was to find you? The IAF killed Jamar's wife and son. There is talk that Hamas and Fatah may unite against Israel now."

"No wonder there has been no word from him." Rashad looked around, "That means he will be even more intent on finding Anne, but not until after the funerals. Tell Ari he only has a day or two."

"This is insane, Rasha. Everyone is on the verge of going mad. Please, come back with me."

Rashad pulled Khalid close and pressed his forehead against his brother's. "I am here for a purpose. I have to do this."

Both of them were silent until Khalid sighed and answered, "Then I will remain as close as I safely can, but it is crazy trying to get in and out of this place. Be careful…you are all I have."

"No, I am not."

"You know what I mean." Khalid turned away when Rashad's guard came back through the tunnel.

✡ ✡ ✡

Anne had met Rachael at one of the brick pavilions located along the Zamir beach. They had ordered a light lunch at a simple café and then strolled along the golden sands of the coastline. It had felt good to tell her all that had happened. Like the nurturer she was, Rachael had just listened and sympathized.

Now that she was gone, everything seemed empty. Anne couldn't bear the thought of going back to her apartment. She smoothed out her blanket and watched the sun make its way toward the horizon.

The wind died down, and the gentle waves called out Ari's name and told his sad story to her. She covered her ears, but the memory of their brief time together in Eilat insisted she face her feelings.

She remembered Moshe's admonition about forgiveness and drew her knees up and buried her head in her arms. Tears burned hot as they streaked down her face, but they brought her back to the feet of the Lord, where she surrendered her bitterness and cried out for forgiveness.

With the anger gone, and assured she was in right standing again, she grieved in a new way. "Abba," she prayed, "what have I done? How am I going to make this right?"

She lifted her head and saw the sun hovering at the edge of the horizon. A path from the pulsing orb streaked across the water toward her and shimmered with the mesmerizing intensity of a desert mirage. Overhead the sky blazed with gradient tiers of reds fading to pink as they swirled through a golden haze.

Anne absorbed the beauty of the moment, wondering at the peace God spoke through His creation. When the sun disappeared, she closed her eyes and sat in quiet meditation, until a chocolate Labrador ran up to her and started licking her face. Startled, she scooted to her knees. She put her hands on the dog's neck and pushed it away.

"What are you doing here?" she laughed, as the overly friendly animal continued to lick her. She heard a whistle and saw a runner approaching them. The dog turned away for a second and then looked back at Anne as though undecided about what it should do.

"Macy! Here, boy."

Anne stood to her feet and watched a man in running shorts and a hooded sweatshirt head their way.

"Sorry about that," he said. He snapped a leash onto the Lab's collar and bent over to catch his breath.

Anne knelt down to pet the dog that had inched over to her again. "So, your name is Macy, is it?" She turned to the owner, "It's okay. He just startled me."

The stranger kept his sunglasses on in spite of the fading light and said quietly, "I was wondering, would you mind asking us to sit on your blanket?"

"What?"

He lowered his sunglasses just enough so she could see his eyes. "Do not react, Anne. We need to talk, but you are probably being watched."

Anne had hoped to meet Ari in a different setting, or at least have had the chance to prepare for a meeting with him. She patted the blanket and found her voice, "I think your dog likes me. Would you like to sit for a while and catch your breath?"

When he walked over, she scooted back and moved her straw bag out of the way to make room. Ari told Macy to lie down between them. The dog was obviously well trained, except for licking Anne's hand every time she tried to pet him. She laughed out loud.

Ari kept his voice low, "It is good to hear you laugh."

"Ari," she whispered back, "I am so sorry for pulling a gun on you in Moshe's camp. I was just so out of it. No…that's a stupid excuse. I was angry, really angry."

"I know," he said. "I am sorry I did not get a chance to explain about Achmed. He was an informer, nothing more. Dov was just as much of a shock to me as he was to you. But there are more serious things to talk about now."

"You said you think I'm being watched. Why? My computer was destroyed. It's over."

"I wish it was as simple as that. Right now my orders are not to have any contact with you. Intelligence is keeping you under surveillance."

Anne reached for the *Magen David*. "Why?"

Ari got to his feet. "Get your things and walk back to your car with me."

She grabbed her jacket and gathered up the bag. Ari told Macy to stay while he helped her shake and fold the blanket. He removed his sunglasses and offered to carry it. For a brief second, their hands touched, and she held her breath.

They walked down the beach beneath the faint starshine. The waves had quieted down and sparkled when moonbeams hit them. Ari tucked the blanket under his arm. "I wish things could be different with us right now. I have not thought about anything else since leaving Eilat."

Anne glanced over at him. "Even after what I said and did?"

"I knew what you had gone through, Anne, and I knew you did not understand."

"Is that why you aren't allowed to see me, because of what happened in Eilat?"

"Actually, I was not supposed to be with you in Eilat."

Anne stopped walking. Macy licked her hand and whined until she petted him. "You mean…?"

"I mean, I went down to find you based on Achmed's report. He was supposed to be supplying us with information, but I found out Jamar had upped the price, and he had turned informer for our enemies."

"What about Dov? I thought he was your friend."

"So did I. I had no idea he was the connection."

"Ari, I caught some of the conversation between Achmed and Dov when I was in the Van. Daniel's name was mentioned and I heard the word *friend*. Do you think he was Dov's contact all that time?"

They had reached Anne's jeep, and Ari held Macy back while she unlocked the door. Without answering her, he asked, "Do you want to get something to eat?"

Anne pulled the key out and faced him. "Are you asking me on a date?"

"It would not be much of a date." Ari put his hand over hers. "We really need to do some serious talking."

"I thought you weren't supposed to have any contact with me. How could we? Ari, I don't want you to get into anymore trouble."

"Give me some credit. I am actually as good as you are when it comes to escaping surveillance." He let go of her hand to pet Macy, who made pitiful whining noises. "Anne, I need to take Macy for a little walk. Go home and wait for me. I will let you know when I am there."

"But..."

He handed her the blanket. "No *buts,* remember? Go, before someone recognizes me and there is trouble."

Anne hugged the blanket and watched Macy drag Ari behind a dune.

✡ ✡ ✡

Macy was on a mission, stopping only a moment to do his business. No matter how hard Ari pulled on the leash, he couldn't get him to stop. He soon found out why when a dark figure stepped out in front of him. Macy crouched low and growled. Ari instinctively pulled out his sidearm. "Careful, Friend," he warned.

Arms went up as the shadowy form stepped back. "It is me, Khalid. I have been searching everywhere for you."

Ari holstered his gun. He smacked Khalid on the arm and pulled him into a hug. "Where have you been? Did you find Rashad? Wait; do not answer that. I am not sure it is safe to talk."

"Yeah, it is. I just saw an agent take off after Anne."

"Then tell me what is going on."

Macy licked Khalid's hand just then. He knelt down and ruffed up the dog's fur. "Nice trick, Ari. Guy takes dog for walk, dog runs to girl, girl thinks dog is cute, guy gets girl and the agents are never the wiser. Right?" He stood and laughed. "Why the cloak and dagger bit anyway?"

Ari started walking. Macy took the lead as they headed back to the parking lot. "General Elon ordered me to stay away from Anne. Thinks I botched up the operation by going down to Eilat on my own."

"What he thinks is, you are too involved with her."

"How did you guess? How did you get here, anyway?"

"Came by bus from Ashkelon. It was not easy getting out of Gaza this time."

"You are crazy. I will not even ask how you found the two of us." He opened the door of a Land Rover for Macy. "Come on boy. In you go."

He turned to Khalid, "You up for eating? I am going back to Anne's apartment and sneak her out so we can talk. I think it is time she met you and is aware of what is going on."

Khalid got in and closed the door. "I am not so sure it is the right thing to do, Ari. Rasha is certain Jamar will get to her and bring her to him to be interrogated. He seems to think he can protect her. If she knows who he really is, it might jeopardize them both."

"I think not. If we can talk to Anne and condition her, Rashad might not have to work at gaining her trust if and when the time comes. Plus, she already has the benefit of Daniel's training."

"Maybe. But are you not concerned for her? Jamar is not known for his hospitality. I met him, Ari. He is ruthless, and right now he is very elusive."

"Do you think I am not aware? We will just have to work that much harder to protect her."

"I told Rasha that Jamar's wife and children were killed in an air strike. He says you only have a day or two to work with."

Ari ran his hand across the back of his neck and winced when he hit the sore spot. "Jamar is going to be furious, and Anne is going to be nothing more than bait."

"But why would our government use her that way?"

"That is the big question, is it not?" He started the Land Rover and headed out to the highway. "Because they will not let an opportunity to take out Jamar slide through their fingers. They think Anne will lead them to him. It will be up to us to make sure she does not become a casualty in their dirty warfare."

"Treasonous talk, Ari."

"Say I am wrong."

Khalid stared through the windshield. "We are in a war, and if we do not win, we will not have a country. And Ari, what if she *does* know something?"

Ari was silent as he watched Haifa's harbor shimmer with nightlife. "That is why I want to talk to her first." He turned off Highway 2 onto Ben Gurion Boulevard and headed up the hill two blocks past Anne's apartment. He parked along a side street directly behind it and tossed Khalid the keys when he got out. "Give me a couple of minutes and then pick us up in back of her apartment."

"Wait." Khalid motioned him back. "They are patrolling the next street over. I just saw a car drive past."

Ari watched through the window of his opened door. The space between houses and apartment complexes was just wide enough to see into the street beyond. When the car parked behind Anne's apartment, he faced Khalid. "Remember my friends, Yosef and Hanna Fendel? Macy is their dog. Take him back and ask if you can trade this for their Mercedes. And get my clothes from Yosef."

"And you are going to…?"

"I will find a way to get to Anne. When you get back, see if there is a vantage point where you can watch. Wait for my call."

"And if it does not work out? What is your backup plan?"

Ari grabbed the door handle and backed up. "Not sure, but if you come up with something, let me know. Text me…do not call."

"You are kidding, right?"

"No, I am not."

Khalid shook his head and slid over to the driver's side. Ari waited until he drove away and then hid in the cover of one of the trees lining the street.

Chapter Fifteen

Anne paced in her apartment. Eluding IDF surveillance didn't bother her as much as wondering what she should wear. She stopped and looked at her jeans and combat boots. A dark v-neck shirt and jacket made her feel like she was ready to go on a covert mission. One look in the hall mirror confirmed it.

"Ugh," she groaned and ripped off the jacket on her way into the bedroom. She pealed off the shirt and held up a shimmery blue top. "Better." Standing in front of the dresser mirror, she picked up a sporty leather cap she'd found at the Panorama Center, Haifa's newest mall. She tried it on and looked at the outfit.

The jeans and boots are probably practical, she thought, remembering all she had gone through up to this point. *It's not like I'll look out of place anywhere we're likely to go.*

She sat down on the edge of her bed and stared at her wedge-heeled sandals. *Do I really care what Ari thinks about what I'm wearing?* With a sigh, she put her arms back into the jacket. Another long look at the sandals and she gave in. She unlaced the boots and kicked them off, removed her socks and slipped into the sandals just as she heard a dog whine outside her bathroom window.

Sliding the window open above the sink, she climbed up onto the vanity and whispered into the dark, "That was pathetic."

Ari answered, "I said you would know when I was here. Are you ready to jump?"

"Are you ready to catch me?"

"I hope so. Anne, turn on your TV, and keep the lights on in your bedroom."

"Okay. Ari? Should I wear sandals or boots?"

"How far can you walk in your sandals?"

"Hold on." Anne jumped down and hurriedly put her boots back on. When she got up, Ari was standing in the doorway. She grasped the *Magen David* and sat back down on the bed. "You should be shot!"

Ari held a finger to his lips. "Not a nice way to greet a friend." He walked over and sat beside her. "Guards are everywhere tonight," he said, his voice low and warning. "Not sure we can do this."

Anne grabbed her sides. "I hope you're kidding. I'm starving." She turned to him, "You just did it. How did you get past them?"

"Very carefully, and I almost got caught. They are bound to be suspicious now."

Anne rolled her eyes and bent forward. "Don't you have a backup plan?"

"The same thing Khalid asked. Why am I the guy who has to come up with all the plans?"

She looked over at him. "You know someone named Khalid? That was the name of the terrorist who got shot on the plane."

"He is not a terrorist, Anne."

She sat up and searched Ari's dark eyes. "It's the same person? I don't understand." It was tense moment, but she loved the way he looked back at her.

"He is an undercover agent for us."

"And his brother, Rashad?"

Ari nodded. "Both of them."

"You mean that whole thing was planned? Ari, someone could have been killed!"

"Hush, Anne. It is the risk we take. Rashad and Khalid needed a way to infiltrate Hamas and find Jamar. Besides, it did accomplish something good, right?"

Anne covered her eyes with her hand. "You said Achmed sold out to Jamar. How do you know these men won't do the same?"

"I just know." Ari took a hold of her elbow and pulled her arm down. "Anne, there is more. That is why we need to get out of here and talk."

"But why can't we just talk here? You're here now."

When he didn't answer, she glanced around the room. "You think they're listening?"

Ari raised his eyebrows with a look that said "yes". Just as he stood up and held out his hands to her, his phone vibrated. He read the message and motioned Anne to the bathroom where he whispered in her ear.

"Khalid says the agents are spooked. They may be on to me. Leave the house now and drive to Abu Yosef's. Hopefully it will give me a chance to get away. You know where it is?"

"Jaffa Street? Um…Paris Square."

"Yes. Enough people hang out there this time of night you should be able to give these guys the slip. We will be in a dark blue Mercedes." He touched the side of her face. "Be careful."

The tone of his voice and the way he touched her stirred the memory of his kiss on the beach in Eilat. She blushed as she zipped up her jacket. "See you there," she said softly. She put the cap back on and pulled the brim down over her forehead.

When she walked to her jeep, something Daniel had always told her echoed in her mind. *"No matter where you are, no matter what happens, you are in control. You can do anything you set your mind to, and no one can stop you."* She thought about how his training had empowered her, maybe even hardened her, until she had met *Yeshua*. While she knew she could still employ the techniques Daniel had taught her, she had found out it wasn't her strength of mind and body that would see her through, but her strength of character and the fact that she had entrusted her life to the Son of God.

"Greater is He that is in you, than he that is in the world." Just speaking the Word encouraged her. She drove down Ben Gurion Boulevard to the port area, praying that whoever was keeping her under surveillance would be drawn away from her apartment.

Ari had been right. The crowds made it hard to find a place to park. She got out and kept her head down as she maneuvered through the throng. The smell of *falafel* and *shawarma* taunted her growling stomach, making it hard to concentrate when she ordered. "Can I get that to go?" she asked the young man waiting on her.

"You are American, eh?"

Anne winced. "Is it that obvious?"

He just grinned at her and told her, "It will be fifteen minutes."

"That's fine," she said, swallowing every time her mouth watered. She paid for the food, but before she could turn around someone nudged her in the side. "Wait until you get your food, and then walk toward one of the tables on your far left. Ari says we have to go to a second plan in order to get out of here undetected. I will cause a disturbance when you come over. Just flow with it, and listen carefully to what he tells you to do."

Anne noticed out of the corner of her eye that he pretended to talk on his cell phone. When he walked away, her knees shook. She had learned to handle situations on her own...this was nerve wracking. She took a deep breath and prayed.

As soon as the food came, she walked toward the tables just as she had been instructed and pretended to search for a seat. A young man with a clipped beard and wearing a baseball cap on backwards stood up from one of the tables and bumped her. He yelled at her in Hebrew and backed into a man and woman, who both jumped up from their table. A shouting match ensued, and a crowd gathered around.

Ari grabbed Anne's hand and pulled her down beside his chair, "Take off your jacket and hat. Put this on." He handed her a navy hooded sweatshirt. She set the food on the table and obeyed. Ari pulled the hood up over her head. "Hand me your keys and then make your way through the crowd and wait in the parking lot. We will come for you."

With all the excitement going on around her, Anne quickly slipped outside. She ducked behind a car and waited. The smell coming from the paper bag drove her crazy. Even with all the excitement, her appetite hadn't diminished. She squeezed her eyes shut and tried to ignore the hunger pangs, just as she heard a car approach. Her heart pounded, but it was only a family leaving. When she shifted her weight to keep her balance, someone grabbed her arm.

"Hurry." The young man who had spoken to her at the counter now helped her to her feet and to a waiting Mercedes.

"Where are we going?" she asked, glancing in the side view mirror out of habit.

"Caesarea, eventually," Ari answered. He tugged on the hood of her sweatshirt. "Did you happen to get enough food to go around?"

Anne squirmed in her seat when Ari parked in front of her jeep. "Wait a minute. What are you doing? I thought we needed to get away from here. I thought you weren't supposed to be caught dead with me?"

"Just watch in your mirror," Ari said, quietly.

A young woman with long auburn hair and wearing Anne's jacket and cap unlocked the jeep. She placed a brown bag on the seat and then got in and started the engine. After she flashed the headlights twice, she backed up and left the parking lot.

Anne turned to Ari with her mouth open.

"Not to worry," he said, "she is a friend who can be trusted. Her name is Mona and she is going back to your apartment to wait for my call."

A voice from the back seat broke into the conversation, "So what did you get us to eat?"

Anne looked down at the bag in her lap. "Sorry…too much going on." She took out a wrapped pita filled with *shawarma* and roasted vegetables.

Ari faced her as she turned sideways and handed the food to the young man in the back seat. "Anne, I think you have already met Khalid."

"Under much different circumstances, but yes, I have."

Khalid removed his cap and took the food from her. "You saved my life. I never got a chance to thank you."

Anne squinted. There was something about the way the lights in the parking lot fell across his face. "You were the driver in the mountains! You took us to Moshe's camp."

Khalid reached his hand forward, and she took it in hers. "Anne," he said, "there is something we think you should know."

She was aware of Ari's touch as Khalid continued, "This is going to be a bit of a shock, and I apologize for telling you like this, but it seems we are related."

"Related?" She looked at Ari and then at Khalid. "Is this a joke? How?"

"Your father and my father were brothers." He set his food on the seat and waited while she processed what he had said.

Her voice was a whisper when she spoke, "All this time I…" Then it dawned on her, "That's why my father looked so familiar when I saw his picture!" Tears brimmed, and she pulled free from Ari's grasp as Khalid leaned forward and put his arms around her. *Family*, she thought, *I finally have real family, and this is how it has to be.* She cried softly against his cheek until Ari cleared his throat.

"I know you would like to have more time, but we are kind of short on it right now."

Anne brushed the tears away and touched the side of Khalid's face. "Cousins. This is all too crazy. That means we have the same grandparents. I just talked to them a couple of days ago."

Khalid looked hard into her eyes, "It would be best if you do not reveal your knowledge of our relationship to anyone and especially do not discuss this with them. Their safety is fragile at the moment."

"I understand."

"I have to find Rashad again. Ari will explain everything."

"You mean there's more?"

He took her hand down and kissed her cheek. "I am afraid so. Be safe, Anne, and be strong. Pray for us."

"I will," she whispered, more confused than ever.

Ari handed her a set of keys. "Come on," he said. "Mona's Kia is on your left. Khalid is taking this. I will get in the back seat and stay out of sight. Head south…it is a half hour drive."

Anne got out and watched Khalid drive away. Ari motioned for her to hurry. "I know," she said. "Caesarea."

✡ ✡ ✡

Khalid coasted down the street in back of Anne's apartment to check on her jeep. He called Ari to let him know it was there before he took Yosef and Hanna Fendel home. They had insisted on going to the café to help if they could. As it turned out, their presence made it easier for Anne and Mona to switch clothes. He had pulled around in front of the restaurant and picked them up afterward. It gave him a much-needed cover for getting away.

When they reached the Fendels' home, he thanked them for all they had done to help Ari and Anne. They pressed him to stay, but he told them he had a friend waiting to help him get in to Gaza City. If all went well, he would find his other contact there and get information on Rashad's recent whereabouts.

With Jamar moving around to keep from getting targeted by the IAF, his only hope of finding his brother again would be through those who risked their lives daily to keep Israel informed of Hamas' operations. He breathed out a prayer and entered the Wadi Nisnas, an Arab section of Haifa.

Chapter Sixteen

Anne followed Ari's directions and headed down the coast to Caesarea. When she handed the bag of food back to him, he took out a pita and unwrapped it for her. While she ate, she thought about what had just happened and what might lie ahead. Ari never answered her about why she was still under surveillance. She brought the Magen David to her lips. *Is that what he wants to talk about now? Why Caesarea?*

He directed her just north of the town to the remains of an ancient Roman aqueduct. She parked the car, facing north and stared through the arches, fascinated by Haifa's lights as they twinkled in the distance. He hadn't said anything the whole way down. Anne broke the silence, "There's so much beauty in this land. I just wish all the hatred and fighting would cease, and people would live together and appreciate what this place has to offer."

Ari got in the front seat. "It is more than just a beautiful land, but the hatred is so ingrained in Arab minds that I have a hard time even trying to visualize such a thing as peace, especially with our government's past actions of all but paying the Arabs to take our land, section by section."

Anne pushed her seat back and faced him. "It was just a wish. I know there won't be peace until Messiah comes back to rule the earth from Jerusalem."

Ari said nothing, but she saw him shift uncomfortably and close his eyes.

She took a chance and continued, "The *Tanach* says He will intervene and destroy Israel's enemies when they join forces and surround her with the intent to utterly destroy her. I almost feel like that could be any day now."

At this, Ari sat up and turned toward her, "Anne, do you know anything about what Daniel was doing? Anything at all?"

His question took her by surprise, and she shook free from her ponderings and focused on his face. His hair, the color of strong Arabic coffee, had grown out since she'd last seen him and formed curls around his tanned face. His prominent nose added to his handsome features, and when he smiled, his teeth were nearly perfect. She got a mental image from the Song of Solomon, as Ari's dark brown eyes drew her in and held her captive. She had heard his question but was completely sidetracked now.

"Anne."

"I'm sorry," she said, pulling back from his intense gaze. She turned her head away and concentrated on what he had asked. "No, he never told me anything about what he had been doing. The whole time we were married I thought he was just a corporate lawyer who had to travel to Washington D.C. for weeks at a time. I did wonder about the nature of his work, though, when he insisted I learn self-defense. You have to understand he wasn't just a smooth talker. He was completely convincing in his reasons why he wanted me to be able to take care of myself. I believed him and worked hard prove that I could."

She looked at him then. "Ari, I knew nothing until you talked to me at Moshe's camp when we first visited. I only had questions."

He looked thoughtful. "When did you find out he had put something on your computer?"

She closed her eyes and forced herself remember. "He had just come home from one of his business trips and seemed paranoid and agitated. He wouldn't let me go out of the house. Didn't want me calling anyone. When I saw him at his desk deleting files from his computer, he was so intent on what he was doing, he didn't know I was standing there. He didn't even notice me leaving. Later that evening I saw him loading his side arm and for the first time, I was scared. Really scared."

She fought the pain of remembering and continued, "I knew that he packed a gun. He said it was just for protection because of how rough D.C. could be. I believed him, even though I had my suspicions at times. But that night, I had a feeling something was wrong. I got on the treadmill and ran for nearly an hour with my headphones turned up as loud as I could stand it. I took a long soak in the whirlpool afterward, and when I went back into the bedroom to get dressed, he was at the computer again. I was too exhausted to think about what he was doing, so I just went to sleep."

Anne opened her eyes and looked past Ari. She barely felt the back of his fingers slide down her cheek. "The next morning he woke me up early and told me to go to my grandparents' home and stay there until he called. By that time I was too afraid to ask why. I quickly packed a suitcase and took my computer and left.

The next night I got the call that he had been in a terrible accident and hadn't survived. I drove home and found the house had been ransacked. His computer was missing, and I had the uncanny feeling I was being watched. I didn't have sufficient pieces of the puzzle to put it all together then, but I had enough to know I couldn't tell anyone anything, not even the police."

She looked down at her hands and interlocked her fingers. "The police told me Daniel's body had been burned beyond recognition, so we had a private burial. After that I stayed with my grandparents. They hired someone to pack my belongings and bring them to their house. Then I put my home up for sale. It wasn't until I was searching the net for housing in Haifa, that I discovered the strange icon on my monitor. I tried every password combination I could think of, but I could never get in."

Ari took her hands and pulled her closer.

"Ari, there's more I have to tell you. Please, let me finish. I have to tell you everything." She felt his warm breath on her face as a sigh escaped his lips.

"It is okay," he said, looking concerned.

Anne's lower lip trembled when she spoke, "Daniel was an excellent driver. I did my own investigation of the crash site and the circumstances they said had caused it. They told me fog and slick roads were to blame. But I checked. There was no fog that night, and even if he had hit the guardrail at a high rate of speed, it wouldn't have resulted in a fiery crash that would have burned him beyond recognition. I believe it was a Mossad hit."

Ari frowned as he searched her eyes, "What made you come to that conclusion?"

She held the back of her hand under her nose. "Because," she sniffed, "because one day, after I was married, I had gone to my parents' house to visit my mom, and I overheard, David, the man I thought was my father, talking to a stranger. Mom had gone to the store, and he wasn't aware I had come in. They were discussing his days with the Mossad and some of the tactics they had used to eliminate enemy spies, but especially Jews who were counter spies. I remember how shocked I felt at the time, but I quietly went out to the kitchen and sat at the counter and pretended to read one of my mother's magazines until she came back."

Ari moved away. A frown still creased his forehead. "I still do not see how..."

"There's more." Anne searched for a napkin from their food bag and blew her nose. "As I walked away, I heard David say to this man, 'How involved do you think Daniel is?' I convinced myself it wasn't my Daniel they were talking about and put it out of my mind, until I pieced together the events leading up to his death. And then I thought about my own parents' tragic accident. None of this made sense until you told me about Daniel. Don't you see? I don't think their deaths were accidental either. And what about my real father? After what I heard David saying that day, I wonder now if he had something to do with Yasir's death. It certainly seems convenient that he just happened to be there at the same time of the crash and then pursued my mother and married her."

Anne watched him suck in his cheeks. "You know I'm right, don't you? In the letter from my grandparents, it says my mother had fears concerning my father's death, and they said they were concerned for me as well."

Ari sat forward and placed his hands over his face. "Anne, you really need to let the past go. Some things are better left untouched and forgotten."

"No!" She grabbed his arm, "Don't do this to me. You know I'll keep searching for the truth. Tell me what you know about all of this." She waited for his response, the silence pounding in her ears.

At last, he spoke, "Yasir was training to be an undercover agent for the IDF. After he brought your mother back from America, his family and David's family spent a lot of time together. Someone found out later that David had fallen in love with your mother. There has been speculation about all that happened, but there has never been proof, Anne."

She let go and turned away. "Is that why David left the IDF and moved to America with my mother and me?"

"Yes, but Mossad had reason to believe he was also involved with counter espionage. They have since found out that he actually recruited Daniel. Your marriage, they believe, was arranged out of convenience."

She pressed the napkin to her eyes and shook her head.

"I am sorry, Anne."

"You don't have to be sorry," she said. "I came here to find out the truth and now I know. I've put you and your mother in danger, and Moshe and his family, and possibly my grandparents, not to mention Khalid and Rashad."

"That is not entirely true. Do not bring all of this on yourself. Things were put into motion long before you were born. It is not your fault."

"But it is! When I met your mother and she told me about you, I was going to use you to find out what I could. The incident on the plane only changed how I felt about your mother and later, you. My intentions in the beginning were selfish and stupid."

She broke down then and cried. In between sobs, she blurted out, "And on top of all that, I'm a Christian. I believe in *Yeshua HaMashiach*. I'm a Jew, an Arab, an American and a Believer, who has just made a mess of everything." She crossed her arms on the steering wheel and buried her head.

There was a period of silence before she heard Ari open his door and get out. Her heart broke, thinking she would never see him again. In the darkness, at the center of serene beauty, it seemed as if her world had come to an end. She didn't know he had opened her door until he touched her.

"Come here," he said softly. He pulled her around and coaxed her out of the car. "Walk with me," he said and took her hand.

Anne grabbed the keys and followed him up a set of stairs to the top of the aqueduct. The glow of city lights from Haifa to the north and Tel Aviv to the south illuminated the sky enough for them to maneuver around the crumbling parts of the structure.

When they reached a cleared spot, they sat on the edge together. The beauty of the Mediterranean tugged at her senses, but she fidgeted with the soggy napkin until he spoke.

"What do you know about this place?"

She pondered his question, wondering where it was leading. "I know it was basically a small seaport, rebuilt by Herod for Caesar Augustus, and that Pontius Pilate resided here. Many of Yeshua's followers made it their home until the Fourth Century, when it converted entirely to Christianity. One of the first Gentile converts to *The Way* was from here. And Paul, one of Yeshua's converts after His death and resurrection, was imprisoned here for two years before he was sent to Rome. I did my homework on Israel, Ari."

"What you may not know is that it was nothing but a dusty little village before it became renowned for its splendor. After that, it went through one violent takeover after another, until the Mamluks eventually razed all its magnificence to the ground. It passed from Jews to Christians to Crusaders to Muslims, and, in the end, it is a cultivated playground for the Jewish elite, surrounded by archeological digs. Guess what it would be like if the Arabs got a hold of it?"

"I don't understand." Anne blew her nose again and shoved the napkin into the pocket of her sweatshirt.

"You talked earlier about the beauty of Israel and people living together in peace. It is not going to happen. It never has and never will. Even today, Arab leaders care less about building a meaningful life and more about annihilating Jews. Our government, in league with the US, forcibly removed our people from Gush Katif and then razed their houses and synagogues to the ground. These were Jews who took barren sand dunes and built a thriving community. They designed hothouses and their produce generated a multi-million dollar industry. After they were expelled, a former World Bank president and wealthy American Jews purchased the hothouses. They gave them to the Gazans, so they could make a prosperous living for themselves and prove to the world that they could be trusted to live side by side with Israel in peace. Have you seen the place today? They couldn't make it work. It is a disaster. The Arabs use the rubble to hide behind while they lob rockets at us.

They gain the world's sympathy, Anne. Millions of dollars pour into their leader's hands…money used to buy weapons to destroy Israel. They do not care about their people, wasting away in squalid refugee camps. Can you not see the madness? You think you made a mess of things? Your personal involvement here, good or bad, is like one little raindrop in the Mediterranean Sea."

Anne pulled out the soggy napkin and pressed it to her nose. "You told me all this to make me feel better? I know what's happening here, but I also know there will come a day when Messiah returns, and the situation will change for the good of Israel."

He got to his feet. "My mother believes as you do. But I honestly do not see it. It is not something I can accept. Not even for you."

Anne took his hands and stood. "I'm not asking you to change or believe in something just to please me. I just want there to be complete honesty between us. I'm fully committed to what I believe, Ari. I look at the stars in the heavens and see what *HaShem* has written there concerning His Son and what's to come. I look at *Eretz* Israel and see the miracle of her rebirth. It's written in the *Tanach* and revealed in the New Testament. It's impossible for me not to believe."

Her words hung in the air like the aftermath of a clap of thunder, but even though she trembled, Anne remained brave and resolute in her feelings, both for Ari and for her Lord. She watched him run his hand across the back of his neck. He faced the sea and looked up. "I do not see anything written in the stars."

She felt a quiver of hope. Maybe he wasn't dismissing this. Maybe he was searching. *"Abba, please help me. Reveal Yourself to him."*

She searched for a familiar constellation, but Ari looked at his watch and turned her around. He pointed to a thin line of deep vermilion stretched across the horizon. "We should go back to the car and get some rest. I will call Mona later. She will meet us at the mall, and you two can change clothes before she takes me home."

That was it. He led her down the steps of the aqueduct. Dismissed and disappointed at how the night had turned out, Anne asked the one question left on her mind, "How do you know Mona can be trusted?" She heard Ari's deep sigh and wondered if she had again stumbled across a personal boundary that would leave her wounded.

"She is Mossad. We have been through some tough situations together. I would trust her with my life…kind of like I am doing now."

When they reached the car, he got in the driver's side and leaned the seat back.

Anne battled her churning emotions. This wasn't how she had imagined she would find out about Daniel or her family. It certainly wasn't how she wanted things to end between her and Ari. She listened to his deep, even breathing and wondered why she hadn't guarded her heart more closely. *Why did I let myself fall in love with you, Ari Milchan?* She got out of the car and walked beneath the arches of the aqueduct to be near the water.

✡ ✡ ✡

Khalid navigated the narrow steps winding down through the alley in the Wadi Nisnas. He counted houses and found the side stairs leading to a stone house familiar to him. A coded knock alerted his friend, Daoud, to let him in.

They both scanned the darkness before he entered and closed the door. Khalid wrapped the young Arab in a hug. "Are you ready?"

Daoud stepped back. "I cannot go, Khalid." He kept his voice low and motioned for him to sit on the sofa. "My father is angry right now. Very angry. They are saying Mossad murdered Fahim."

"That is not true!" Khalid got up and jammed his hands into his pockets.

"I thought as much, but I cannot convince Father. He does not want me out of the house at night anymore. Tensions are running high here among the youth, on both sides, especially after the attempted bombing last week and the week before. Do you know who is responsible for Fahim?"

"Hezbollah. They plan these kinds of things to incite the Arabs. That is how ruthless they are. They use their own people against each other for their own advantage. They want war to happen while they have the international elites on their sides so Israel will take the blame."

Daoud clasped his hands behind his head. "I know they do. Listen, I am sorry, but until I can get my own car and a place to live, I must honor Father's wishes. He took my phone and my papers."

Khalid stopped pacing. "It is not your fault. Your father is a good man and he wants what is best for you and his family. I just need to figure out a way to get in to Gaza."

"If it helps, you are welcome to stay here for the night," Daoud offered. "You should be safe, as long you leave before everyone wakes up in the area."

"Maybe. I mean it makes sense." He sat back down on the couch. "I could call Ari in the morning and meet him at the mall where he is supposed to hook up with a friend. Are you sure you will not get in trouble?"

Daoud moved next to Khalid and faced him, "My father only knows I have a friend I occasionally go on trips with. He knows nothing else. I will tell him you came by to visit, and I felt it safer if you stayed the night."

"You are a true friend, Daoud. We could use more men like you."

"I am seriously thinking about it. Israel is my home, too. The only way there will be peace for those of us who truly want to live together, is to find a way to defeat the militants. There is so much mistrust and suspicion right now that it is hard to live any kind of a life, let alone a secure one."

"Yeah, I know. But remember the Scriptures we studied? Jesus said things would get worse until He returns. Have you had any success getting that across to your family?"

Daoud shook his head. "I have tried, but family, traditions, peer pressure…it is a hard wall to break down. I think they would at least come to the meetings if they felt safe. You know going against the Muslim faith is punishable by death."

"All too well. It is not easy being an Arab Christian, but do not give up."

"Not to worry. So, how are your grandparents? Are they still in Bethlehem?"

"I just heard from *Sitti*. They fear for their lives and have decided to move to Jerusalem as soon as they can. Perhaps there they can find a place to live out the rest of their lives without being threatened every time they go out the door."

"That has to be hard. I remember my parents taking us to Bethlehem when it was a spiritual place. People from all over the world walked up and down the streets, buying souvenirs from shops. Now… The militants are crazy, Khalid. They leave death and destruction in their wake. How can the world side with them?"

Khalid placed his hand on Daoud's shoulder, "Because it is Satan's world for now, and it is in God's plan. We have to be prepared for what lies ahead and be willing to stand for what we believe, even in the face of death."

"Noble words."

"But you know they are true." Although his friend agreed, Khalid saw sorrow glisten in his eyes.

Chapter Seventeen

Ari woke with a start and checked his watch. The empty seat beside him threw him into a panic. He turned and looked in the back and then bolted out of the car. Through the arches he saw Anne's silhouette on the beach. She had fallen asleep, sitting up, with her head resting on her knees.

He paced in front of her, mad that he had slept so soundly she could have slipped away without his knowing. The fact that she was safe didn't diminish the dread he still felt, knowing Jamar or his agents could have taken her. He kicked at the sand and stared at her. *Why do I love you so much?*

When she stirred, he knelt down beside her. He wanted to take her in his arms and never let go. *Forget the army. Forget Jamar...* He reached out to touch her and stopped. *What am I thinking?*

Anne opened her eyes and groaned as she stretched out her legs and turned her head sideways. "Ari?"

"C'mon, Anne; it is late. Mona will be waiting." He held out his hand, but she got up by herself and brushed off the sand. She walked silently beside him, and Ari sensed the barricade between them from the night before loomed larger than ever. He reached for her hand, but she drew it away. "Anne, I..."

"It's okay, Ari. It's better this way, for both of us. You said as much yourself." There was no bitterness in her voice, just the sound of resignation and acceptance. She got in the driver's side of the Kia and waited. When he sat in the passenger's seat instead of getting in the back, she gripped the steering wheel and stared ahead. "I really don't want to talk anymore."

"We have to talk. In fact, I should have talked to you about this when we drove down here. Head back to Haifa, but listen carefully."

"What...you aren't going to hide in the back?"

"They will not be looking for me now. Listen, Anne, we have reason to believe you are still in grave danger."

Anne turned the Kia around and got back out on the highway. "You keep saying that, but it must be common knowledge by now that my computer was destroyed. These people aren't stupid. They have informers. I'm nothing to them."

"The fact that they are not stupid is exactly why you are in danger. Do you really think they are going to believe Daniel put information on your computer and never told you anything?"

Anne clenched her teeth, "I *don't know* anything."

She kept her voice controlled, but Ari saw the way her green eyes sparked. Riled or not, she had to hear him out. "These are ruthless men, Anne, determined to find out if that is really true. We can try to protect you, but Rashad thinks Jamar will find a way to get to you, sooner or later."

She glanced at him, "Rashad?"

"He is in Gaza."

"With Jamar?"

Ari pursed his lips. "I am afraid so. Jamar knew that Rashad had dealt with you on the plane. He wants him to interrogate you, once his men find you."

There was a long moment of silence. Ari watched her breathing become erratic. He ordered her to pull over.

The minute the car stopped, she fumbled for the zipper on the sweatshirt. "I can't...breathe," she cried, struggling to take it off. She pounded the steering wheel and rested her forehead on her fists. Her sobs were dry and heart wrenching.

Ari rubbed her back. "You are tired." He waited until she calmed down. "Let me drive." She nodded and switched sides without saying anything.

"I am sorry, Anne," he said, when they were back on the road. "I know this is hard for you, but you need to be strong. It is the only way you are going to survive if you should somehow be captured. Rashad, Khalid... we are all going to do everything we possibly can to keep you safe. Do you understand?"

She sounded frustrated and sleepy when she answered. "Yes. But if it happens, my trust will be in Yeshua's deliverance, not yours, and not my cousins'. The Almighty is the One in control. My confidence will be in Him. In His strength. Adonai is my light and my salvation," she murmured. "Whom shall I fear..."

Ari glanced over. She was sound asleep. Though her answer had stung his heart and wounded his pride, he thought about the Psalm she had just quoted. It was one he had recited many times when going into battle as a young soldier. *"What has happened, HaShem? What has happened to me? I used to believe in You and trust You the way Anne does."*

He thought back to the last time he had entered a Synagogue. It was for Rani's funeral. Feelings of abandonment and betrayal flooded his mind. Feelings he had never really dealt with but that had shaped his life afterward. They were always there, haunting him, surfacing whenever he thought about G-d. He wanted to know more about *Yeshua*, but pride kept him from searching it out. He looked over at Anne again. He couldn't deny his growing love for her, but what if he couldn't set aside his doubts long enough to examine her faith? Would it be a wall between them forever? One he couldn't breach?

When they got to the Grand Kenyon, Anne woke up and sat forward. She grabbed her purse and opened the door. Without looking back, she quietly said, "Thank you." Nothing more.

Ari ignored his training and obeyed his heart. He jumped out and ran around to her side of the car. Knowing what he was risking, he held on to the door and knelt down in front of her. "Do not leave like this, Anne."

He couldn't read her expression when she looked at him. She leaned her cheek next to his, "I don't need your sympathy, Ari. Be careful," she whispered, "there's a soldier close by."

She got out and stepped around him before he could respond. He looked over his shoulder and saw her walk toward the mall. On her way, she gave the soldier a cordial nod and then disappeared into the entrance.

Frustration burned through his being, unlike any pain he had ever known. He put his head down and waited for Mona.

✡ ✡ ✡

Anne slept until two o'clock in the afternoon. When she woke up, she turned onto her side and leaned on her elbow while she waited for her head to clear. Thoughts about the last week and what had happened surfaced. She shivered as memories of the whole ordeal caught up with her. She rolled back and stared at the ceiling, putting each day together like pages in a scrapbook. So much had happened in such a short time. Safe and secure in her bed, she wondered if it had all been a dream. *More like a nightmare,* she corrected herself. *Well, at least, parts of it.*

Her eyes brimmed with tears when she remembered her last conversation with Ari. *"I know there is something between us, Abba,"* she prayed, *"but I don't see it going anywhere unless You remove the veil from his eyes about Your Son."*

"Oooh, this is so crazy!" she said out loud. Martha and Phillip's offer to stay with them sounded tempting. "Maybe I do need to visit them and just get away from all this right now." She threw back the covers and dialed their number while her feet searched the floor for her slippers. No one answered, so she left a message and wandered out to the kitchen. As she rummaged through the refrigerator, the only thing that sounded good was chicken salad. She called the one person who would understand.

Just the sound of Rachael's voice gave her hope that all would be well. Their time together at the beach had given them both a chance to talk about their faith in *Yeshua*. Rachael told her she had already known in her heart. Now there was something else Anne wanted her to know.

Rachael's invitation: "I made all this salad for Ari yesterday and he took only a few bites. You want to come over and help me eat this, right? Of course, right!" made Anne laugh out loud. She got dressed and hurried to her Jeep.

When she arrived in front of the house, Rachael stood waiting for her at the door and pulled her into a hug. "Anne," she whispered in her ear, "take a little walk with me. We will not be long. I promise. "

She linked her arm through Anne's and headed down the street. "I am not sure we can talk freely in my house. I think the government might be spying on me."

A neighbor two houses down was outside watering plants and interrupted her. "*Yom tov*, Rachael."

"Good day, Alyona," Rachael answered.

"The government? But I really need to talk to you, Rachael."

Rachael turned and placed her hand on her cheek. She whispered, "Not to fret. I have an idea. For now, be careful what you say around Mrs. Walinski. She is well meaning, but she has seen you and Ari at my house...at the same time."

"Ah, Rachael. And who is this?" Mrs. Walinski asked.

"This is my friend, Anne. She makes *Aliyah* from the States."

Rachael's neighbor embraced Anne. "This is a good thing, *nu*? We need more young people to move to Israel, especially now with all that is happening around our tiny little nation." She dug a handkerchief from the pocket of her dress and dabbed at her eyes. "It is holocaust all over again. I do not know if I can survive a second time. I barely made it out of Poland as a young girl, and now..."

Alyona Walinski could have been an actress. Anne didn't know whether to be amused or sympathetic. To her surprise, Rachael agreed with her neighbor.

"Now, now, Alyona, nothing happens that escapes the Almighty's eyes. *Yeshua* said this would all come to pass before His return."

Anne took Rachael's arm, "Have I missed something?"

Alyona looked at the two of them in disbelief, "You have not heard what has happened? Rachael, you must bring Anne to our meeting Thursday night."

"What meeting?" Anne asked.

"The Am Yeshua Centre, not far from here," Alyona proudly stated. "We meet with Messianic Jews, Christians, Arab believers. It is a beautiful place of worship and fellowship, founded to promote peaceful relations among different nationalities. Russians, Orientals, Arabs, Americans...we all come together to worship God."

"But what's just happened?" Anne persisted.

Alyona didn't hesitate, "The border between Egypt and Israel has been breached again by the Gazan's, before the Egyptians are planning to put a new wall in, and all-out war is taking place in the Negev. The IDF have killed several top Hamas leaders and their families. Arabs are accusing the Mossad of killing another prominent Hezbollah terrorist." She barely took a breath while Anne stared. "Now, Lebanon and Syria are allied to Russia and are amassing for war in the North with Iran's backing. All this, and our government leaders are weak and give in to our enemies. We have so little land, and yet they agree to give more away while the people are silent. So few are passionate anymore. We are anathema to the world." She dabbed at her eyes again.

Anne watched Rachael put her arm around her neighbor. "All this is true, but Anne is very hungry, and I promised her some chicken salad. I will speak to her some more about coming Thursday. Remember, we can leave all this in *Yeshua's* capable hands, my dear friend. Maybe you should not watch so much news, eh?"

Alyona sniffed and blew her nose. "Yes, yes, you are right. Forgive an old woman her fears. Not many of us are left who lived through the holocaust and remember it well enough to see the same thing happening today, only throughout the whole world, not just Poland."

Anne smiled in sympathy and reached out her arms to Alyona, who pulled her close for another hug. "*Baruch atem b'Shem, Yeshua.* I can tell you are good for Rachael, Anne. Come see me again."

"I will, and blessings in His Name to you, too."

Rachael said good-bye to Alyona and took Anne's arm. "Hurry," she whispered, "before she thinks of something else. I do not want to have to answer questions right now about you and Ari."

"So what she said is true?" Anne whispered back.

Rachael patted her hand. "It is as I said: all has been prophesied and must come to pass before His return, *nu?* Come, we will eat chicken salad, and I will tell you my plan."

Seated at Rachael's kitchen table brought on a wave of nostalgia. Anne missed the warmth of home and family. Rachael hovered and flitted and seemed to enjoy every minute of preparing a lunch for the two of them, just as Anne's mother had done when she was younger…when life wasn't such a mess. She placed her elbows on the table and covered her face with her hands. Her mind waged a battle with her emotions, and she fought to stay in control.

Rachael placed her hand on her shoulder and lowered a plate of chicken salad to the table. "Anne, I was thinking; we should go down to the Louis Promenade when we are done. It is beautiful and calming to walk on level ground and look out over the port of Haifa." She placed a writing tablet to the side of the dish and wrote: *We can talk there.*

Anne looked at what she'd written and wrote back: *Can we talk now about what Alyona said?*

She slid it over to Rachael, who took bites of her salad and wrote: *You mean about what has happened here in Israel?*

When she nodded, Rachael said, "You know, I think you were gone when the IAF learned the where-a-bouts of several Hezbollah leaders in Lebanon through Intel, and then on a secret mission they destroyed the houses where they were hiding. It has the leaders of Hamas in Gaza City running scared. Since the first time Arabs tore down the border fence at the Rafah crossing between Gaza and Egypt, it has been nothing but chaos. They now fire on Jews in the Negev with rockets more powerful and dangerous than the ones they launched against Sderot for eight long years."

Anne placed her hand over the *Magen David* and pressed it against her heart. Rachael looked up, "It is a good thing you got back here when you did. Who knows what could have happened while you were wondering around in the mountains. They love to take Jews and Americans hostage. But you are safe now, and that is what counts, *nu?*"

The chicken salad tasted just as she knew it would, but Anne couldn't finish. She thought about the responsibility that had been placed on her shoulders. Convinced she needed Godly counsel, she asked, "Can we take that walk now?"

"Of course we can." Rachael put the salad away and held out her hand.

By the time they reached the Promenade, Anne was ready for level ground. Rachael's stamina down the steep hill surprised her. "Do you come here often? This is going to be quite a walk going back."

"True," Rachael agreed. She took hold of Anne's arm and steered her to a wrought iron bench "I usually come here early in the morning, and by lunch time I am hungry enough that I do not mind the walk back up. I just want to get home." They sat beneath a shade tree and looked out over the harbor. "This was built by the parents of Louis Ariel Goldschmidt in his honor. Arie Gur'el was mayor then."

Normally Anne would have loved to listen to the history of such a place, but she couldn't wait any longer. "You said you had a plan. What did you mean?"

Rachael glanced around before answering, "My cousin Marni's daughter, Shira, is getting married the day after tomorrow. They live in Ein Karem. Come with me. It would do you good to get away for a while, would it not? Invite your friends in Jerusalem if you like. She wants me to stay the night, and they have plenty enough room."

Anne thought about what she said. "So, Ari will be there?" She felt a slight nudge in her side and turned to see Rachael point at a family who walked by.

"Tourists," she smiled, "look at how awed they are by all of this beauty. Americans have such a twisted view of Israel until they come here and see for themselves." She pressed her forehead against Anne's and whispered, "*Baruch Bat*. Of course he will be."

Anne repeated the phrase to herself. *Baruch Bat. Blessed daughter.* She hadn't felt this loved in a long time. "Rachael," she took both of her hands and asked, "what would you do if you had a secret two different people wanted to know, and both were willing to do whatever it took to find it out...only you felt neither one should have knowledge of it?"

Chapter Eighteen

Ari had just walked in the door of his house when Khalid called. He flipped it on speaker while he took off his jacket.

"Ari, I am still in Haifa, on foot. Are you at the mall? Sounds like trouble is brewing here."

"No, I am home now. Trouble *is* brewing. We just put Patriot Batteries in place close to the city. It makes me wish we had more control over what is going on. We need new leadership or at least someone not afraid to face down our enemies. So what happened to your ride?"

"Come get me, and we will talk."

"I seriously need a shower first and some coffee."

"Make it a fast shower. I will have hot coffee waiting for you."

While Ari got ready, his thoughts focused on Anne. *This is so dangerous,* he reminded himself. It didn't help. He couldn't get her out of his mind anymore. Her remark concerning her trust in God hadn't been arrogant or demeaning, yet it continued to work on him, like a dull knife sawing through raw flesh. She had strong convictions and faith, yet she was human enough to show her fears. For that he admired her…no, he loved her.

For the first time since Rani's death, he felt a driving force motivating his will. Before he had met Anne, he had just gone through the motions of living day to day and not caring about himself or anyone else besides his mother. He devoted his time and his life to his country, and his only goal was to serve in whatever capacity he was able to, for the purpose of eliminating as many terrorists as he possibly could. Now, he was determined to see Anne safely through this nightmare until they could get Jamar and end the madman's obsession with finding out any secrets Daniel had uncovered.

He checked the time and headed for the door. Once again, his phone rang. It was his mother. He decided just to listen to her message on his way to the car.

The usual fifteen minutes to get to the Wadi Nisnas district, turned into twenty-five, due to traffic. Curious onlookers had come out to see the missiles, only to be turned away. Ari turned off Histradut Street and wound his way over to Ben Gurion Boulevard. A quick call to Khalid, and they were soon sitting outside a small café with a morning coffee and walnut baklava.

Khalid shifted nervously in the wrought iron chair. "Are you sure this is wise, sitting out in the open like this? I had a table inside for us."

"With that beard, and your hair pulled back under your cap, I hardly recognized you. Not to worry. I like to be out in the open and know what is going on."

Ari lifted his sunglasses so he could rub his eyes and check out the area. "Binyamin said he would drive you to Jerusalem. I have received orders to stay close to home and keep an eye on the situation with the missiles."

"That does not sound good. What is up?"

Ari studied Khalid for a moment before he answered, "Nobody is saying, but I am sure we will find out soon enough. Right now, I am more worried about what is going on in our government."

"That is even more unsettling."

"I know." Ari leaned forward, "I am not sure who we can trust anymore. A couple of men have come to me with their concerns about our government officials, one MK in particular."

"Maybe we should get in touch with Moshe."

"Yeah, that has been on my mind. I think I will give him a call. So what happened last night?"

Khalid sat back in his chair and looked around. "Daoud's father got spooked and said there was trouble afoot. Took his keys and phone, would not even let him go outside. I ended up spending the night."

"You think he knows more than he is letting on? I was under the impression that he was loyal."

"Daoud is loyal enough. I am not sure what his father knows," Khalid said. "There is a lot of chatter right now about all the terrorists our government recently freed, making their way through the major cities to recruit spies and suicide bombers. It could be that he overheard this or maybe someone threatened his family. It is not easy being an Israeli Arab nowadays. One's loyalties might lie with Israel, but if terrorists threaten a man's family, blood ties generally win out over devotion to a country."

Ari was thoughtful while he ate the last of his pastry and washed it down with hot Arabic coffee.

Khalid finished his cup and pushed it away. "Daoud is ready, though. I told him to call you."

"Are you sure? We could use him now, in an unofficial capacity. He would have to be very careful."

"He can handle it. I have known him for a long time. He is a Believer, and he has a friend who is already helping us."

Ari flinched. *Another Believer in Yeshua. What are you trying to tell me, HaShem?*

"Speaking of Believers," Khalid said quietly, "my grandparents are moving to Jerusalem. The PA has made it clear they are not welcome in Bethlehem. *Dhimmitude* against Christians is widespread now, especially there, yet the Arab's spin it off as Israel's fault for putting up the wall."

"Of course. Everything is our fault. I am sorry to hear about your grandparents, Khalid," Ari said, and he meant it. "Hopefully, it will be better for them. Although, with talk of dividing Jerusalem, one has to wonder." He quickly scooted his chair away from the table and got out his wallet.

"I can see Biny's car," he said. "Walk toward Ha Maginim, then slip through to the City Center and meet him at Yaffo. He will pick you up there."

Khalid obeyed without question. He said good-bye and strolled down the street. Ari left a tip on the table and got in his car. The sun shone through the windshield, but these days he lived under a dark cloud of doubt and fear…fear for Anne's life and for Israel, his beloved country.

He took out his phone and called his mother back. "What about the wedding?"

✡ ✡ ✡

Anne had watched Rachael's expression when she asked her what she would do if she had a secret. In her wise way, she had patted her hand and told her *Yeshua* was the only one who could direct her paths.

She had been ready to tell Rachael everything, but at the last minute, she felt a familiar nudge by the Holy Spirit…a warning to spare her friend needless worry. Rachael's knowledge would inevitably place her in personal danger. Anne ached for wanting a confidant, but her love for Rachael led her to keep her secret a while longer.

She had hugged her and thanked her, and the two of them had managed the climb back to Rachael's home. They both had decided on the way that they were hungry enough to finish the chicken salad when they got back.

While Anne sliced avocados and cut slits in the sides of the pitas, Rachael turned on the small television on her counter. Both of them stopped what they were doing and listened to the breaking news report.

Rachael turned to Anne with a wide-eyed stare. "Rockets from the North again? How much more can this country take before our leaders are broken to the point of committing the unthinkable and plunge us into a nuclear war?"

The station showed a plume of smoke rise from a rocket blast on the beach near a high-rise apartment building. "They are messing with our minds," she fussed. Anne moved closer. "They glory in terrorizing us and instilling fear. What kind of a government do we have that allows this to happen time after time? The US fights terrorism with force daily and yet orders us to act with restraint. It is not right."

Anne clutched the *Magen David*. *"What should I do, Abba?"* she prayed. *"Is the answer within my grasp? Or will I unleash a Pandora's nightmare?"*

Sirens broke the silence and startled them. They both shrieked when an explosion rocked Rachael's home. The blast came from the northeast, and they hurried to the back door to see how close it had hit. Other neighbors gathered in their doorways. They could see and smell the smoke.

Anne ran back in to the kitchen to check if they were reporting on this recent blast. Rachael came in behind her, her face white. Anne helped her sit in a chair while she grabbed a washcloth and ran it under some cold water, but Rachael was on the phone by the time she handed it to her.

Fear for Ari gripped her as she tried to remember where Rachael had said he lived. When a reporter mentioned Nesher, she turned and watched. Scenes of damaged buildings and a car on fire made her catch her breath.

She heard Rachael speaking in Hebrew but couldn't concentrate on what was being said. This wasn't the first time Haifa had come under attack. She saw the looks on people's faces, heard the despair in their voices. It didn't take an understanding of Hebrew to know what they were saying…their hand gestures and body language said it all.

Rachael grabbed her hand just then, "Ari says it is just falling debris from the rockets. Patriot Missiles exploded them before they could hit anything and inflict real damage."

"He's all right?"

"Yes," Rachael said, her voice still shaking. "He was just going to call me."

"But it looks awful. The people, the pictures…I don't understand."

"They are explaining it to the public now," Rachael said. "The pictures are from the last time and make it look worse than it is. Ari told me they just put the Patriot systems in place this morning. I say it is about time our government gave us some measure of defense."

"This makes you feel secure?"

"Of course not, but it helps to know we are not taking this without doing something about it. The situation is getting worse. I can hear it in Ari's voice. He is frustrated that we seem to be easy prey, that our hands are tied from turning the table on our enemies."

Anne sighed. Rachael squeezed her hand. "Stay with me tonight, if you want. Tomorrow we can pick up clothes and whatever else you need for the wedding."

Anne let go of her locket and looked at the imprint left on the inside of her hand. "Ari thinks it's okay to travel?"

Rachael got up and wrapped her in a hug. "Yes, we will be safe. It is hard, when this happens, but let us not forget we have *Yeshua* with us, *nu*?"

"Yes," Anne murmured, "but all these people don't. They are going to trust in a weapons defense system that could fail them. What is going to have to happen for them to realize *HaMashiach* has already come? That He is their only defense?"

Rachael gave her a squeeze before releasing her, "The nations of the world will gather around Israel before God destroys them and His Son is revealed. That has not happened yet. It is just terrorists right now, nipping at our heels like little foxes, trying to wear our resistance down. We must stay strong and get to as many as we can with the truth about *Yeshua*."

"Rachael, I am a warrior when I feel threatened or my life is in danger, but dealing with this situation and trying to sort out my feelings for Ari, especially knowing that he doesn't believe..." She closed her eyes in an effort to find the right words. "I'm just not sure where I fit in to all of this."

"You have to deal with the moment, Anne. *Yeshua* will reveal His will, as you need to know it. As for Ari, I talk to him whenever I can. It is all in the Almighty's hands. He is the only one who can open his eyes. Just remember, there is still time to love and to be loved."

Rachael's phone rang again. Anne reached her hands behind her and gripped the counter top. She was right. Trust and faith. It didn't always resolve the situation, but it made it easier to go through times like this. She closed her eyes and prayed for guidance until Rachael was done talking.

"That was my cousin. She says Shira and her fiancé, Aaron, have decided to have their wedding in spite of what is happening. We will go on with life. It is the best way to show our enemies that we are not afraid of them." She grabbed Anne's hands from the counter and held them up to her chin. "So. Do we need to go shopping for something new to wear?"

Anne couldn't believe the twinkle in Rachael's eyes. "After all this? You're kidding, right? A minute ago you went white from thinking Ari was in harm's way. Now you want to go shopping?"

Rachael pointed to the food still waiting on the table. "What? Would I kid you?" she said with a teasing smile. "We will eat and then see what bargains we can find today. HaCarmel has the most amazing shops. The news just said we have silenced our enemies for now, so we will enjoy the rest of the day, and you will see. All the shops will be open, business as usual, with sales to celebrate. Just like we are going to do." She pulled a bottle of wine from the small rack on her counter and proudly waved it in the air. "*L'Chaim!*"

Anne still shook from the ordeal, but Rachael's enthusiasm engulfed her and chased away the dread of what had just happened. She picked up their glasses and held them out to her. "To life," she said, her eyes misty.

"And to love," Rachael added with a wink as she removed the cork.

Chapter Nineteen

Khalid had Binyamin take him as far as the East Gate in Jerusalem. A friend of his resided in the Old City and would give him a place to clean up and change. From there he could make his way to Bethlehem.

He and his brother were only two of many Arab Israelis who formed a network of spy and surveillance teams for the Israeli Defense Force. It was their selfless devotion to the cause of disarming Hamas and Hezbollah terrorists that helped the IDF and Mossad thwart many of the attacks and bombings in Israel. They were willing to sacrifice their lives rather than see the Muslim extremists prevail.

Bethlehem was one place Khalid could get into easily with special papers from the IDF. *If only it was that simple for Gaza.* Tensions were high as he made his way to his grandparents' home. From a distance he could see the front door had been torn off its hinges. Broken glass from the windows littered the small yard. He battled the feeling in the pit of his stomach and nonchalantly walked close to the building.

Stones lay scattered about. He picked one up and threw it at the house. A quick peek in the window confirmed his fears. If his grandparents had left anything behind, it had all been looted by now. He walked toward Manger Square and prayed for their safety, hoping they had managed to escape before the violence had erupted. Muslims terrorized Christians and killed any of their own who converted, then down played the diminishing Christian population, blaming the wall of separation as the reason for their leaving.

Bethlehem's high-rise buildings and downtown hustle and bustle appeared too modern for its religious image promoted at Christmas, but that was before the last Intifada and the construction of the wall by the Jewish government to separate it from Israel. Too many terrorists and suicide bombers had entered Jerusalem from Bethlehem, and this was the only way the Israelis could protect themselves. It had accomplished its task, but it had also evoked the chastisement of the world. "Apartheid" they called it. *What do they call the carnage left by the suicide bombers?*

Khalid studied the stone streets and buildings that looked as if they had been etched into the landscape with white chalk. This was his town. He loved that it had been the birthplace of his Lord, but even back then it had known its share of violence when Herod had all the infants two years old and younger slaughtered after his visit from the Magi. *Not much different than today. The madness continues and innocents suffer on both sides, and will until You come back and make it right, Lord.*

He stopped when a group of Franciscan Friars crossed the street. They were the only ones he knew of, who didn't take sides. They just lived peaceable lives and continued their Order's ancient tradition of guarding the Holy Sites in Israel. They were a likable bunch of men who helped anyone in need, no matter who they were.

As he watched the robed monks smile and carry on as though they hadn't a care in the world, he wondered what that feeling was like. In his intense life, the only peace he experienced was that of knowing his Lord and Savior, who was with him through times of terror and conflict. He prayed for His presence to be with him through the next couple of days.

While he stood there, he scanned the pedestrians for his friend, Ahmad, and hoped he hadn't missed him. An arm came around his shoulder. He tensed until he heard a voice say, "Khalid, my friend. You are late, and I am hungry."

Khalid grinned and smacked Ahmad on the back. "So what else is new in the Holy Land?"

Anne tried on her new dress and twirled around in her bedroom. Yesterday after the rocket attacks, it had been just as Rachael had predicted: the shops were open and ready to do business. They spent the afternoon trying on dresses and shoes.

Her bargain was a simple mid-length dress of pure shimmery silk in a pale avocado color. The sleeveless top crisscrossed the bust line and was gathered to a wide empire waistband. A biased cut skirt, finished in a softly ruffled hem, draped gracefully from the bottom of the band. The look was definitely

Grecian. After trekking through the mountains in Ahmad's jacket and boots and wearing a hooded sweatshirt and combat boots the night before, it was a strange sensation to feel feminine.

"I love these ivory heels. The narrow piece that crosses back and forth from the toe up to the ankle strap adds to the Greek style, don't you think?"

Rachael sat on the bed with a dreamy smile playing across her face. Anne watched her in the mirror. "What is it? Do you think Ari will like what I'm wearing?" She was surprised to see her smile slowly disappear. "What's wrong?"

"Anne, I had hoped that Ari might be able to come. But, do not give up hope," she added quickly. "If I know my Ari, he will try, especially if he knows you are going to be there."

Anne sat down on the bed beside her, "So, does he know?"

"Yes. I told him yesterday when he called."

"What did he say?"

"He said nothing. It was so crazy, then, you know, with the sirens and all that was happening. I think he worries about where all this escalation is headed. An all-out war would greatly change things, especially here in Haifa. Lebanon did much damage to us last time."

She reached over and patted Anne's arm. "Oh, but not to worry. I should not carry on so. We will go and have a wonderful time, and if he can make it, he will, *nu?*"

Anne took off her heels, "No. He won't be there."

"Now, now."

"No," Anne insisted, "he's been ordered not to see me anymore, and now that he knows I'm going to be there, he won't come." She felt bad as she watched the expression on Rachael's face turn to one of confusion.

"Rachael, he went to Eilat without authorization and his general feels he messed up somehow," she tried to explain. "When he got back, he was ordered to stay away from me. And if that wasn't bad enough, we didn't leave on good terms the other night after I talked to him about being a Messianic Jew." Rachael wasn't stupid. Anne's only hope was that her explanation would satisfy any questions about her involvement in the whole scenario. The day before at the beach, she had told her about her kidnapping, but she had left out the details as to why. It hadn't seemed to matter then...she hoped it wouldn't now.

A long moment of silence passed before Rachael looked at her, "There is more than meets the eye here, this I know. And things I should *not* know, true?"

Anne could only nod. "I'm sorry."

"No, no, do not be sorry. My son is in Intelligence. I am used to being told it is in my best interest not to know details." She nodded her head as if agreeing with herself. "Like I said, God will deal with Ari's heart in due time. Besides, I doubt anything you could say or do would change his feelings for you. I may not be able to help, but I can always pray."

Anne didn't know how to respond. "I am so blessed by your friendship, Rachael. And yes, that would be what is needed the most at this point."

Rachael stood up. "Then, you and Ari have my prayers. The Almighty is in control, is He not?" She dismissed their conversation with a wave of her hand, "But it is late, *nu*? And we should get going." She picked up a bag that Anne had thought was a wedding present for the couple and handed it to her.

Anne took out an exquisite lace shawl and held it up. She was speechless.

"It was mine when I was much younger and wore such lovely things," Rachael said. "I want you to have it. Besides, it matches your shoes, and you might need it with the nights becoming chilly. Soon the fall festivals will be here."

Anne hugged Rachael. "Thank you. It's beautiful and means even more to me that it was once yours." She slipped back into her heels and gathered her purse and overnight bag. By the time she locked the door, Rachael was waiting for her in the car.

They headed to Ein Karem, a suburb some seven miles southwest of Jerusalem. The small village overlooked the Sorek Valley and was rich in Biblical history. It was famous for being the home of John the Baptist, where Mary had visited her cousin, Elizabeth, after she found out she was going to bear *Yeshua HaMashiach*.

Rachael told her how, when she was younger, she had explored some of the caves in the hillsides of the Sorek valley. She also told her that the valley had, at one time, been home to the infamous Delilah, who had caused Samson's downfall.

Anne knew some of the history already. Martha and Phil had taken her there, and she had purchased several pieces of art for her apartment. With its beautiful wooded hills and unique artisan shops, it was the perfect setting for a wedding. She couldn't wait to visit again.

As they drove toward Tel Aviv to get on highway 1, Rachael grew quiet and turned up the radio. Anne didn't give it much thought until the news report mentioned something about the rocket attacks. As soon as she heard the word, *Intifada*, Rachael quickly turned the radio off.

Anne turned to her, "What is it?"

Rachael's lips moved silently before she answered. "The rocket attacks against the Negev have intensified, and there was an incident in Jerusalem. They are on high alert there."

"I heard them say *Intifada*, Rachael," Anne pressed. "Are we in danger?"

"There is the threat of danger everyday when you live in Israel, Anne," Rachael said with a sigh. "This day will be no different, except we have the Almighty on our side. It will be all right."

"*Intifada* is an organized uprising on all fronts. That's a lot different than sporadic attacks out of Gaza. It means war."

"Yes, and *Yeshua* said there would be wars and rumors of wars, but the end is not yet," Rachael countered. "Anne, you have much to learn about our way of life in this country. We live within the parameters of war everyday. The extremists hate us. They do not want peace and co-existence. They want us dead or expelled, so they can take over the whole country. Not only that, most of our own people are apathetic and care not about the land that God promised us, including some in our government. The whole world is against us and our officials seem to be on their side. Besides, they did not say the third *Intifada* had erupted, only that it could."

Anne realized she had upset Rachael and remained silent, but Rachael continued, "Life here is a fragile balance between acceptance and resistance-- acceptance of what *is,* right now, and resistance to the fact that it will always *be* this way. That is our way of life, and it will not change. Things will get worse until our people realize *Yeshua is* the Messiah and they cry out for Him to return. Only then will He rescue the remnant of those who believe and silence our enemies."

Tears threatened as Anne looked out at the countryside going by in a blur. For the first time since she had arrived in Israel, she felt like an outsider. Even with all she had been through, she had never questioned if she really belonged here...until now.

The mission to find out who she was had unraveled with each event that had taken place, and she wasn't sure if she understood anything anymore. The weight of what she carried was now a burden instead of a mystery to solve. Suddenly she felt tired and alone. She lowered her head to her hands and cried.

Rachael pulled off the freeway and stopped. She slid her arm around Anne and apologized, "I am afraid I was too harsh with my words. I meant not to hurt your feelings, Anne. Please do not take it to heart so."

Anne shook her head. "It's not just that, it's everything that's happened. And all the things that I can't tell you."

Rachael opened her purse and offered some tissues. She waited until Anne was composed and then tilted her chin with her hand. "When I first met you, you were a woman in charge of your life. Oh, I knew you were afraid inside, but you had such a fight in you, so ready to take on the Israeli Army. You stood up to the Arabs, you stood up to my son, and I thought, 'This is what Jews used to be like.' You gave me hope, Anne, with your *chutzpah*. But something has happened since then."

Anne pressed the tissues against her eyes. "That's because I had on rose-colored glasses. You just threw them away and gave me black and white ones."

Rachael took her hand away. "When Christians and Jews come visit Israel, they already have on their rose-colored glasses. That is the way they want it, so we accommodate them. They are shown all the wonderful sites and sounds and smells, and then they fly back to the safety of America or wherever they have come from. But you live here now. You are a part of the land. It is time you faced the harsh reality of our existence, *nu*? Whatever is toying with your emotions, you need to give over to *Yeshua* and let Him bear it for you."

Anne used the tissues to blow her nose. She couldn't tell her what was really wrong, but, in a sense, it was just an excuse. "You're right. I let my emotions get away from me, and gave into the fears threatening my future."

Rachael brushed the hair away from the side of Anne's face and spoke softly, "Never give into fear. You are basically telling *Yeshua* you do not trust Him. Place your trust in His Word. He keeps His word." She took a hold of Anne's chin again and gave it a little shake. "You will be fine, true?"

Tears brimmed in her eyes again as Rachael pulled her into a hug. She patted her back and declared, "You *will* be fine. Now, we must get on, or we will be late for the wedding!"

Anne said nothing when they passed military convoys headed in the direction of Tel Aviv, but Rachael prayed each time a unit went by. "You know, Anne," she said, "just because you have an Arab for a father does not mean you are not a true Israeli. It comes from within. Having a deep abiding love for this land and for the covenant made by God with Avraham makes one an Israeli, whether they are Jewish or not." She looked over at her, "And you have that love. It emanates from your heart. It shows in your eyes."

Anne blinked back the tears threatening to spill over again; only this time they were tears of gratitude. She smiled through them and laughed when Rachael teased her. "You really need to save some of those tears for the ceremony. I know my cousin. It is going to be absolutely, breathtakingly beautiful."

Anne relaxed against the seat. She needed something breathtakingly beautiful to lift her spirits, like the trip through the Jerusalem forest to Ein Karem. The winding drive up through groves of cedars and olive trees didn't just inspire her, it brought on a soothing and restorative feeling that reassured her. The natural beauty of the Sorek valley and the calming order of the terraced hillsides spoke peace to her heart. She thought about the ceremony and prayed for Ari, wherever he was.

Chapter Twenty

Rachael and Anne arrived at Marni's home a little after two in the afternoon. The house sat on a small hill away from the narrow road. A four-foot-high stone wall lined the edge of the road and followed the property around the house. Large palm plants raised their branches high above bougainvilleas, which draped the landscaped hillside in a riot of bright purples and magentas.

Enchanting was the only word Anne could think of as they drove up the curved driveway beneath the shade of tall cedars. A gnarled olive tree grew close to the house. It was the focal point of a Spanish tile patio that had been laid out in a square around it and extended all the way to the entrance. They walked to the front door beneath a pillared portico, much to Anne's delight. The house, she learned, was a preserved historic home, built from Jerusalem stone, replete with brick arches framing the windows. She noticed a railing on top of the roof. It was one she had seen on many homes built out of the same kind of stones. Rachael told her it was a design carried over through the centuries.

Anne was fascinated. "To think, John the Baptist could have been born and raised in such a home!"

A lovely woman a bit younger than Rachael answered the door, and they were greeted with bubbling enthusiasm, "Shalom, shalom, Rachael!"

Rachael kissed her on both cheeks and pulled Anne to her side, "This is Anne Sheridan. Anne, this is Marni."

Marni gave Anne a hug and gushed, "How beautiful you look." She turned to Rachael, "Has she met Ari? Rachael, she should meet Ari!"

Rachael merely smiled. She winked at Anne and hurried to change the subject. "Should we not be off to the wedding?"

"We have time." Marni waved her hand in the air and Anne thought how much she looked and acted like Rachael. "Everything has been moved ahead an hour to accommodate the Rabbi," she went on. "He has been detained in Jerusalem. You heard about the stabbings last night, did you not?"

By the look on Rachael's face, Anne had a feeling that she had heard it on their way over.

"I am sorry, Anne," she whispered, "I thought it best not to mention it at the time."

Anne bit her lip and stared at Marni as she continued, "One of the young men, Nehemiah, is Aaron's best friend. He is in stable condition in the hospital, and Aaron and Shira are stopping by to see him. Aaron was crushed by the whole ordeal, but Nehemiah has insisted that they continue with their wedding. He told Aaron to make sure to tape it for him and to send him pictures on his cell phone."

Marni looked at Anne and gasped, "I am so sorry. I did not mean to go on. You are probably not used to the things that happen here like we are. Well, I mean, we are not *used* to them." She stopped and beckoned to someone coming from behind, "Binyamin, come greet Rachael and her friend, Anne."

Anne turned around and faced Marni's husband, who nearly choked on whatever he had been drinking. He set his glass down and greeted Rachael first. When he held his hand out to her, she had the oddest feeling he had been taken by surprise. She searched his gentle, blue eyes. "Have we met before?"

Binyamin picked up his glass without answering. "You look a little upset by what Marni just told you. Maybe some fresh air would help."

He spoke to Marni, "You and Rachael should catch up. I will take Anne outside to see our infamous view."

Before Anne could react, he took her by the elbow and guided her outside. They followed the patio around to the back. The Spanish tiles surrounded the house on all four sides and the patio enclosed several trees in the same manner as it did the ancient olive tree out front. Here and there spaces had been left open for landscaping with large stones, flowers and shrubs. "I'm impressed with your low maintenance yard."

"Well, I am not home on a regular basis, so this is perfect. We stayed with native plants that do not have to be watered, except when there is a severe lack of rain." He pointed in the direction of Jerusalem and told her to take a look.

Anne walked over to the stone wall, a continuation of the one at the bottom of the hill. It ran along the length of the patio and defined the edge of their property. She gazed out over the Sorek valley.

"This is breathtaking," she murmured, totally entranced.

Binyamin stood beside her. His tall lanky frame reminded her of the pictures of British soldiers who were stationed in Israel before it became a nation. His short sandy hair and his skin, tanned by the desert sun, emphasized those charming eyes. *Why does he seem so familiar?* she mused.

He looked sideways at her. "I am sorry if my actions in the house seemed strange, Anne. Ari and I work together, undercover. In fact, I was with him in Eilat after you were kidnapped."

Anne tensed and stared at the hills beyond. "That's where I saw you. You were with him at Moshe's, weren't you? I don't know what to say. Does Rachael know you work together?"

"No, and neither does Marni. It is just better that way because of the nature of our jobs, especially since we are family."

"I see," Anne said. She slowly turned and faced him. "Then you know he's not supposed to see me."

"Yes, I do." He took a drink and looked away.

Anne thought for a moment. "Why did you tell me about you and Ari, if your own wife doesn't know?"

"Ari and I are friends. I know everything about you. I felt it would be best, in case anything should ever happen and I am involved. And," he turned and searched her eyes, "because I knew Daniel. I am sorry about what happened. He was a nice guy."

Anne felt her face color at the mention of her late husband's name. She reached for the *Magen David*. "How can you say that?"

Binyamin leaned his elbows on the wall's capstone and held his glass with both hands. "He *was* a nice guy, when all of us knew him before he moved to the states. I cannot imagine what influenced him to turn against his own people after that."

"He was a nice guy until after we married." She let go of the locket before it left another imprint in her hand. "We became strangers. He was hardly ever home. We seldom talked, and now that I know what he was, what he did, I..." She took a deep breath. "The only positive thing he ever did was teach me how to defend myself and elude anyone who might be after me, which didn't work the last time."

"I am sorry, Anne," he apologized, "I did not mean to upset you. I just thought you should know I will be looking out for you if there is any trouble."

Being careful not to get her dress dirty, she placed her hands on the wall and braced herself. "Do you think there's any chance that Jamar will just leave me alone?"

She watched Binyamin shift his stance. His silence was his answer. She heard Rachael and Marni's voices, and dusted off her hands.

Binyamin caught her arm, "Anne..."

"Don't worry," she said. "I won't divulge your secret."

They both turned and smiled when Rachael and Marni walked around the corner. Anne pulled Rachael to the wall. "I may change my mind about where I want to live," she said. "It's so peaceful and quiet up here. And there are no words to describe this view."

Marni took her husband's arm and addressed them, "We should probably get ready. Help yourselves to food and drink. Rachael, you know where everything is."

Binyamin looked back when they turned to leave. Anne nodded in response to his smile. There was an unspoken trust between them now, though she felt uncomfortable with the secrecy.

After they were gone, Rachael stood at the wall and sighed, "I know what you mean about this place. This is what makes Israel so beautiful, *nu*? The trees, the terraces, the olive groves. You should see it in the spring when the almond trees bloom." She swept her hand out in front of her, "And there is something calming and rewarding to the heart when taking in all those hills in the distance. That is, if our leaders do not give them all to our enemies."

Rachael peered over the edge, "Such a stunning view of the valley with the brook and Avshalom Reserve. Did I tell you this is the valley where Samson went down to get Delilah?" Before Anne could answer, Rachael turned around and took hold of her hands, "Binyamin is not in the habit of stealing beautiful young women away to secrecy, I am thinking."

Anne looked away, "He knew my husband. A long time ago."

"I see." Rachael let go and patted the side of Anne's face. "Come on. We will have a good time tonight and forget such things, *nu*?" She took her arm as they headed toward the house, "He works with my Ari, you know."

"What?" Anne stopped and stared at her.

"Oh, I know I am not supposed to know these things, but a mother just does. Marni suspects as well, I am sure. Our men give us not enough credit, eh? But we say nothing."

Anne ducked her head and bit her lip to keep from smiling. When she looked up, Rachael studied her. "He told you as well."

"Yes...he did. And I promised I wouldn't tell anyone."

Rachael laughed and leaned her head against Anne's. "So. We will not tell anyone, will we? Are you thirsty? Marni has the most wonderful drink. It is a mixture of sweet wine with the barest hint of mint from fresh leaves. She adds crushed whole grapes that have been frozen. You will love it. It is very refreshing."

Anne shook her head. *What else do you know or suspect, my dear Rachael?*

✡ ✡ ✡

Khalid and his friend, Ahmad, discussed the best ways to get into Gaza without arousing suspicion.

"It used to be easy," Ahmad mused, "but the Sufa crossing is shut down, forever, I am thinking. There is no way in except through the tunnels, and that is dangerous either way now. One collapsed a week ago, killing five men and three children...they had smuggled weapons in from Egypt."

"That, plus tensions are running high on both sides," Khalid added. "I was just in a tunnel under Gaza, by the way. Found out fast I was not meant to be a rodent. Had to go south and bribe guards so I could come in through Egypt. Just in time, too. Next thing I knew, there was another border incident."

"Yeah, well, I hope I never have to go into one. Do you know they force children to labor in those death traps?" He looked around and lowered his voice. "I am not understanding why you cannot have the IDF alert the guards at the crossing to you somehow, so they will let you pass."

"It will not work this time. It is totally closed off to ordinary people because of the renewed rocket fire. I need a way to get in without drawing any attention to my presence. And it has to be now."

"I understand." Ahmad leaned closer, "My cousin is a driver for the Red Cross. At least, whenever they are allowed to transport aid into Gaza City. Maybe he could get us a job as helpers."

"Sounds like our best bet if it is soon...like today." Khalid finished his meal and casually glanced around the room while Ahmad made a call to his cousin. Being in public made him nervous. Too many things could go wrong too quickly.

In a matter of minutes, Ahmad was back and set his phone on the table. "You have luck on your side, it seems. A shipment is scheduled for early tomorrow morning, and I mean early, like five o'clock. They want to avoid any problems. Seems that this is too dangerous for most who volunteer, so that left us an opening."

Khalid saw his own opening. "This is God at work on our behalf."

Ahmad gave him a crooked grin. "You think everything is touched by your God."

"I know it is." Khalid took every opportunity to witness to his friend, but time was short. "What about Hassan, our contact in Gaza?"

"I already alerted him that we might be coming. I just need to let him know the details."

"He is good friends with my brother, Rashad. What is his cover these days? Is he still driving that taxi?"

"Not so much. It was crushed into retirement by an IDF bulldozer when they razed the building where two Hamas leaders were hiding. He recently found an old four-wheel-drive junker of a jeep that he fixed up. He painted it black and then sprayed, 'used taxi--reduced rates' on it in orange Arabic letters."

Khalid laughed, but he turned serious when Ahmad added, "Scary business--and times, right now. He has had a lot of close calls, and his family desperately wants to get out of Gaza. You have seen the conditions there."

"Yes, and barely got out in time to warn the IDF about the rockets Hamas had stashed close by."

Ahmad put his head in his hands and rubbed his face, "It is not a good situation anymore, and I do not know what it will take to turn it around. Gazans just want a normal life, like the people here. The international community has to back off and let us work all this out. The Israel my father and grandfather knew would have taken care of this matter and made short work of it while they were at it. Now their hands are tied, and we suffer for it."

Khalid understood his friend's frustrations. "I know, but no matter what happens, or who is in charge, there's only one solution to all of it."

"Yes, yes, I know. Your God. But I just cannot believe all that yet. Still sounds too much like a fantasy."

Khalid grasped Ahmad's wrists, "Ahmad, prophecies written thousands of years ago are being fulfilled daily. It is not a fantasy. It is our only hope."

Ahmad looked thoughtful. His eyes twinkled when he answered, "I know you believe this with all your heart, Khalid, but if you do not let go of my wrists, I will have to find another way to defend myself while I wait for your God to come to our rescue."

Khalid let go and grinned. He reached forward and pulled the cord that was wrapped around Ahmad's *kaffiyeh* down over his eyes. "One day soon, you will believe as I do. God will open your eyes."

"If I have any left," Ahmad retorted. He adjusted the cord and stood. "Come, let us pay for this. We will go outside and call Hassan."

While Ahmad connected with Hassan in Gaza, Khalid searched the main street of Bethlehem. He studied the looks on the faces of the city's inhabitants and wished he could stand up and proclaim *Yeshua*-Messiah Jesus to them. The most important thing gone from their eyes was hope. The Israeli built wall oppressed them from the outside, and the Palestinian Authority oppressed them within. It was a no-mans-land of despair, and despair was Satan's playground.

Ahmad hit his arm, "Hassan will be waiting. Another contact will be at the loading docks to take your place when you slip away. You have a white t-shirt on under that tunic?"

Khalid nodded.

"Good. Your double will be wearing a white t-shirt and a checkered *kaffiyeh* with a gray cord holding it in place. I hope you are not fond of that tunic and cap." He laughed as he put his arm around Khalid's shoulder and shook him. "Ready to go? I know a way back to East Jerusalem. Maybe though, you should first pray to your God that we do not get caught." Ahmad grinned at Khalid, but his eyes weren't smiling this time.

He wasn't getting into Gaza as quickly as he had wanted, but Khalid had to believe the timing for all this was in God's hands. He could take the long way around to the south and enter underground near Rafah if things had finally settled down, but the tunnel system wouldn't get him to where he suspected Rashad might be. Besides, he was sure Ahmad was beginning to take seriously his preaching about Jesus, and he wanted more than anything for his friend to know the truth and accept it.

As the two young men ducked in and out of alleys and finally out into a rocky field, Khalid thought about his family and friends. He prayed for mercy and grace.

Chapter Twenty-One

Anne sipped the special drink Marni had made for them. It was as good as Rachael had said: slushy with just enough mint to make it thirst quenching. They wandered around the house, admiring the beauty and simplicity of the furnishings and decorations while they waited for Marni and Biny. "I want a house like this someday."

Rachael responded to Anne's sigh and put her arm around her, "All in God's time, *nu*? But I must say, my cousin knows how to decorate. I love the open windows with no curtains, just a beautiful drape of sheer material over the top. And these tile and wood floors and the adobe look of the paint on the walls. So simple and yet so elegant."

"It is," Anne agreed. The warmth of the interior impressed her as much as the landscaping outside did. The barely-pink glow of the walls, set against the rich color of the cedar used for the stairs, the banister, and the trim around the windows, put her in a dreamy mood. "Do you ever wonder what it's going to be like when *Yeshua* comes back? Everything will change. Even the land, which means that homes such as this one will be gone. What will we wear? What will we live in then?"

"I do not give it much thought, Anne. The *Tanach* says there will be a lot of devastation before that day comes. I just have to keep an open mind and know that no matter what happens until then, it will be wonderful when *Yeshua* is King and rules in Jerusalem."

"I know. Still, I like to imagine. I've never been able to entertain the silly notion of cloud sitting while I learn to play a harp. I like the prophets' visions of *Yeshua's* thousand year reign, and then a new earth, cleansed from all the

163

mess we've created." She stopped to admire a silk hanging above the couch, when Marni and Binyamin walked down the stairs.

"It is time," Marni said with a nervous laugh.

Rachael went to her side, "Are you going to be okay?"

She said yes, but there was a watery sparkle to her eyes. "I think it is all beginning to sink in now." She turned around, "How do I look?"

Rachael hugged her, "*Oy!* You look every bit as lovely as your daughter. Not to worry. It will be the most beautiful wedding ever!"

Anne braced herself for the onslaught of emotions headed her way. Maybe Ein Karem wasn't the perfect place after all. She needed fresh air. She needed the beach and the sound of water. "Would you mind if I walked?" she blurted out. "We passed the restaurant on the way here. It's not that far."

Binyamin reacted with a firm, "No!"

Rachael took her arm and walked her to the car, "What are you thinking? You would ruin your shoes. Besides, we must arrive at the same time and not spoil the moment for Shira."

On the way, Marni explained, "Shira loves traditions, and since some family members are Conservative, and some are Karaites, she and Aaron are going to incorporate a few of the more traditional wedding practices, hoping it will help unify both sides."

Rachael leaned over and asked, "Are you familiar with the Karaites?"

Anne nodded. "They adhere to the teachings of Moses in the *Torah*, instead of following the rabbinic traditions and oral interpretations of the *Tanach* and *Talmud*."

Rachael looked impressed. Anne shrugged. "I told you I did a lot of research before I arrived. I just wish I would have had more teaching on my heritage, but David didn't seem to care, and my mother must have been conflicted by her beliefs. I know why now. It also explains a lot about my grandparents."

After they parked in the space reserved for the bride's parents, Biny joined a group of men who were standing outside around Aaron. Anne followed Rachael and Marni inside. She learned that the owner of the restaurant was a good friend and had closed just for the wedding.

When all the guests had arrived, Rachael told her the men would take Aaron into a room to sign the *ketubah* in the presence of witnesses. It was customary after signing the contract, for them to hoist the groom to their shoulders and carry him to the receiving room where she and Rachael were now. They heard them coming with loud singing and clapping. Aaron's family and friends entered the room and let him down in front of the prospective bride.

Shira sat like a princess on a satin chair decorated with lace and flowers. Aaron leaned down and kissed her before he pulled the veil over her face, to signify she was the one he had proposed to and wanted to marry.

Rachael whispered that the significance of the veiling custom dated back to when Jacob had been deceived into marrying Leah after he had served seven years for the right to marry her younger sister, Rachael. "What am I doing? You already knew that, *nu?*"

Anne smiled and whispered, "Not exactly. I know a few things. Would you believe I never attended a traditional Jewish wedding? I've never even been in a synagogue."

She sat on the right side of the room with the women who were related to the bride and watched Binyamin walk over and place his hands on Shira's head. The festive singing and clapping, or *simcha*, as they called it, continued. It was hard to hear Biny recite a blessing and tell his daughter how much he loved her. When he was done, he walked backward and joined the men who lifted Aaron onto their shoulders and carried him away again.

After the women had all greeted Shira, they joined the men in the dining room. Tables had been set up to form an aisle, which led to the stage at the far end. Attendants seated each family member and the guests according to the names that had been written on place cards.

Anne and Rachael sat at a table for three, but she knew the third person wouldn't be showing up. She hid her disappointment and focused on the centerpiece. A crystal bowl filled with roses and floating candles, sat in the middle of a square mirror. Several stems of lavender, tied with lace and a ribbon, graced each place setting, along with a wedding program, which explained the ceremony and the traditions.

Rachael picked one up. "These used to be called *benchers*. Originally they were prayer booklets, but much has changed within the religious sects of Zion. Now they can contain anything the couple wishes."

The *chuppah* on the stage caught Anne's attention. The silk canopy had been draped over four white poles wrapped with satin ribbon. Large silk tassels hung from the four corners of the covering.

"I think it is a beautiful symbol of God covering us with His banner of love," Rachael said as they discussed it.

Anne agreed. "It reminds me of the wall hanging in Marni's living room."

"It is the same design. Marni invited family and friends to a betrothal party for Shira and requested that they not bring gifts. After refreshments, she brought out this large square of white silk, and the rest of the time was spent designing and cutting it into different sizes. Each person then took home a strip and decorated it with embroidered blessings and Scripture verses. Marni said she and Shira enjoyed sewing the pieces all back together. Shira and Aaron said it was the best gift any of their friends could have given them."

"Incredible." Anne felt the familiar ache in her heart. "What a precious time for them to spend together as mother and daughter before the wedding. I can't think of a more beautiful way to constantly remind the newlyweds of their family and friends' love and support." She lowered her voice, "My mother was unhappy that Daniel and I had eloped, instead of having a traditional wedding. Now that I think about it, David probably paid him to do it, but I'm glad. It would have been such a lie, had we given in."

Anne knew Rachael understood by the way she patted her hand. She leaned over to thank her, just as a young man and woman stepped up to the microphones on either side of the stage and sang a love song in Hebrew.

"Not just any love song," Rachael whispered. "It is from the *Song of Songs*. Solomon was quite the romantic, eh?"

The rabbi walked down the aisle and took his place on the stage behind a small table also draped in white silk. Three groomsmen entered next and stood to the left, facing the stage. The best man followed.

The song ended and everyone remained quiet while Aaron, escorted by his parents, walked down the aisle. They each held a candle and led him to the left side of the stage. As soon as Aaron stood by the best man and groomsmen, they all turned to face the guests. Anne barely felt Rachael pat her arm when she recognized Ari.

Three bridesmaids came down the aisle next, followed by the matron of honor, Shira's best friend. They waited to the right of the stage, and everyone in the room watched Shira approach with her parents, who also carried candles. Just before they reached the stage, they each kissed her, and she walked toward Aaron by herself to signify she was ready to leave her parents and enter into marriage. The couple stepped up onto the stage together.

An older man approached the mike on the groom's side and sang Psalm 19, acappella. Aaron stood in the middle under the *chuppah* with his eyes closed and his hands raised and upturned, while Shira slowly circled him seven times. The rise and fall of the deep baritone voice, singing the Word of God, had Anne reaching for her shawl. She drew it around her shoulders as she watched Aaron and Shira's lips move silently. It was a perfect picture of humility and worship, and suddenly, she understood. When it ended, she looked at Rachael, who smiled. "They are Believers," she said. "They wanted this to be a testimony to their faith."

Shira stood at Aaron's right side now. The rabbi read the *ketubah* to them and poured wine from two glasses into one for them to drink. At that point, Aaron's grandfather, his father and one of the groomsmen stood at the mike on the left side. Binyamin, the other two groomsmen and his best man, Ari, stood at the mike on the right side. They recited the *Shevah Berachot* or Seven Blessings in Hebrew, with Ari speaking last. Anne closed her eyes and listened to his voice, wishing it would last longer.

The couple then read the vows they had written, after which, Aaron slipped a solid gold ring on Shira's first finger. She held it up to the cheers of the guests. Another shared drink of wine sealed the vows. The rabbi nodded his consent and Aaron placed the glass under a cloth and broke it with one stomp from his right foot.

"*Mazel Tov!*" Anne shouted with the others. She wiped away tears and was swept up into the crowd as they sang and clapped and escorted the newlyweds to the room prepared for their *Yichud*. The rabbi stationed two witnesses outside the door to ensure their privacy for the symbolic seclusion and consummation of their marriage.

The crowd resumed their festive singing and dancing on their way back to the dining room. Everyone helped rearrange the tables into a semi-circle with a large open space in the middle, while a live band set up their equipment on the stage.

In all the excitement, Anne barely felt a hand reach around her waist. Ari whispered in her ear, "You are even more beautiful than the bride. Say nothing. I will look for a time when we can be alone…we need to talk." He kissed the side of her face. "I love you, Anne."

She quickly turned her head, but he was gone. Rachael found her then, and together with family and friends, they stood on opposite sides of the aisle and raised their arms to form an arch.

When the ten minutes were up, the Rabbi sent word to the two witnesses to call forth the couple. Aaron and Shira ran through the long arch, with everyone shouting blessings. At the end, they stood together with the rabbi, who introduced them as Mr. and Mrs. Aaron and Shira Shaufer.

The couple kissed and separated, a cue for the band to start a lively tune. Shira took her mother's hands, and the rest of the women formed a ring around them while they danced. Aaron grabbed his father's hands, and the men formed a ring around them.

Anne took off her heels and totally immersed herself in the dance when she joined the ring. At one point, they all linked arms on either side of Shira, while the men did the same with Aaron. Moving to the fast paced music, the lines met in the middle long enough for the newlyweds to kiss, and then surged backward. After three kisses, one of the groomsmen brought out chairs for the couple. To help them stay together, Marni handed them a white cloth to hang onto while they were hoisted up above the crowd.

The dancing continued until a signal from the rabbi ended the music. The newly weds were lowered and led to their table, where they toasted their guests and thanked them for sharing in their special day.

Ari sat with the wedding party during the meal, but he and Anne seldom took their eyes off each other. Forgotten was the fear and anxiety of the past several days…all that mattered to Anne was Ari's declared love for her.

At the close of the meal, Aaron stood to make an announcement. "We are going to end this day of celebration at Shira's parents' home, where we can watch the sunset together. Afterward, those who want, may join us at the hospital to visit Nehemiah."

Without any prompting, the guests raised their glasses and spoke a blessing together in Hebrew in remembrance of those who had been attacked.

Rachael leaned over and told Anne what had happened. "Nehemiah and two of his friends were walking through the Old City in Jerusalem after visiting with his grandparents. Several Arabs attacked them with knives, and Nehemiah is the only one who survived. I did not realize at the time I heard it on the radio that he was Aaron's friend. Marni explained it to me when you were outside with Binyamin. She said Aaron called Ari and asked him to take Nehemiah's place as his best man."

"How awful, Rachael." The news played on her already sensitive emotions. She thought about the life and death drama encountered here on a daily basis and marveled at the strength needed just to exist. Exhaustion followed on the heels of sadness, but she remembered what Ari had said about meeting later. She had to remain alert. The time was close when they could get away alone, and this was one moment with him that she didn't dare miss.

Before she knew it, Binyamin herded them to the car and drove them home. Aaron and Shira greeted them when they arrived. Anne took a moment to congratulate them on their marriage and express her condolences for what happened to Nehemiah and their friends.

When they left to change their clothes, she asked Marni if there was anything she could do to help. Marni gave her a hug. "You are wonderful to ask, but I am fine," she said, "We are only providing drinks, which are made already. You go enjoy the evening with the others." She winked at Anne. "Off with you now. Biny went back to supervise the clean up. He will help me when he gets here."

Anne hurried to change into her jeans. She'd brought along the shimmery blue top she had worn on her daring caper with Ari and Khalid…it seemed fitting to wear it now. She touched her cheek where he had kissed her. Something had changed in both of them since that night. Whatever it was, it gave her heart permission to share her burdensome secret with him, no matter what the outcome.

Rachael had already retired for the night and sat on the edge of the bed, reading. She looked up when Anne opened the door. "There you are. I was hoping to see you before you went out with the others." She patted the side of the bed, "Please, sit for just a minute."

Anne sat next to Rachael, wondering at the serious tone of her voice.

"I saw the way Ari looked at you tonight, Anne," Rachael said, as she closed her Bible. "His heart so open, and his love for you so evident, I thought my heart would burst with joy for the both of you. But I knew if it was obvious to me, it certainly was to anyone else who saw you two, and I remembered what you had said about him not being allowed to see you." She looked at Anne, worry in her eyes, "I know he will try."

Anne wanted to tell her everything, but she answered carefully, "Rachael, he got close enough tonight when we were all dancing to whisper in my ear that he loved me. I know now that I love him just as much. If he does try to make contact, we will be careful. I don't want him to get in trouble because of me. I need him right now, more than you can know."

She saw the tears in Rachael's eyes and gave her a hug, "Pray for us. We both need your prayers that the Lord will watch over us until the matter is taken care of."

Rachael pulled away, "So. It is that serious, then?"

Anne nodded, "I wish I could tell you everything, but it's best that you don't know until it is settled."

"All right, then." Rachael put her hands around Anne's face, "I love you like you were my own daughter. I will pray for both of you. Be strong, Anne. And be safe."

"I will." She kissed Rachael on the cheek, "I love you, too." She quickly changed, laced up her boots and grabbed her jacket.

✡ ✡ ✡

The air had turned chilly when Anne walked outside to join the others who had arrived. She pulled her jacket on and stared at the sunset. Fiery crimson clouds danced across the face of the disappearing sun and then faded into lavender tendrils across the sky. Aaron and Shira stood at the wall with their arms around each other. Several of their friends gathered next to them and placed their hands on them. Anne joined them, adding her benediction. She lifted her hands and prayed silently for wisdom and grace and protection for these newly weds, who faced an uncertain future.

When she opened her eyes, the sky had already darkened. One by one, stars appeared across the sacred expanse, their lights a comfort to her heart.

She searched for her favorite constellation and whispered a prayer for all those she had come to love in such a short time, but especially for her beloved Israel.

Since the Hadassah Medical Center was just a few minutes drive from the village, Aaron and Shira waited until everyone arrived before they headed up to the hospital to see Nehemiah. Anne stepped in with the crowd when a shadowy figure appeared at her side. A hand engulfed hers and led her around to the backside of the house.

"Have you been here long?" Anne asked.

"Shhh," Ari whispered. He pulled her close and wrapped his arms around her. "I have no idea how much time we have, but I had to see you. I love you, Anne. I care not about all the reasons or excuses that say why it should not be, or why you should not love me back. I just know I love you in a way I have never loved anyone before."

Anne slipped her arms around Ari's neck and rested her cheek against his, "I love you, too."

He turned his head and when their lips met, she kissed him with all her heart. Tender, lingering, it was a declaration of unquestionable love. A love that could not be destroyed by any outside pressure, nor deterred by any barrier set in their way. A love that would grow as time allowed.

Ari broke away first. He held her even tighter. "Anne, I will do everything within my power to keep you safe. But if the worst happens...if Jamar does get to you, and if you know anything, he will find a way to extract it unless Rashad can intervene."

"I know. But I'm not afraid anymore. If this is my destiny, if God has planned this for me, He will keep me safe."

Ari buried his face in her shoulder, "Help me believe, Anne. I want to believe. I cannot lose you. "

There was so much she wanted to tell him, but only one thing burned in her heart, "Ari, God says that if you seek Him, you will find Him. He knows your heart. He will reveal the truth to you. But there is something I have to show you." She reached for the chain that held her *Magen David* and saw flashing lights.

Ari kissed her and pushed her behind him when soldiers surrounded them from both sides of the house. "Anne, trust no one but your cousins and Biny and Moshe. Do you understand? No matter what happens."

Two soldiers restrained Anne as Ari was led away. "No, wait. I have something...Ari!" In desperation, she kicked both soldiers' legs and brought her wrists down with a sudden snap. She ran after him, only to be intercepted by more soldiers. Once again she was dragged away before she could get to him. "I can explain," she yelled, as two men forced him into a black sedan.

Anne saw Binyamin run up the driveway past the car that held Ari. When he reached her side, he showed his credentials to the officers who appeared to be in charge. "Let her go," he commanded. "I will take care of this."

The outside lights came on. She heard Rachael and Marni's voices. "Binyamin, please," she begged. "Call General Elon."

Biny grabbed her arm. "You do not understand. There is nothing I can do now. Ari will probably be locked up."

Anne held out her hand. "Not if intelligence can decipher the information I think I have."

He stared at her and then at the necklace. "Are you sure?"

"I think I saw Daniel insert a chip beneath the opal."

Biny took out his phone and pulled her down the driveway. "I will explain as soon as I can," he called back to Marni and Rachael.

Anne looked over her shoulder and saw Rachael lift her hand. "Pray, Rachael," she whispered. "Pray for us."

When she got in the car, Biny put his headset on. He turned to her, his look one of disappointment. "Why did you wait so long?" he asked.

Chapter Twenty-Two

For two days Rashad had stumbled in and out of a maze of tunnels that appeared to have no end. No one seemed to know where Jamar was hiding. Along the way, several places in the underground system collapsed from overhead bombings by the Israeli Air Force, and he and Jamar's bodyguards had to dig their way out. The last bunker they led him to, was reinforced with concrete.

Although they were finally safe, Rashad had no way to get word to the IDF. He leaned against one of the walls. Most of the cement Israel had allowed to be delivered to Gaza for humanitarian relief had been confiscated by Hamas to build bunkers such as this one instead of much needed housing and sanitation. He would have to pinpoint the location and trust God to get him out when the time came.

Inside help would make it easier, but discovering the operatives within the Hamas ranks and revealing himself to them would be next to impossible. *"Lord, lead me and guide me. Make my way clear,"* he prayed. *"Keep Khalid safe and cause our paths to cross. I need him."*

When they entered the bunker, men hurried back and forth, stacking boxes of ammunition. Others loaded rocket launchers and stood them up against the walls. A group of men leaned over a table stacked high with maps. Khalid glanced around, "Where is Jamar?" he asked. "Why is he not here?"

His question got their attention. "Who are you?"

The guard who had led him there stepped forward. "He is working for Jamar," he informed them.

One of the men pointed to a map of Gaza, "He is caught here, between Khan Younis and Deir al Balah, which was under heavy fire from the Israeli Air Force earlier. We do not have a way to get him safely to the bunker. The tunnels have collapsed."

"They are collapsing everywhere." Rashad took a closer look at the map. "Is there no one in the area who can help?"

The Arab who acted in charge answered, "No. There is no way to tell who is who, and these incessant attacks by the IAF are wreaking havoc with our communications."

"That is not the only reason," one of the other men added. "Any cars or trucks that were there have been destroyed. We were just discussing how to get to the area and extract him. We need access to a vehicle by someone we can trust."

Rashad saw the opportunity he had been praying for. "I think I can help, if you show me where we are," he offered. "I have a friend in Gaza City, who owns a jeep he painted black to use as a taxi. It would be less conspicuous. I know he will be glad to offer his services."

One of the men pointed out their location. They were less than a mile away. Rashad tapped his finger on the map. "I can be there and back with Jamar within an hour if all goes well."

The men argued and finally insisted two of them should accompany him. Before Rashad could come up with a valid excuse why they shouldn't go along, one of the Arabs made a convincing argument that he would be more successful if he traveled alone. The man didn't have to say any thing more... Rashad knew he was the answer to his prayers.

As soon as he was clear of the bunker, he ran through the darkness into Gaza City. When he got to Hassan's home, Khalid stepped out from behind the doorway. Rashad pulled him into a hug, but Khalid cut their reunion short by saying he had bad news. The two took a walk outside.

"What is up?" Rashad asked.

"Biny called a few minutes ago. They have taken Ari to Jerusalem. He is under arrest for disobeying the General's orders not to see Anne."

Rashad sat down on a chunk of cement from a demolished building. "What do you mean, they arrested him? What are you talking about?"

Khalid slapped his forehead, "I am an idiot. I forgot you have not talked him since we got back from Eilat. Not only did General Elon blame Ari for the botched up loss of Anne's computer and Dov's death, he gave orders for him to stay away from her. I think I mentioned it when we met in the tunnel."

"So what happened?" Rashad asked.

Khalid sat down beside his brother, "Biny's daughter got married this evening. Ari was called in to be best man at the last minute, and his mother brought Anne to the wedding. The two of them met up afterward at the Feldmans' home. Biny suspects someone spotted them at the wedding and called the general."

Rashad tried to piece it all together. "Where is Anne now?"

"With Biny. He said something about her having important information to give to Ari. He is taking her to the police station in Jerusalem, hoping whatever she has will get him released."

"She is alone with Biny? Khalid, if Jamar's men know where she is, they will probably make their move tonight. We have to do something to change the circumstances, but first we will need Hassan's help."

"Wait, Rasha. Ari believes someone in the government is involved. He told me to trust no one but Biny and Moshe."

Rashad put his arm around his brother, "Are we surprised? It explains the way things have been handled lately. We will rely on the Lord's wisdom, then. He will show us what to do."

✡ ✡ ✡

When Rashad explained the situation to Hassan, he was more than willing to loan the two brothers his taxi. He even offered to go along. Rashad put his hands on the operative's shoulders. "No," he told him. "As soon as we leave, get your family ready to travel by morning light. Take them to the Erez Crossing. Tell the soldiers it is an emergency, and take only enough of your belongings with you to avoid arousing the suspicion of the factions roaming the streets. I will find a way to let the border guards know you are coming."

Hassan understood. He handed his keys to Rashad with a blessing, "May God keep you safe and give you success."

Rashad drove the jeep through the darkness to the location Jamar's men had given him. Hassan had gone over the garish orange letters with a quick coat of black paint. It was hardly a stealth vehicle, but both brothers prayed for God's cloak of protection.

On the way, he rehearsed his plan with Khalid. They kept the windows down to listen for any incoming missiles and wrapped their *kaffiyehs* around their faces to keep out the dust. Just outside of Khan Younis, he had to maneuver around massive craters in the road. Twice they swerved just in time to miss getting hit by an explosion.

"Those are not Israeli missiles," Khalid yelled.

"I know. They are fighting against each other now. Jamar has his hands full with all the chaos." Rashad hit his brother on the arm, "But we have Jesus on our side."

He radioed Jamar to get the exact location and told him to be ready. As soon as they pulled up to the site, the Hamas leader came running from cover with three masked and armed guards. One of them had to stay behind. Rashad didn't wait for instructions; he turned back to Gaza City and drove with a prayer in his heart that he was doing the right thing.

When they parked outside of Hassan's home, Jamar stuck his rifle in Rashad's face. "Are you crazy? You are leaving us out here in the open. You might as well put spotlights on us and whistle for the Jews and everyone else who wants us dead, to blow us up!"

Rashad pushed Jamar's gun away and kept his voice low, "Follow me," he challenged, "if you want to get to safety." He led the way through the rubble of a demolished apartment with Khalid at his side. Neither of them looked back.

The minute they were safe inside the bunker, Jamar grabbed Rashad and kissed both of his cheeks. He did the same with Khalid. "I should never have doubted you. I am in your debt. You risked your lives for me." He waved his hand in the air, "Name your price."

Rashad held back his disgust when he answered him, "It was not for money."

"Then, whatever you want, I will see to it personally." His cell phone rang and he turned around. One of his men directed him to a camouflaged opening close to the top of the bunker. When he finished talking, he walked back to Rashad, "It seems my men have learned the whereabouts of our elusive Mrs. Sheridan Weis."

✡ ✡ ✡

Anne sat still and listened to Binyamin's side of the conversation with the undercover agents who had apprehended Ari. They were too far ahead for him to catch up to, especially on the winding road that led to Jerusalem. He looked tense and unhappy. Another call to Khalid made her stomach tighten. She listened to Biny explain what had happened.

It was all her fault. She clutched the *Magen David* in her left hand in an effort to try to pray, but her mind wandered. She thought about Ari and the kiss they had shared. It was a possessive kiss, leaving no more doubts as to how they felt about each other. There were issues they would have to work out in their relationship, but now they could do it together. If only her mother...

Her fingers uncurled from around the pendant and she released the catch. When she looked up from her mother's picture, they had turned into the roundabout. Three men, armed and wearing black masks, ran into the middle of the road. Anne cried out. Biny hit the brakes.

Before they came to a stop, the terrorists converged upon the car and forced them to pull off to the side of the road. Anne heard Biny give a quick distress call. She kept her eyes on the gunmen while she eased her hand toward the console.

Two of the men forced Binyamin out of the car and threw him up against the opened door. Anne saw one of them slam the butt-end of his weapon into the back of Biny's head. Before he crumpled to the ground, the other terrorist ripped off his headset. The third man pulled her out of the car and led her away.

"Aba, please, don't let them kill Biny." She heard intense arguing in Arabic and then a round of gunshots. Just as her knees buckled, someone grabbed her from behind and placed tape over her mouth. One of the men pushed the barrel of a gun into her right side against her ribs. Pain shot up her arms from the ruthless grip of her captors, and she fought to stay in control of her senses.

They continued for some time on foot. In the darkness, she could tell only that they were following a path and descending into the valley. When they reached a road, the men stopped and forced her to wear an *abayah* over her clothes. She was then handed a *burqa*.

"Put it on and keep your head down," a voice commanded. As soon as she pulled the material over her head, she was shoved into the back seat of a plush sedan, with two of the terrorists on either side and the other one in the front seat with the driver.

The men took off their masks. The one on her right slipped his arm behind her and placed his hand at the base of her neck. With his free hand, he made sure her face covering was secure. "Head down. Do as you are told."

Anne complied, but she quickly glanced at the driver before she was forced to lower her head. The distinguished looking man wore a business suit.

Though she couldn't see, she prayed and listened to the voices around her. The men spoke Arabic, and she heard the name Beit Jala, an Arab city south of Bethlehem. With the checkpoints recently dismantled due to pressure from America, getting through this sensitive area was now possible. It mattered little that it put Israeli lives in grave danger. The Arab on her left side eased his hold on her arm when she shivered.

As soon as the car stopped, Anne was warned again not to look around. She stared at the sidewalk and counted the steps leading up to a door. Her mind focused on what little of her surroundings she could see. When they got to the second floor, they walked down a hallway, where she was taken to a room and shoved inside.

She swallowed when she saw the bars on the window. There was a narrow bed beneath and a side table with a wooden chair. A decanter of water sat on the table.

The same young man who had eased his grip on her arm in the car stayed behind after the others left the room, and Anne backed up to the table, tensing for the inevitable. When he approached her, she was ready, but he grabbed her wrist and twisted her arm up. "Do not try anything foolish, and you will remain free, without restraints." As he let go, he slipped a tiny piece of paper into her left palm. He closed her fingers tightly over it.

On his way out, he turned and warned her, "There are many guards. Your room will be watched closely." He held her gaze for a moment. Suddenly she understood. She placed her right hand over her closed fist and lowered her head.

The minute the door locked behind him, Anne peeled the tape away from her mouth and got a drink of water. She pulled the *burqa* over her head, but before she took it off completely, she read the note. *Better you do not escape. Trust me. Swallow this.*

With a prayer on her lips, she rolled the paper into a ball and swallowed it with another drink of water. When she set the decanter down, the objects in the room blurred. Dizzy and confused, she fell onto the bed and curled into a fetal position. She grabbed the edge of the cotton spread. "Aba, help...me."

✡ ✡ ✡

Biny came to and stared at the fuzzy, but familiar sight of Israeli uniforms. Two IDF officers helped him get up. He grabbed his steering wheel and sat on the seat, facing the men. "How long have I been out?" he asked.

A lieutenant answered, "Just minutes, Sir. We headed back here as soon as we got your call and heard what was going on."

The other officer opened a medical kit from their jeep. Biny accepted the instant icepack and held it at the back of his head. "You *heard*?"

"Yes, Sir. We believe an Arab operative may have been with the men who captured Mrs. Sheridan." He held up Biny's headset. "Must have dropped this so we could hear what was happening."

"Captured her? Do you know where they took her?"

"I am afraid we do, Sir."

Biny resisted the pain and read the soldier's name on his uniform. "Something you are not telling me, Lieutenant...Rohnen?"

The lieutenant bent down and looked him in the eye. He motioned the other officer over. "This is Staff Sergeant Oleny. They took her to Beit Jala in a Member of the Knesset's car."

Biny took a moment to process this information before he asked, "An MK? What, exactly, did you hear?"

"After you made the distress call to us, the one we think was an operative, argued with another Arab about staying behind to kill you. It sounded as if he had won the argument, but the other Arab yell the MK's car would be waiting, and that they should hurry. The operative ordered his partner to make sure Anne did not scream. Then we heard gunshots. From the way it looks, he fired into the dust beside you."

When Biny lowered his head, the ice pack slipped out of his hand and onto the floor. "Lieutenant, do you know who this MK is?"

"No, Sir. We only have our suspicions."

"As we all do, *nu*?" Biny rested his elbows against the steering wheel and placed his head in his hands. "Are you sure you were the only ones who heard this?"

"Yes, Sir. We called the agents to let them know we had gotten a distress call from you and were turning back to try to find you and Mrs. Sheridan."

The throbbing at the back of Biny's head started up again. He leaned over to retrieve the ice pack, when he saw the edge of Anne's silver chain on the floor beside the seat. He picked up the locket and slipped it into his pocket. "Lieutenant, Staff Sergeant, what you just told me is classified. Can I trust the two of you?"

The resounding "Yes, Sir," made him reach for the back of his head. "I need to get to the police station so I can talk to Ari."

Lieutenant Rohnen glanced at his partner before he answered, "We just got a call from the station. They are going to question him but not hold him. General Elon wants us to take him back to headquarters in Tel Aviv."

"Instead of the agents?" A number of thoughts raced through Biny's mind. Was it possible that General Elon was involved in this conspiracy as well? How far up did it go? He had to reach Ari and fast.

"Lieutenant, can you...?" He saw Rohnen hold up his phone and answer.

"Yes, Sir." The lieutenant motioned Biny out of the car. "The car is empty. Looks like a lot of shots were fired."

He looked at Binyamin when he answered again, "Uh, yes, Sir. There are tracks everywhere, but they disappear into the brush." He took a deep breath, "No sign of any keys, Sir. They may be planning to come back for it."

Biny closed his eyes when he heard the officer finish his conversation with, "Yes, Sir. We are on our way."

"What can we do?" Lieutenant Rohnen asked.

Biny pointed under the car. "I dropped the keys and kicked them under the front wheel when they made me get out."

After the staff sergeant retrieved his keys, Biny shook the soldiers' hands. "I am grateful, but be careful," he warned. "We do not know yet who to trust."

Lieutenant Ronen handed him some pain medication. "These will not make you drowsy, but they will help the pain. What do you plan to do?"

"I am not sure."

"I have an idea," Sergeant Oleny offered.

Chapter Twenty-Three

Ari waited in the station while Avram Hershel, the police chief, conferred with General Elon by phone. Handcuffed and standing between two guards, his only thoughts were about Anne. Now that he had time to think, he remembered her mentioning she had something for him.

The locket...that has to be it. Anne had been trying to give it to him when the soldiers surrounded them. He breathed a sigh of relief, glad he had not thought of it during his interrogation.

He remembered seeing Biny run past the agents' car as they were driving away. He knew his partner well enough to believe he would have found Anne and questioned her. Hopefully she would trust Biny enough to confide in him. It was possible the two of them could get to the station in time, and if the *Magen David* contained the information the government was determined to uncover, they might overlook his transgression and allow them both to go free.

Ari twisted his hands and felt the frustration of being restrained. He had always been the one in control of his life, but falling in love with Anne had changed everything. Once again, he would be unable to protect her should Jamar somehow find her.

He thought back to what she had said about G-d. *"if you seek Him, you will find Him. He knows your heart; He will reveal the truth to you."*

"Adonai, HaShem, Elohim, G-d, I know you by all of these names. I just do not know if I am ready for one more."

The chief of police addressed him, cutting his prayer short. "Ari, I have known you for a long time. I am sorry it has to be this way, but I have my orders." He nodded to the soldiers standing guard, "Take him outside. The dispatch is here."

Ari bit his tongue. He had been trained well enough to know that words wouldn't do him any good right now. Avram had been a friend of his father's, but the suspicion of corruption in the government made him wary. He had told Khalid to trust no one but Biny and Moshe. Now he had to follow his own advice.

Outside, two Army officers helped him into a jeep. Biny and Anne never showed up. He had no hope of talking his way out of this. Why weren't the agents the ones taking him to Tel Aviv? Was Biny ordered not to take Anne in to the station? What if she gave him the necklace, but he didn't trust anyone enough to turn it in? His mind searched for answers, but nothing made sense.

Ari looked back at the empty street in front of the station. He watched the lights of Jerusalem fade into the darkness. Traveling to Tel Aviv was never safe at night. He squirmed and fought against the handcuffs. It was then the soldier guarding him released his seat belt and told him to turn sideways.

✡ ✡ ✡

Moshe answered his phone. "Biny!"

He looked around in the darkness. "They have Ari? What happened to Anne?"

"No, I am here. I moved my family to Laqiyya. Khalid just called. He said Ari might need my help, so I am on my way."

"I know I said I would never move into one of those death traps. I do not like it, but Ari convinced me it would be better for my family's safety. My brother already lives there with his. It was not long after we moved that Khalid called. What is the word you always use for things that mysteriously work together?"

"Yes, providential. Well, it seems as if this was all meant to be, does it not?"

He checked his watch. "About fifteen minutes. I am close to Beit Shemesh. You had better have a good plan, and it had better work, or I am going after Anne, myself. She means a lot to me and my family."

Moshe went over the details Biny had worked out with the two Army officers. Ari would be in on the plan by the time Biny picked him up on the highway near Sho'eva. Once again he thought about Anne's beliefs and her strong convictions. "If You are really God's Son, *Yeshua*, then I ask that You keep her safe and help me find a way to free her."

✡ ✡ ✡

Anne heard voices around her. Someone helped her to a sitting position. "Wake up, Mrs. Sheridan. Do you understand me?" one of them asked in English.

The dizziness made it impossible to respond. This time, someone pulled her to her feet. "Can you walk? We need to leave. Now."

Her tongue sat in her mouth, swollen and unmoving. "N...No," she managed. She forced her eyes open. The room blurred and her knees buckled. Strong arms picked her up.

The voices she had heard at first sounded angry now. She thought she heard gunfire. They were running, but no matter how hard she tried, she couldn't control her body. She desperately wanted to go back to sleep, but the jerking motion of going down steps forced her to fight the drowsiness. In a matter of minutes, they were outside.

The wind blew hard enough to make Anne catch her breath. She felt raindrops on her face. When she opened her eyes, she recognized the Arab who had given her the paper in the room. He hurried toward a military jeep and shoved her inside.

"*Yel-la, yel-la, yel-la!*" he shouted to the men who got in the front seat. She didn't need an interpreter to know he was in a panic and telling the driver to hurry, but who was pursuing them? Could Ari have found her already?

As her mind cleared, the feeling rushed back to her hands and feet. An overwhelming thirst made it hard to swallow. "I need water," she begged.

When the driver yelled from the front seat, the Arab beside her forced her head down. "There is no time for a drink; you will have to wait," he said. His voice was gruff, but he sought out her hand and squeezed it gently. His actions confused her. She had thought earlier that the Lord had sent him to protect her. After being drugged, she wasn't so sure.

The jeep passed through a second checkpoint, and the Arab eased his grip on the back of her neck. Anne strained to see but it was still too dark. She thought about Biny. She had prayed for his life to be spared. Had God used this Arab to keep him safe as well? If he had found her *Magen David* and had gotten it to Ari in time, there was a chance that the police would have let him go. What about Khalid and Rashad? She held her head as thoughts about Ari and her cousins merged into confusion.

A small beam of light drew her attention away from the pain. With her head down, she could see the Arab had taken out a cell phone and was texting a message in Hebrew.

One of the men in front spoke up. He said something about Hebron, but that would mean they were headed south. *Why south? Where are you taking me?*

Questions tumbled through her mind, but her unbearable thirst blocked her concentration. She closed her eyes and fell into a fitful sleep until they stopped. Once again she heard voices. Once again, her Arab protector grabbed her hand and pulled her out of the jeep. After he guided her into a building and led her down a short hallway, he pointed to a door at the end. "Use the facility to get a drink and take off your garments. You must hurry."

Anne glanced at the Israeli soldier standing by with his weapon poised. He had come in with them, while the driver had stayed outside with the jeep. Something wasn't right. Her nightmare wasn't over. She had a feeling it was just beginning.

Nothing made sense. She tried to think back to when they had been in the house in Beit Jala. She was positive there had been only Arabs. She assumed from the man standing guard that the IDF had found and rescued her. But if they had, then who was the Arab still guarding her, and why weren't they taking her back to the police station?

✡ ✡ ✡

"Who are you?" Ari asked, when the soldier unlocked his handcuffs.

It was the driver who answered, "I am Lieutenant Rohnen. This is Staff Sergeant Olney."

Sergeant Olney handed his personal belongings over and Ari shoved everything into his pockets before he strapped on his holster.

Lieutenant Rohnen watched him in the mirror. "We are working with Binyamin Feldman right now. You need to stay buckled in, Sir. We are about to be run off the road."

"You saw him?" Ari rubbed his wrists where the handcuffs had left a mark and fastened his seat belt. "When? Where? Did he have a woman with him?"

"There is no time to explain it all, Major. But, no, Mrs. Sheridan was not with him. We have reason to believe Arabs who work for an MK abducted her. We overheard them say they were going to Beit Jala"

"An MK? Did you find out which one?" Ari lurched forward when Lieutenant Rohnen slammed on the brakes. A loud thud rocked the jeep. It careened across the center of the road and flipped onto its side. When it skidded to a stop, he heard someone call from outside. "Ari, are you okay?"

He searched for the release button to his seat belt. "I am fine…I think."

"Olney? Rohnen?"

The lieutenant answered, "We are okay. A little banged up, but nothing serious."

Ari grabbed the lever on the seat and pushed it forward. A familiar voice greeted him when he stumbled out onto the ground. "What are you waiting for? We have to rescue Anne."

"Moshe?" Ari grabbed his friend's hand and stood up. "How in the world?"

"Do not ask. It is providential, as our friend here would say."

Biny helped the soldiers. "I am sorry. I guess I rammed you a little too hard. If you are sure everything is intact, give us twenty minutes and then radio for help. You know what to tell them." He grabbed Ari's arm. "I will explain on the way. We have to hurry."

As soon as they were in the car, Biny clicked on his police radio. He turned to Ari and reached into his pocket. "Anne believes there is something embedded in this that will give our government access to the information they are after. I think she dropped it in my car on purpose when we were attacked. I assume my men told you everything that happened?"

"Yes. Have you heard anything more?"

"Not yet."

Ari took the *Magen David* and released the catch. Anne had never shown him the picture, but he had heard about it from his mother. The likeness intensified the ache in his heart. He pushed the locket closed and ran his thumb over the opal.

Moshe put his hand on Ari's shoulder. "I know what you are thinking, but right now we need to make sure Jamar does not get to Anne. Only then will you be free to unlock the mystery."

Moshe was right. Ari slipped the chain over his head and asked Biny, "Why did you not get this to the police before they sent me off to headquarters?"

Biny seemed frustrated, "I have no idea who to trust anymore. If they ordered you not to see Anne and arrested you in the dark when they could not possibly have known you were at my house, then someone in the department has to be an informer, or worse, a traitor. I just could not risk it."

"Well, for Anne's sake we will have to find someone we can trust to decipher this information."

Biny held his fingers to his lips and pointed to his headset. His tires squealed as he made a u-turn on the highway. "They have Anne."

Moshe leaned forward. "Who?"

"Our own military. They rescued her, but are now headed for the Erez Crossing."

"They are going to use her to draw out Jamar." Ari felt the points of the locket press against the inside of his palm. "If they were in Beit Jala, they may head down toward Hebron and cut over to Kiryat Gat. We will not get to the crossing in time."

"Turn here," Moshe called out.

Biny got off Highway 1 and headed south toward Beth Shemesh. "We have to try, Ari. Unless you have a better plan."

✡ ✡ ✡

Khalid watched Jamar pace inside the bunker as the night wore on. The leader seemed preoccupied with keeping in touch with his men who were holding Anne. At one point Khalid heard him cursing. He glanced over at Rashad. His brother's eyes were closed, but his lips moved. He closed his own eyes and prayed as well.

When word came through that the IAF had stopped bombing, the men went to work bringing in new supplies. Khalid and Rashad helped. The tunnel from the bunker led up through the floor of a demolished building on the outskirts of Bayt Hanun. It was the closest city to the Erez crossing.

"I am not liking this," Rashad whispered when they were out of the bunker. "It is too quiet."

Khalid felt his cell phone buzz against his side. He had slipped it into the inside pocket of his jacket earlier. "I know." He took the phone out and read the text message from his friend, Daoud. He nudged Rashad and handed the phone to him. Daoud's contact in the West Bank had learned that the IDF had rescued Anne and were headed to the Erez Crossing with her.

"We need to get a hold of Biny," Rashad whispered. "Find out what is going on with Ari, and see if Moshe found them."

One of Jamar's guards headed over to them just then. Rashad hid the phone and walked away through the rubble.

"Where is he going?" the guard demanded.

Khalid turned to face him, "Something is not right. The way the bombing ended so abruptly. It is just too quiet. He went to check it out. I think we should let Jamar know in case he needs to get out of here fast."

The Arab didn't waste any time getting to the tunnel opening. As soon as he disappeared, Rashad stepped back through the wall. "It is a ploy by our government to get Jamar out into the open. Anne is the bait. Biny did not explain, but Ari and Moshe are with him. They are trying to get to the crossing first."

"What are we going to do?"

When they heard their names called, Rashad handed the phone back and put his arm around his brother. "We will trust the Lord to frustrate the enemy's plans," he whispered.

✡ ✡ ✡

Jamar didn't seem the least bit concerned when they returned. Maps had been cleared from the table. Food and drink had been laid out. "We are celebrating," he said as Rashad looked around.

Unlike the many Gazans who had to scrimp to make ends meet, men in the Hamas ranks ate well. The money they charged those who dug tunnels into Egypt to get supplies was pure profit. Some of the better supplies that were hauled back ended up on their tables. The humanitarian aid that did get through rarely reached the civilians. It was a simple but clever plan. The Jews closed the crossings when the militants fired upon Israeli towns. The Israelis were then blamed for the impoverished condition of the Arabs, which brought them condemnation from the world. It was the innocent who suffered the most, and it all worked in favor of Hamas and Hezbollah terrorists.

Jamar gestured toward the food. "Eat," he said. "Not to worry about the IAF. I know why they stopped bombing. Besides, we have Mrs. Sheridan Weis on the way to us. And she will tell us everything."

Rashad grabbed a piece of bread and tore off a chunk. "So," he asked, "what do you suspect she knows? It would help to have some background when I interrogate her."

Jamar sat on a crate to eat his food. Between mouthfuls, he explained, "Daniel Weis' contact, Dov Stedman, relayed any information he obtained on Israel to Hezbollah headquarters in Lebanon. I handled the information until they sent me to Gaza to help Hamas take control. I made contact with Dov through my own informant. Unfortunately, they were both killed in a crash a few days ago. The last message Dov said Daniel sent, before the Mossad eliminated him, was that he had gained Intel on Iran's nuclear program and their plans for wiping Israel off the face of the earth. Iran has forged ties with Russia and Syria, and Daniel's information on all of this, as well as what he knew about Israel, came by way of a member in the Israeli government."

"So why not get your information from this traitor?"

"Because he had a heart attack very suddenly and very conveniently died... after Daniel's death, no less. Does not matter, though, another has taken his place. But the information we need right now is in our little American's head."

Khalid spoke up, "What if she does not know anything?"

"Oh, but she does!" Jamar jammed his knife blade into the crate. "Dov was sure of it when he saw her computer. She was protecting the information, when she gave the wrong password in Eilat. She is sly. Daniel trained her well, and Dov was convinced that she worked together with him."

Jamar stood. He nodded toward the tunnel entrance. "You and your brother need to be at the crossing to escort her here. She knows you. It will be easier for you to gain her trust."

His eyes glimmered in the garish light of the bunker. "The IDF thought they could trick me, but my men ambushed them when they tried to rescue her. They are on their way here in the soldiers' jeep, wearing their clothes and carrying their papers."

The Hamas leader pulled his knife out of the crate and waved it in the air. "The Israeli government thought they could lure me out into the open, but they will find out too late their plan backfired. Once through, my men will cover you while you get her to this bunker."

"But, I do not understand," Khalid said, hoping to stall. "Why would the Israeli government give her up? Why not try to extract the information from her themselves?"

"Because my informant was a double agent. He convinced one of our allies in the Knesset that she knew nothing, then told him he believed I thought she did, and that I would do anything to try to capture her."

He pointed the knife at Khalid. "Right words, spoken at the right time to the right people, make for a powerful force. We will soon see who is so clever."

Chapter Twenty-Four

The predawn did little to enhance the layered landscape of the Hebron district when the soldier and guard escorted Anne back to the jeep. It had been quiet enough, but an outburst of angry shouts from a gathering crowd had the Arab shoving Anne into the back seat. Rocks pelted the outside of the vehicle. The two soldiers cursed as they careened down the road.

"What's happening?" Anne whispered.

"We stopped in Halhul outside of Hebron proper. Guess it was not far enough away from all the trouble. It is Jewish settlers and Arabs in their on-going clash over the land. A dispute about housing in Hebron has everyone up in arms. The military is a favorite target. Too late, I think, the Jewish settlers rebel against their leaders who betray them at every turn. They are out for Palestinian blood. Unfortunately, the Arabs outnumber them and are tired of the IDF and police looking the other way while angry mobs of Jews go on rampages. It is a never-ending feud. Palestinians maim and kill. Israelis oppress. Palestinians retaliate. Funny how it comes down to basic weapons."

Anne ducked her head so it was below the seat and looked over at the Arab, not understanding.

"Rocks," he said. "Rocks kill as sure as bullets."

Tears threatened as Anne thought about what he said. Check points, concrete walls, death, all of them a daily reality for both sides, with neither giving in. What a mess her beloved land was in, and she was a prisoner in the midst of it all.

"They're taking me to him, aren't they? I don't know anything," she said, her emotions surfacing. "I can't tell Jamar anything."

The conversation between the two soldiers in front grew less intense as they turned southwest. The Arab put his finger to his lips. "You must be strong," he whispered. "It is the effects of the drug wearing off that make you feel this way."

Anne suppressed the urge to cry and closed her eyes. He was right. *"You are my strength, Lord,"* she prayed. *"You alone. Direct my steps."*

She glanced at the Arab and got his attention. "What is your name?" she asked.

"Abrahim," he said in her ear.

"Why did you drug me?"

The Arab frowned. "Not me. It must have been the water on the table. I heard the others say Jamar did not want you alert and possibly escaping."

Anne pondered what he said. It made sense.

They passed several villages, one of them Kiryat Gat. Now that they were headed west, the thought of Gaza loomed before her like a medieval fortress with a dungeon of horrors soon to be her demise if Ari or Moshe or someone didn't hurry up and rescue her.

✡ ✡ ✡

Ari locked his hands behind his head. The agony of knowing they might not make it to the crossing before Anne got there was worse than anything he had ever experienced. The madness of it all gnawed away at his heart and mind, leaving holes of despair. Had he stayed out of trouble with the army and the government, he could have ordered a helicopter, and they would have been there by now.

Moshe's hand gripped his shoulder. "You, my friend, are slipping. You have fallen in love with her, have you not?"

Ari didn't answer. He unlocked his fingers and banged the dash with his fist. "Biny, let me have your phone."

"Are you crazy? Who are you going to call?"

"I love her. I will not let them do this. Let me have your phone. Stop the car and get out. They can do what they want to me, but you do not have to go down for this."

"You *are* crazy!" Biny pulled over and reached for his phone just as it buzzed. He read the text. "It is from Khalid. The government does not have Anne. It is Jamar's men!"

Ari grabbed the phone and called IDF headquarters. "This is Major Ari Milchan...put me through to the general."

Biny pulled back onto the road, his tires throwing dirt and sand as he accelerated.

Ari placed his hand over the receiver. "What are you doing?"

"We are in this together, remember?"

Ari started to protest when his call was transferred. "General, this is urgent. I am turning myself in. I will explain what happened later, but you have to listen to me. You have been double-crossed. Your men are most likely dead. Someone informed the Arabs before the soldiers arrived, and they now have Anne and are close to the Erez crossing. You cannot let them get through."

Biny pressed his headset. "General, this is Binyamin Feldman. Ari is telling the truth. Khalid just sent a text. He and Rashad are supposed to meet Jamar's men when they arrive with Anne. Jamar plans to take out your border guards."

Ari listened to Biny explain that they had the information with them. "We believe it is a chip embedded in the *Magen David* she wore as a necklace. Sir, we can do this; we are moments away. We can save Anne. We can get Jamar's location for you. You can have him and the information Anne has… just tell the guards to stall until we arrive."

Moshe tapped them both on the shoulder. "Sderot is not far from here. What did the general say?"

"Rashad called in and confirmed our story. General's giving us a go. Moshe, what can you see?"

Moshe held up his binoculars and scanned the area. "It is too foggy that way to tell. This is not a good thing. Although," he lowered the glasses and looked at Ari, "it could be to our advantage. We could use the element of surprise on our side."

✡ ✡ ✡

The dim morning light faded into foggy gloom as they neared Sderot. Anne thought about the beauty of the landscape as they traveled from Halhul in the West Bank across to the southern portion of Israel. Orchards, vineyards, green fertile terraces. Driving through them as the emerging sun swept across them like a spotlight, produced a calm and peaceful vision of the land, but she knew it was a facade. Hatred and counter hatred ran beneath the surface like an electrical line with frayed and damaged wires. When exposed to the right circumstances, they could spark unspeakable violence on both sides. It was evidenced physically by the roadside work of Israeli bulldozers as they cut through the landscape to form bypasses around Arab villages and made road blockades to keep them from entering Israeli towns.

It's Ishmael and Isaac. The feud has lasted for thousands of years, passed down through Jacob and Esau...a fulfillment of the prophecy given to Rachael when she carried the twins in her womb. Neither side understands the real reason for the conflict. It is not about land, or peace. It is about Satan's rebellion against God, carried out now by militant Arabs. She closed her eyes. *"And it will only end when You return, Lord, in power and in might. When Your people finally believe You are their Messiah."*

Abrahim squeezed her arm. She saw his phone light up with a text. "Do you trust me?" he whispered.

"Yes, I do."

"We are going to be caught in the middle of a rescue attempt when we reach the crossing. Be ready, and stay beside me."

"Okay." She didn't care who her rescuers were. If she could get away, maybe she'd have a chance to speak on Ari's behalf. She prayed for angels... legions and legions of angels.

✡ ✡ ✡

Khalid and Rashad headed out into the morning haze. It was on a day like this that an Arab militant had slipped through the crossing in the dense fog and had breached the wall around the *Erez kibbutz* before getting caught.

"This weather is an answer to our prayers," Rashad whispered to his brother. "We need all the help we can get if this is to go down without anyone getting hurt. Where are Ari and Biny now?"

"They were going to come in along the east side of the *kibbutz* and drive into the parking lot. The guards have been instructed to detain Jamar's men until we are all there."

"Do you think Abrahim is up for this? He is so young."

Khalid didn't answer until they made it to the gate at the entrance of the tunnel through which anyone entering or leaving Gaza had to pass. Once there, they could feel the heaviness of the fog, as though God had gathered all the cool moist air in from the sea and kept in that one spot. "Pray for him," he replied. "He might be young, but he is capable."

As soon as the gate opened, they broke into a run. It was too early for anyone else to be around and they hurried through the tunnel to the first door. The saturated air intensified the squalid stench of urine...the Arabs' crude protest of the insanely long hours of waiting in line to get through to work in Israel.

"I am not sure about this." Khalid covered his face with his arm. At that moment, the door opened and two IDF soldiers grabbed the brothers.

They were searched for weapons and explosives and then whisked through to another door and into a small room. The soldiers escorted them into the main part of the building. The sound of their footsteps echoed through the enormous hangar. Rows of bulletproof glass vestibules, designed to herd thousands of Arab workers through the structure at the same time, looked like an eerie scene out of a science fiction movie.

Khalid felt his phone buzz. He took it out and read the text before he stopped one of the soldiers. "We have a problem. The men posing as IDF soldiers have explosives. They are suicide bombers, waiting until we take Mrs. Sheridan through before they blow themselves up along with the guards."

"Wait!" Rashad turned to the soldiers, "Warn the guards, but tell them not to react yet. Khalid, call Biny. They need to know what they are up against before they confront them."

Khalid held his phone up, "He is not answering."

✡ ✡ ✡

Ari saw the empty jeep on the other side of the parking lot when Biny stopped the car. Jamar's men had walked up to the first guard post and were talking with the person behind the glass. Anne and a young Arab stood behind them.

Moshe opened his door and slid to the ground. Using the car for cover, he trained his rifle on Jamar's men. Ari could see that Anne was too close to them. Although he had the utmost confidence in Moshe's aim, he felt fear seep into the every fiber of his body. One wrong move...

When he reached for the handle on his door, Biny grabbed his arm and whispered, "Wait. I missed a call from Khalid earlier. He is texting now."

"Ari! Jamar's men have explosives..."

Ari didn't hesitate. He unbuttoned his shirt and threw the car door open. He stumbled out, yelling in Arabic, "What is wrong with you stupid people! Get me back to Gaza!"

Biny jumped out and ran around the car. He slammed Ari up against the door. Ari pushed him away from the car and went after him. As they scuffled, he kept an eye on Jamar's men, who stopped talking to the guard at the post and whirled around with their rifles pointed their way.

Ari looked at Anne and saw the recognition on her face. She opened her mouth, but the young man next to her grabbed her arms. He stepped back and pulled her away from Jamar's men, who were now in Moshe's sight. In that split second, he pushed Anne to the ground just as Moshe fired two lethal shots.

When Jamar's men went down, complete chaos erupted. Soldiers emerged from the hangar. Amid the shouting and confusion, Ari ran for Anne. As soon as he reached her, she buried her face against his chest. He held her close and leaned his chin on her head. His voice trembled with emotion, "It's over… it's finally over."

"It was a miracle, Ari. The fog. And you arriving just in time."

"I know," he said. "I experienced my own miracle last night."

He let go of her and lifted the chain with the *Magen David* from around his neck. "I believe this belongs to you."

Anne wiped the tears from her eyes. She held her locket close to her heart for a second before opening it. When she lifted out the picture of her mother, she handed it back. "This is your defense. After all I've been through, I'd feel better if you kept it safe with you."

Ari closed his hands around hers, "I have no idea when you will get it back."

"Doesn't matter," she said, "as long as I get *you* back."

"Ari, Anne!" Rashad and Khalid ran toward them. Armed soldiers swarmed the parking lot with their weapons trained on Biny and Ari.

Rashad reached Anne first and pulled her out of the way into a strong embrace. He kissed her forehead before letting Khalid hug her. Ari watched the three of them stand in silence with their arms around each other. When Anne looked back, he and Biny had been handcuffed.

Overhead, an Israeli gunship approached and fired a missile. Anne covered her ears. This time it was Moshe who wrapped his arms around her. The massive secondary explosion left no doubt that they had successfully located Jamar's bunker.

Ari heard Biny tell Moshe he could use his car to get everyone back to Tel Aviv. At least now they knew they could trust General Elon. Hopefully, the information contained within the chip and the elimination of Jamar would expedite the investigation and result in his and Biny's release.

He watched Moshe hold the car door open for Anne. Before she got in, she turned around and mouthed, "I love you."

"I love you, too," Ari said out loud, not caring who heard.

✡ ✡ ✡

Anne met with General Elon and a quickly assembled group of military advisors. Satisfied with her story about Daniel and her sworn testimony that she knew nothing about what was contained within the chip, they dismissed her. A military review board released Biny and Ari after hours of interrogation.

Abrahim, Khalid, Rashad and Moshe were questioned next. The meetings took place secretly without any public knowledge due to the nature of the situation.

Rachael and Marni were there to greet them when they came out of headquarters. They gathered around in the parking lot under glowing clouds, a welcomed end to a day that could have ended so tragically. Marni whispered in Biny's ear. He put his arm around her and got everyone's attention. "We would like to invite you to our home. We have plenty of food, and room for you to stay for the night. It would be a great way to wrap all this up emotionally. We have been through a lot together."

The invitation was discussed. Moshe declined. He politely told them it would be a pleasure to spend the evening with them, but he preferred to return to his home to be with his family.

Abrahim spoke up, "I will go with Uncle since we live in the same town."

Anne turned to the young Arab. "You are his nephew?"

Moshe placed his arm across Abrahim's shoulder. "My brother's son. I taught him everything he knows! That is why he pushed you to the ground and protected you at the crossing."

Abrahim grinned. "I saw the barrel of his rifle on Biny's car and knew what he was going to do. I heard many times how he and Ari had used that tactic during the war. Actually, given the circumstances, it was the only thing he could do."

"Abrahim is done with his two years in the IDF," Moshe bragged. "He already graduated from the university at Tel Aviv and wants to get into a government position. He could make a real difference there and help our people."

Ari pulled the young Bedouin into a hug. "I owe you," he said. "If you ever need anything, let me know."

Ari and Biny agreed to take the Bedouins to Laqiyya. Marni talked Rashad and Khalid into going to Ein Karem with them. "You can shower and change into clean clothes while the men are on their way."

Anne could see it was a desirable proposition for her cousins. "Besides," she encouraged them, "it will give us some time alone. We have a lot to talk about."

She walked over to Moshe and threw her arms around him. "You saved my life again, Moshe. I love you. Give my love to Nila and Jale."

"I would gladly have given my life for you, little Zhura. You are welcome in our home, anytime." He held her close and kissed the top of her head before he whispered in her ear, "You will be good for Ari. He needs you."

Anne placed her hand on his leathery face. "Thank you."

She hugged Abrahim next. "How can I thank you for all that you did for me?"

Abrahim returned her embrace and kissed her on both cheeks. "Uncle told me about you. I was afraid for you for a while, but I could see you were strong. We got through it with no problems."

"No. It wasn't my strength. It was God's," Anne insisted. "It was a miracle how it all turned out."

He laughed and said, "So Daoud tells me."

More seeds, Anne thought and thanked *Yeshua* for her Bedouin friends.

✡ ✡ ✡

Rashad and Khalid sat around Marni's kitchen table with Anne. "Feels good to be dust free," Rashad told her. "I cannot tell you how many times the Lord protected me in those tunnels."

Khalid held out his hands, "Us, you mean."

Anne looked at both of them, "All of us. It felt like I was in a tunnel when I was trapped in the desert. On top of that, I found out a lion had been tracking me."

"The point is, He obviously has a plan for each of our lives," Rashad said, "And, He honored our prayers for each other."

Anne showed them the letter from their grandparents and they became so engrossed in discussing family that they didn't hear Biny and Ari arrive. Marni came in to tell them. "If I know these two at all," she said, "they will want to clean up before seeing anyone, even if they are starving."

When she left the room, Rashad placed his hands over Anne's. "Ari is not a Believer, Anne." His voice held concern. She understood.

"I know. He's not one *yet*. We've talked about it. He said he wants to believe, and maybe what just happened has opened his eyes."

Khalid seemed thoughtful. "What is it?" Anne asked.

"We have not said a lot to him, but he knows what we believe. People of faith, who know Ari, have known better than to talk to him about it. But, perhaps God has sent you here, at this moment, to complete what we started."

Rashad agreed. "One plants, one waters, and yet another reaps the harvest."

Anne looked at both of them, amazed. "Did your grandparents teach you that?"

Khalid exchanged grins with Rashad. "When we were young, we would sneak away and go to our grandparents' home. They would read the Bible to us. It made more sense than what was written in the Quran. Your father would spend hours helping us understand. He was our favorite uncle."

"Our grandparents got to plant, water, *and* harvest," Rashad told her. "If it had not been for them, we probably would have become suicide bombers, like most of our friends, killing as many Israelis as we could. Instead, I went to university and met Ari."

Anne leaned forward, "Is that how you both came to work for the IDF? Through Ari?"

"In a roundabout way," Rashad answered. "Both his family and ours suffered at the hands of extremists. We vowed to do something about it. When Ari told us he was going into the Intelligence division, we asked if there was a place for us there."

"Yeah, but it was hard on our grandparents," Khalid added. "They understand, but they do not believe violence is the way to stop violence. For us, we try to do as much as we can without using force."

"I can't wait to finally meet them."

Rashad brushed a tear from the corner of her eye with his finger, "We can call them tonight and make arrangements. They do not live far from here."

Ari joined them and pulled up a chair next to Anne. The look in his eyes melted her to her knees.

Rachael, who had stayed in their room until then, appeared with Marni and Biny. After Marni brought plates of food to the table, they all joined hands. Biny prayed. His gracious words filled the room with thankfulness and praise, and Anne's heart sang when Ari kissed her hand at the end.

As they recapped all that had happened to bring them to a place of safety, with no casualties, it was even more evident how God had miraculously orchestrated all of their steps. "His love for all of us seems almost overwhelming at times," Anne said. The others agreed, but Ari was silent. She hoped it was because he was considering all that had been said.

When they finished eating, and the table was cleared, Biny took Marni's hand. "Anne," he said, "when we came in, we heard you talk about seeing your grandparents. You should consider doing it first thing in the morning. I hate to be the bearer of bad news, but after we took out Jamar's bunker, Hezbollah completely took over Gaza. Now that the government has the information from Daniel's chip, there is talk of going to war, and that could mean increased violence from Arabs in the West Bank and East Jerusalem."

Anne tried to process all that Biny's information implied. She shuddered when she looked at Rashad and Khalid.

"That is why we wanted to have everyone over tonight." Marni told them. "It does not appear there is going to be much of a respite from all of this for us."

Biny looked around at all of them. "We are exhausted and going to bed. May God continue to protect us, guide us and give us wisdom," he said. There were only nods from everyone. The silence was palpable.

Rachael stood then. She brushed the hair back from the side of Anne's face and kissed her cheek. Then she moved to Ari and kissed the top of his head. She seemed too emotional to say anything. When she turned away, Anne got up and pulled her into a hug. "I'll be in later," she said.

Rashad and Khalid both scooted away from the table. "There is a fire going in the living room if anyone is interested," Khalid offered.

"That sounds wonderful," said Anne. "I'm not ready to go to bed, yet."

The living room was warm and inviting. Ari pulled her down beside him on one of the couches. She curled up close and listened while the two Arab brothers and their Jewish friend filled each other in on all that had happened. Rashad had gotten word that Hassan and his family had made it to the Erez crossing, but he hadn't heard anything about the operative who helped him in Jamar's bunker. Khalid put his arm across his brother's shoulder, and Anne's heart went out to her cousins.

As they pondered the future of Israel and what would come of an all-out war with Iran, Ari spoke of the passages in the *Tanach* about how God promised He would come to Israel's defense and defeat her enemies. Anne was amazed at how much he had changed since their talk that night at Caesarea. When he quoted a portion of Psalm 2, Rashad and Khalid came alive.

She had never thought of using that particular Psalm to explain Christ, God's Anointed, to a Jew. The passion of her cousins surged through her. She had no idea what Ari was thinking, but she knew they spoke God's Word and that it would accomplish its purpose in his life. To her surprise, he didn't argue; he simply asked if there were more passages like it.

Khalid looked around, and Anne jumped up. "I have a Bible in my room," she said.

When she came back and handed it to Khalid, he and Rashad pulled chairs up to the couch. Ari leaned forward.

Though she longed to stay, she listened to the still small voice of the Holy Spirit and slipped away to bed. It was her first peaceful sleep in days.

✡ ✡ ✡

Voices woke Anne in the morning and drew her to the kitchen. Rashad and Khalid sat at the table, drinking coffee with Biny. Ari wasn't with them.

"Is Rachael still sleeping?" Biny asked her.

"She was just starting to stir when I got up."

"Good, Marni should be down soon."

"Are you ready?" asked Rashad. His eyes twinkled.

Anne thought him even more handsome than when she'd first seen him at the airport in Eilat. She still marveled at the fact that they were related. She ducked her head and smiled. "I'm a bit nervous, I think."

"Not to worry." Khalid pulled her close. "We will be with you."

Biny held out his cup as though to toast Khalid's statement, "I would say that is better than an entire army."

Anne nudged Khalid in the side. "I didn't mean I was afraid." When the men laughed, she asked the question that had been on her mind since coming to the kitchen. "Where's Ari?"

Biny cleared his throat. Rashad set his cup down. "He went for a walk. Said he needed more time to wrestle with what we showed him in the Bible last night. It is a good thing, I think. We did our part. Now, God will have to open his eyes to the truth."

Anne did her best to hide her disappointment, but she knew he was right. "So. When do we leave?"

Biny checked his watch. "Now."

As they drove down the road to Jerusalem, Anne couldn't help but look for Ari along the way. Rashad must have noticed, for he placed his hand on her cheek and turned her head to face him. "Trust and faith, Anne. You must let go of him and let God do His work in his heart."

Anne's lips trembled. "I know." She leaned against him and drew strength from this man she had come to love so deeply.

✡ ✡ ✡

Ari sat just below the wall around Biny's house and looked out over the valley. He loved this place. Loved thinking about how his ancestor, the King of Israel, had once roamed these hills. David had loved and lived life to the fullest, and as the Psalmist, he had been given revelations of the Messiah. But was the Messiah he wrote about the same *Yeshua* that Anne and his family and friends believed in?

HaShem, I need to know. Show me, somehow. With that prayer in his heart, he headed up to the house. Biny's car was gone by the time he walked up the driveway. He struggled with the disappointment of not getting to be with Anne and encourage her before she left, and then decided maybe it was for the best. She might have asked questions he wasn't ready yet to answer.

Rachael handed him a cup of coffee when he entered the kitchen. "Your phone rings constantly. Did you see Anne? They just left."

Ari didn't answer. He sat the cup down and ran for the bedroom where he had purposely left his watch and phone so he could think without interruption. It was Moshe who had been calling. He returned his call and found out there were reports of unrest in East Jerusalem. As Moshe filled him in on what was happening, Ari raced through his received calls to see if the army had contacted him. They had.

"Listen, Moshe, I need to go. Anne is on her way to see her grandparents in Jerusalem."

Rachael and Marni had taken their coffee out to the patio. Rather than cause them worry, Ari said only that he had urgent business in Jerusalem and asked to use his mother's car. He kissed her and left before she could ask any questions.

He forgot where they said they were going and called Anne. When there was no answer, he tried the others. His frustration grew. Desperate, he called Moshe back, "I am not getting a hold of anyone. Can you call Daoud? He knows the Sayyids' grandparents. Maybe he can tell me where they might meet."

After several phone calls, Ari made his way to the Old City. Trouble was brewing too close to East Jerusalem, and the thought of Anne being in the midst of danger again was more than he could bear. As he fought through heavy traffic, his conversations with Khalid and Rashad from the night before refused to give him peace. "I cannot deal with this right now," he said out loud.

You must. To believe in Me is to believe the truth. The voice seemed real and filled the air around him.

Ari pounded the steering wheel. "Leave me alone!" He looked around. "Great, now I am hearing voices and talking to myself."

I cannot leave you alone.

The light ahead of him turned red. He screeched to a stop and put his hands over his ears. "Why? What do You want with me?"

Nameless faces surged through the intersection, but one of them stopped and looked at him. The man's gaze pierced Ari's soul, yet his eyes were warm with compassion. Something clicked in his heart, and in that moment, he understood. Everything he had been shown from the scriptures about *Yeshua* suddenly made sense. His eyes blurred. Forgiveness flooded his being and stilled his repentant heart.

When the light turned green, Ari searched for the stranger but saw no one around who looked like him. Cars behind him beeped and reminded him where he was going.

✡ ✡ ✡

The minute Anne saw the Jaffa gate ahead, her burden for Ari lifted. She felt a stirring in her heart. Excitement took over at the prospect of seeing her father's parents for the first time.

Biny dropped them off close to the Kotel and said he would wait for their call to come pick them up. Khalid reached for his phone. "Good thing you said that. I forgot to turn it on this morning."

Anne thought about her own phone still charging on the nightstand at Biny's. She brushed aside the thought that Ari might be trying to call her and geared up for the walk down David Street to the Western Wall.

Visitors and residents crowded the main street, soaking up the warmth of the sunshine. The Wall was a symbolic meeting place, and it would make her first encounter with her grandparents even more special. Anne got caught up in the excitement as they neared the Temple Mount, but the enthusiasm turned to panic as chants of "death to Jews" roared toward them from the Arab Quarter.

Rashad grabbed Anne's arm. Khalid moved closer until she was sandwiched between them. He took out his phone and tried to talk above the chaos that now enveloped them. As they looked for a way of escape, Rashad pointed toward an older couple who huddled together, looking confused and afraid. Anne knew them at once. She broke away and ran toward them before Rashad or Khalid could stop her.

Police from the Shelem police station used riot shields to ram their way toward the scene. IDF soldiers swarmed the area. Hysteria escalated when Arabs picked up rocks and hurled them toward the masses.

As she fought to reach her grandparents, Anne saw an Arab man shove his way toward her. He wrapped his arms around his bulky shirt, and the scene in Haifa with the young suicide bomber flashed through her mind in slow motion. She turned her head to look for Rashad and Khalid, but was thrown to the ground just as an explosion went off.

Sharp pain ripped through her right hip and leg, the only parts of her body not covered by her protector. Shock and confusion gave way to tears when she recognized who had saved her life. She pulled free from Rashad, who had wrapped his arms around her, and stroked his still face, while her cries for help dissipated into the bedlam. It was then she saw Ari crawling around bodies to get to her. Two soldiers stopped to help him, and when they set him down beside her, he pulled her close. She wrapped her arms around him and cried, as he whispered over and over, "You are alive."

Soldiers rushed passed them, firing rubber bullets. Police threw stun grenades into the Arab mob and were able to push them back. Barricades went up around the area to allow ambulances into the Kotel.

Khalid had found Namir and Qasim, and they rushed to her side. Though covered in blood and visibly shaken, they assured her they had not been injured. It was not the meeting any of them had looked forward to, but they were together, and together, they prayed and mourned.

They each kissed Rashad goodbye before the medics arrived and covered him with a sheet. Anne longed to comfort Khalid and her grandparents, but she was told her injuries would require stitches. Khalid called Biny and they promised to meet her at the hospital.

Ari had sustained the worst injuries. The medics applied a tourniquet to his leg and gave him a shot for the pain, but when they placed him on a stretcher, he grabbed Anne's hand. "*Yeshua*. I saw Him," he said, his voice fading.

She leaned closer, not understanding. "The second Psalm," he said. "Tell Khalid…I believe."

Epilogue

Anne dragged the tops of her feet through the wet sand along the shore of the Red Sea. They left a line of toe marks that teased the incoming waves. The wind kissed her long sundress, and the silk material hugged her tanned body in response. Deep side slits revealed her legs as she walked. Even with the scars left from the shrapnel wounds, she felt free and elegantly feminine. She took off her straw hat and shook her hair loose.

Life had not accommodated her as she had imagined it would when she first arrived in this country of dreams and hopes. She thought back over the events that brought her once again to Eilat. Through her ordeal, she had learned that barriers, whether of race or religion or ideals, couldn't corral love. She had learned also that while love transcends all adversity, generations of hatred fueled by ambitions and greed would ever be around to battle until *Yeshua's* return. It was an experience she would never trade, though she wished it could have turned out differently. She knew she would write about it someday. For now, she decided to let it mellow and age gracefully, allowing time to replace the harshness of death and sorrow with acceptance and fond memories.

Her love for Rashad would ever be deep with admiration and respect. He had risked everything for her and for his Jewish friends he had loved so intensely. In a selfless act, he had given his life for the dream that his people could exist in peace alongside Jews.

But peace seemed out of reach. Ceasefire agreements remained fragile at best, and often broken by Hamas. Russia had made an alliance with every enemy north of Israel and grew more aggressive. Turkey beefed up relations with Iran. The threat of all-out war, perhaps even the widely discussed Gog-Magog war of Ezekiel 38, loomed on the horizon. If peace did come, it likely would be a false peace--one short lived.

New leadership in Israel gave them hope, but the recently elected administration in the United States seemed to work against the very mandates that God had firmly stated in the *Tanach* and the New Testament. She and Ari prayed daily for America and for their beloved Israel.

Times were uncertain, but they knew life must go on. Their wedding ceremony took place on Biny and Marni's terrace in the spring, when Ein Karem turned white with its own bridal veil of almond blossoms. Afterward, she and Ari bought a house on the outskirts of Eilat and remodeled it. When they finished the additions, they moved her grandparents and Rachael in with them.

Khalid persuaded Daoud to join forces with him in the Intel division of the IDF. He visited as often as assignments allowed. Abrahim worked for the government on strengthening ties with the Bedouin population.

Since Ari's wounds required him to retire from the military, he bought the Red Sea Jeep Safari business from Dov's wife, Havah, and convinced Moshe to join him as a partner. Their explorations into the Edom Mountains made it easy to discover places that could be used for refuge should there be a need to escape someday.

Ari had come a long way in his relationship with his Messiah, and through his knowledge of the *Tanach*, Anne had learned things about the Lord that drew her into a deeper understanding about God's plan for His people and for the ones grafted into the Hebraic root. Their vision of having meetings in their home to study the *Tanach* and the New Testament Scriptures together had already gotten off to a good start, thanks to Rachael. Anne's grandparents had much to offer by way of godly advice and knowledge.

If only Rashad could be with us still. She missed him terribly.

When she sighed out loud, Ari took her free hand. He examined the silver and gold ring on her finger, before he brought it to his lips. His hand slid to her waist and he leaned down and kissed the side of her neck. She smiled and tussled his hair.

"You are awfully quiet," he murmured next to her ear. They stopped walking, and he pulled her into his arms.

Sheltered in his embrace, Anne felt loved and protected. She looked up at him, but she couldn't put her feelings into words.

Ari held her gaze for a moment. She loved the way he could search her heart and know what she was thinking. He kissed her tears away before his lips touched hers.

"I miss him, too," he said.

The End